Wrinkled Heartbeats

A Novel

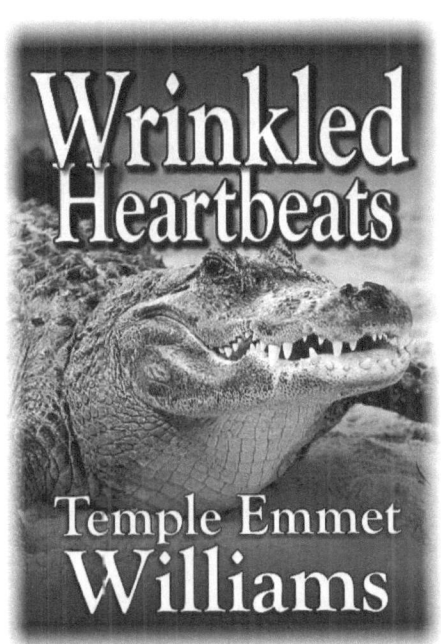

Published by Templeworks Properties LLC
3755 Mykonos Court, Boca Raton, Florida 33487
(561) 241-6323 Fax: (561) 241-6358 (office)
http://www.templeworks.biz
mail to temple@templeworks.biz

Williams, Temple Emmet
Wrinkled Heartbeats: A Novel
1. Thriller-General 2. Mystery-General 3.Action 4. Military
ISBN-13: 978-0-9908433-6-8

Library of Congress Control Number: 2015912842

Dedication

To **Lewis Scott Williams**,
_who was a hero at the start
and at the finish line.
Rest in peace, dear brother._

Books by Temple Emmet Williams

Fiction: Wrinkled Heartbeats
        Poison Heartbeats
        African Heartbeats

Non-Fiction: Warrior Patient
            Warr4iore Patient Heartbeats

Contents

Author's Note

Prednisone Flashbacks

Flashbacks to the Korean Conflict, often called "The Forgotten War," are a revealing backdrop to this novel. The flashbacks result from a steroid named Prednisone, given to the hero of the book. The author, an ex-Marine,  had Prednisone flashbacks in his award-winning memoir, *Warrior Patient.* It inspired his use of the steroid as a literary device in this book.

History records the Battle of Chosin Reservoir as a great victory for the United States Marine Corps. It becomes a revealing allegory in the novel.

Wrinkled Heartbeats is the first novel in the author's Heartbeats Series, which will eventually include six books. The second novel, *Poison Heartbeats*, was published in October 2016. *African Heartbeats* was published in 2020.

They are standalone works of fiction. You don't have to read one to enjoy another.

Chapter 1

A Farm In The Mountains

At the start of June, early mornings remain cold in the Appalachian mountains of Virginia. Clouds smother the Jackson River, but not its sound. The valley that the river runs through remains hidden, waiting for the sun to lift the clouds. The spring rains are gone, the flooding finished, but the music of the river's rapids still drifts up through the mist to awaken Torbjorn Petersson. He yawns and stretches on the second floor of a log cabin built into the side of the mountain.

It is not a store-bought cabin, not prefabricated. It is almost 220 years old, stable, well-maintained, built by Torbjorn's great-great-grandfather, who escaped from the crushing, starving poverty of late 18th century Sweden to become a landowner in the new world.

The sky starts to show daylight as Torbjorn gets up, dresses, and goes downstairs.

He knows that the creak on the fifth step from the bottom will awaken his grandmother, the only other person in the house. *Creak.* He hears her stir.

At the foot of the steps, he waits to hear one of two words from her bedroom between the stairs and the kitchen: pancakes or eggs. She sings out: "Eggs," her voice much younger than her 84 years.

Her request requires a multiple-choice reply from Torbjorn: "Scrambled, poached or fried, Gammy?"

"Sunnyside up," she answers. She does not say bacon or toast or biscuits or orange juice or coffee. Those remain a given. Eggs and the pancakes change places, but not every day. Sometimes Ernestine "Gammy" Petersson goes a week without shouting for flapjacks, blueberry, strawberry, or plain. Blueberry pancakes usually win.

The kitchen smells like breakfast when she appears, wearing the same pale blue housecoat she has worn throughout her grandson's memory. Ernestine Petersson bears the weathered look of Appalachia. She has always been old, and she was born old, tough, and mountain smart.

They eat at a small table in the kitchen, pushed up against a window, looking down on the clouds lifting off the Jackson River. In silence, they enjoy the sounds of the mountain waking up, mostly crickets, an occasional wild turkey, and always the whip-poor-wills that had put them to sleep the night before — their rooster, a quarter of a mile off, struts around the hen house, announcing sunrise.

"We got us two whistle pigs down by the fork in the river," Gammy says, talking about groundhogs she saw the previous day. "Gonna lose another cow, you don't shoot 'em, son." Cows break their legs, stepping into groundhog holes.

She calls Torbjorn "son" instead of "grandson." Her actual son, his father, did not last long. Like her husband, a war in a foreign land stole his life.

Every morning, every night, she touches her husband in a small hallway in the mountainside cabin. The hall has two doors. One opens onto steps into the basement under the cabin; the other leads to her bedroom adjoining the kitchen. She touches her husband twice a day by brushing her fingers over the medal that hangs on the wall separating the two doors, a Bronze Star. Above it, framed, is a handwritten letter from a Captain George McKlane, explaining to her that her husband was a Marine Corps hero who saved the lives of many men at the price of his own.

It is a neat, nicely-handwritten letter. It comes from a military hospital in Japan, dated January 26th, 1951. Sixty-five years earlier, she irons the message before she puts it in a simple wood and glass frame. The heat of the iron turns her tears into permanent age spots on the paper.

Her husband, Jackson Petersson, dies in Korea in the bitter winter of 1950, without ever knowing or holding the child she bears. When their son, Jack Junior, is nineteen, he also enlists in the Marine Corps. In boot camp at Parris Island, he wins the Dress Blues Award as one of the top Marines in his company. He receives a meritorious promotion to Private First Class. He trains further at Camp LeJeune in North Carolina, becoming a demolition expert. He gets a meritorious promotion to Lance Corporal. He takes tests that show he has an innate understanding of engineering and spatial relationships. He turns down the chance to become an officer in MARCAD, the Marine Cadets, where he would have learned to fly helicopters or jets. He does not want to sign up for another five and a half years.

His rejected selection of MARCAD angers his commanding officer, whose appointment to Major depends on the achievements of his men. Suddenly, new orders are cut for Jack Junior, sending him to Vietnam. He dies there trying to create a safe path for his fellow Marines through a minefield in Quang Binh province.

He receives no recognition for exceptional service or bravery. A Marine drives out to the farm one day and says he is sorry. He gives Ernestine Petersson an American flag.

Her grandson, Torbjorn, also enlists in the Marine Corps, and he survives the war in Afghanistan without a scratch. Death does not stalk its messengers. It does not kill Marine Corps snipers.

Torbjorn Petersson gets up from the breakfast table and walks through the living room. He takes his M2010 sniper rifle off the gun rack, grabs its gear pack, and steps out onto the screened porch facing the Jackson River. The clouds have lifted off the valley floor, melted by the sun. The smell of a paper mill stains the air, drifting up from Covington, twenty-two miles south. Good, he thinks, the groundhogs at the fork will neither see nor smell me coming. He will feed the chickens and clear out their eggs later.

"Groundhog stew tonight, Gammy," he says, opening the screen door and stepping off the porch. She smiles as she washes the breakfast dishes and answers: "Whistlepig stew, son." She says it quietly to herself.

Torbjorn walks along the edge of the thick forest that sweeps down from the mountainside to the cleared land on their farm. The upper fields are mostly flat, outlined by barbed wire strung along the top of the gray, split-wooden fences. The property is clear of rocks and planted in corn, or wheat. A worn-down ridge runs through the middle of the farm, and the open ground turns to pasture as it slopes towards the Jackson River. They own 526 acres, carved out of the valley by their Swedish ancestors almost two and a half centuries earlier.

Torbjorn sees a white-tailed deer near the edge of the forest, stepping into the corn. There's a break in the barbed wire. He'll have to repair it.

Downwind, he creeps within eight feet of the doe before it jerks its head high and scampers back into the forest. Torbjorn learns to walk that quietly.

The deer knows precisely where to jump over the fence, at the break in the barbed wire. With softer shoes, Torbjorn might have touched the animal.

He comes to a clear water stream, which will eventually widen into a fork, spilling into the Jackson River. He steps through the rows of corn and then walks up and down "V" steps over the barbed wire that stops their cattle from chewing on the farm crops.

The cows lift their heads, recognize Torbjorn as no danger, and go back to grazing.

Torbjorn sets up his M2010 sniper system on the ridge. He attaches the sound suppressor and muzzle brake, which reduces sound, recoil, and jump. He sets the bullet drop. Then he starts scoping the apple orchard.

In Afghanistan, Torbjorn Petersson always had a spotter with him, another Marine, who would use an independent scoping device to tell him how close he came to hitting his target. He rarely had to take a second shot. His nickname in Afghanistan was "One Shot."

Only once, in two tours, did it require a second and a third shot, and that came at dusk near the Pakistan border, in the shadow of Noshaq in the Hindu Kush mountain range.

In the apple orchard, he uses the rifle scope to spot both groundhogs, twenty feet apart, watchful at the entrances to each of their burrows.

They are about five football fields away, a relatively difficult shot, even for a Marine Corps sniper. Torbjorn waits for one of the groundhogs to move at least twenty feet from its burrow. He scopes back and forth from one to the other, a tiny move through the telescopic sight.

He knows one will race for its den as soon as the first kill shot echoes through the valley.

He scopes the apple trees. A gentle wind ripples their leaves, pushing directly towards him. He squints at the groundhog closest to its burrow, and then a small shift back to the entry to the other one's den. He practices the slight move five times. Then he takes a deep breath and starts to squeeze the trigger slowly. The first shot is easy, at the groundhog closest to its burrow. The whistle pig drops before the sound reaches it.

The second shot is more complicated than the first.

It requires firing a split-second in front of the second groundhog as it races towards the safety of its burrow. The second shot echoes down the valley. Both groundhogs are clean kills.

Torbjorn trots towards the prey, leaving his weapon system on the ridge. He needs to cut the glands out from under the groundhogs' armpits quickly before their death spoils the meat.

After that, he kicks in their burrows, finding additional entrances, and kicking them in as well. Now the cows can graze in the orchard without breaking a leg, stepping into one of the holes.

He ties the groundhogs together with rope. They're young, small, about six pounds each because the apples have not yet ripened and fallen from the trees. They'll make an excellent stew when Gammy gets hold of them.

He hangs them around his neck.

Back at the log cabin, his grandmother cleans what she calls whistle pigs, as Torbjorn does his daily chores. He finishes his work by lunchtime. His grandmother makes sandwiches with homemade bread and thick slabs of beef from a reasonably young cow that stepped into a groundhog hole earlier that year.

Torbjorn takes his sandwiches and disappears through a door on the southern side of the cabin.

He walks into a large room that had once been the master bedroom. Now it has no beds, and Torbjorn covers all the windows with heavy, black shades.

A dim light shows a series of rectangular shapes surrounding a huge U-shaped desk. Torbjorn throws a switch, and a generator starts to hum softly outside the cabin. He turns on a bank of uninterruptible power supplies and, once they are all showing solid lights, he turns on the six computers attached to them.

Most of the computers have three monitors; some have four. The six primary monitors, one for each computer bank, spring to life, and they go through their setup very quickly. They are powerful computers. He types in a password, different on each primary monitor. When done, each series of monitors have a name on their screen.

One bank of monitors is called Canada, followed by England, Turkey, South Africa, Brazil, and Mexico. The names identify the proxy addresses that each computer will use to access the Internet. No one can trace the addresses back to their actual physical location.

The proxy addresses change every day, internet ghosts that hide in the black hole of cyberspace. Although his modems permit WiFi, he never uses it. Everything is hard-wired and difficult to trace. Torbjorn builds each of the computers himself. He has an innate understanding of the mechanics and physics involved, and he is self-taught, an untraceable geek.

He has installed a high-speed, fiber optic, broadband cable connecting the computer system to a satellite dish at the top of the mountain behind their cabin, still on the farm's property. No hunter will cross onto Petersson's posted land.

Torbjorn buries the cable six inches deep in a narrow trench almost a half a mile long, snaking up the mountain. The system catches a perfect signal, even during bad storms. Nobody knows where the satellite dish is, except for the Peterssons and some wild animals that sniff at it from time to time. Nobody looks for it. Nobody cares.

Torbjorn Petersson is a professional killer.

Palm Beach County, Thursday Morning.

At The Royal Coconut Yacht & Country Club in Boca Raton, Florida, thirty-five miles north of Miami, Captain George

McKlane talks to his bagel. "My son wants me to sell the house and move into assisted living." He does not look up at his friends sitting around the clubhouse breakfast table. George McKlane focuses on getting the strawberry jam to stay on top of the cream cheese already smothering his bagel. His hands shake, the right one worse than the left.

"I should have done the jam first."

His friends lean forward to hear what he says. His voice is weak, but slowly recovering the baritone timbre stolen by his recent trip to the hospital for hernia surgery.

"Don't do it, George. The kid just wants your money."

"Yeah, well, nothing wrong with that," George McKlane says. His kid is a full colonel in the United States Marine Corps, who will probably become a brigadier general in less than a year. His son's latest assignment moves him from the headquarters base of the Marine Corps Wing in Cherry Point, North Carolina, to the Pentagon in Washington, D.C. George McKlane laughs at the strawberry and cream cheese mess he creates. It's a pleasant, familiar sound.

"Bagels are a young man's game," he says.

"What the Hell is he talking about?" Ralph Broadslate asks from the other side of the table. He sticks a finger in his ear, pushing on a hearing aid. Someone tells him that George is going to move into an old persons' home.

"Tell him to get a dog instead."

Ralph Broadslate is a retired lawyer and a former federal judge. He remains a not-so-silent partner at the Broadslate & Barnes firm in Trenton, New Jersey.

George McKlane smiles at the judge. "Ralph," he says, "I'm not going to spend my time following around a piece of fluff on a leash, with a bag to pick up his droppings."

"George would rather move into a home for the aged and just follow around old bags," a man named Gunther Klein says. Some people call him "Doctor Jokester," honoring his wit as well as the profession from which he retired many years earlier. Doctor Gunther Klein winks at his wife, Rachel, but she does not laugh at his old bag joke. "Old Bag" — it's his nasty nickname for her behind closed doors.

Rachel Klein, a dietician for many years, would love to put her husband, Doctor Gunther "Jokester" Klein, in an old person's home. She just can't figure out how to do it.

George McKlane, an ex-Marine, shakes a friendly fist at Doctor Klein and tells him to be kind to his wife.

"You'll miss her soon enough," he says.

"Unless he drops dead first," Rachel Klein says. She turns and smiles sweetly at her husband.

Although George McKlane's large hands shake more than they did just a few weeks earlier, before his hernia operation, they do not wobble when he makes a fist. George McKlane suffers from essential tremors, a chronic disease that runs in his family, relatively harmless, according to Doctor Gunther Klein, and shared by many people over 40.

As a physician, Gunther worked as the Head of Neurosurgery at Bassett Hospital in Cooperstown, home of the Baseball Hall of Fame. He often jokes that he should have practiced in Canton, Ohio, home of the Pro Football Hall of Fame, "the Hall of Battered Brains." Then he would have been much more famous.

"The Baseball Hall of Fame in Cooperstown didn't even have a decent beanball section," the Doctor likes to tell anyone who will listen. He swears that he tried to get his neurosurgery wing at Bassett Hospital in New York named after the baseball pitcher Nolan Ryan, famous as one of the game's best, fastball-throwing headhunters.

George uses both hands to get his bagel mess to his mouth. His steadier left hand anchors the move, but it still leaves creamed cheese on his nose. Doctor Klein reaches into the napkin holder at the center of the table and passes a few of them to George.

They've been friends and neighbors for years.

"It's a big house," George McKlane says. "Feels pretty lonely, rattling around the place alone since Agnes died."

The get-a-dog ex-judge starts to open his mouth but remains quiet, thinking better of it. The table goes silent.

"Some of those assisted-living places are very nice," Doctor Gunther Klein finally says. But the tone of the table changes, saddens. They will lose George, and they like him. He'll visit for a while after he moves, but then he'll disappear into another life: the end game.

"I miss Agnes," George says to Rachel, after swallowing some of his bagel. That's when the magic happens, a secret that he has kept to himself since returning from the hospital.

It's a click in his head. He feels it, almost hears it. The magic noise drops him into another time of his life, an instant replay as real as the half-eaten bagel that falls on the napkin in his lap.

North Korea, Yudam-ni, On November 21, 1950

"It's the damned wind off the lake that makes it colder than Hell," Staff Sergeant Raymond Chapman says.

Captain George McKlane looks at him, smiles, and says: "I wish we were in Hell, sergeant. At least it would be a whole lot warmer."

"I suppose so, captain," says the sergeant. "You hear what Corporal Smartass calls us?"

Smartass is a Stars and Stripes reporter, a stringer, assigned to the 1st Marine Division in North Korea.

His real name is Corporal Jackson Petersson, a youngster from the Appalachian Mountains of Virginia.

The corporal tries to grow a mustache to look as old as he feels after just three months in Korea.

Jackson Petersson has an exceptional talent, but it is with an M-1 rifle, not words.

"So, what does he call us?" Captain George McKlane asks, scanning the road in front of them.

There's a jeep on the left, a quarter of a click away, maybe less, burned-out with a dead Chinese Communist Forces' (CCF) uniform frozen in the driver's seat.

"He calls us the Chosin Few," Sergeant Raymond Chapman says, referring to the 1st Marine Division's retreat from the reservoir on the edge of their perimeter.

The UN troops operate off Japanese maps in North Korea. The Japanese translation of Changin Lake becomes Marine Corps history as the Chosin Reservoir.

"He's a clever writer," the captain says.

"And an even better shot," the sergeant says.

Corporal Jackson Petersson qualified "expert" at the top of his company on the rifle range at Parris Island. He tells friends he can shave the whiskers off a squirrel at 200 yards.

The sergeant watches the frozen CCF uniform in the jeep. "Two hundred meters tops, captain.."

There's no need to whisper against the bitter wind, but the sergeant still does it.

"Get Petersson up here," the captain says. He does not lower his binoculars.

Corporal Petersson appears.

The captain keeps his back to him, watching the jeep and the CCF uniform.

"Where's your typewriter, Smartass?"

"In my head, sir."

"See dead China in the jeep up there?"

Captain McKlane, twenty-three years old, calls the enemy "China" instead of some of the other labels they put on the Chinese Communist Forces that try to wipe them out. Respect the enemy. Just make sure they're dead.

"Yes, sir," the corporal says, squinting at the jeep.

"Shoot him."

Staff Sergeant Raymond Chapman, thirteen years older than the captain, bends slightly in front of the corporal, a shoulder prop for Petersson's M-1 rifle.

The weapon's effective range is three hundred yards.

Corporal Petersson loops the web strap of the rifle around his arm.

He rests the weapon across the sergeant's shoulder. Petersson takes a deep breath, gently squeezes the trigger.

In his mind, he's shooting a groundhog on the family's farm back in Bath County, Virginia.

Before the M-1 fires, the frozen enemy suddenly comes to life. "Burp gun," Captain McKlane says, his voice matter of fact, unhurried.

The Soviet Shpagin submachine gun holds seventy-two rounds, with a cycle rate of over 700 rounds a minute.

Some Marines call it The Squirt Gun, trying to minimize its deadly purpose.

The CCF regulars use the Shpagin because it is cheap to make, simple to operate and reliable in any battlefield condition, but only at close range.

At 200 meters, even a barn door has a pretty good chance at survival.

As the chatter of the submachine gun reaches them, Corporal Jackson Petersson squeezes off two shots from his seven-round clip.

The first hit the Chinese soldier in the chest, the second in his neck as he falls. The CCF's Shpagin continues to fire until empty, harmlessly sending bullets into the ground.

"Finger must have had frostbite," the sergeant says.

"Let's move," Captain McKlane tells the sergeant. "Good shooting, corporal. Make sure you get his weapon." They continue their retreat during the Chosin Reservoir Campaign, the Chosin Few, survivors of the Frozen Chosin, part of the 1st Marine Division.

They fight their way through communist Chinese lines in North Korea in what has become the most celebrated military retreat in the history of the United States Marine Corps in the early winter of 1950.

With other UN troops, the Marines effectively destroy seven Chinese divisions that try to stop their escape to the port of Hungnam. Marine Corps deaths number 836, with another 12,000 wounded, mostly by frostbite.

They estimate casualties for the Chinese at 35,000 killed, with many more wounded.

The Battle of Chosin Reservoir becomes a decisive victory and strategic reversal for the United Nations. But it does not end the war. It just stretches it.

The captain feels an unexpected tug on his shoulder. He reaches for it, feeling hollow, expecting blood.

The Royal Coconut Yacht & Country Club on Thursday

"George," Doctor Klein says, "wake up." The doctor's wife, Rachel, says: "You're snoring, George. Agnes told me that you were a terrible snorer, just before she died."

Her husband glares at her and shakes his head.

What an old bag.

George's eyes come back into focus. He sees his friends, recognizes his current life. Judge Broadslate asks: "Are you all right, George?"

The old ex-Marine looks around the table, feels his shoulder. He slowly stands up. "Petersson never made it," he says. The group looks puzzled. "He was a helluva shot, saved a lot of lives."

"What's he talking about now?" Ralph Broadslate says, louder than necessary. "Tell him to get a dog." Doctor Gunther Klein reaches down, picks up George's uneaten bagel, and puts it on an empty plate. "Blood sugar," he says, but nobody hears the diagnosis.

George starts to walk away, stops, turns. "I love you all, but I'm going to sell the house. It's time to retreat."

The table remains silent with confusion.

His friends have not been part of George's blackout.

"Only Marines can snatch victory from the jaws of retreat," George says.

He gives them all a casual salute.

Chapter 2

Coming Back Home

13752 Coconut Palm Court, Boca Raton, FL on Thursday

George presses on the garage door button in his Mercedes 500SEL, and the iron metal gate swings open into his driveway. A heavy walnut door slides up in the garage. His heart stumbles when he sees Agnes' black BMW. He pulls into the garage, notices a thick blanket of dust covering her car. Agnes is dead for almost a year now.

He sits quietly in the car, turns it off. He and Agnes shared over 51 years of laughter, heartache, anger, adventure, and division, with one son late in their marriage, a surprise, almost a duplicate of himself. With Agnes, there was always love, always hope. He remembers her last words, simple, obvious, surrounded at home by equipment that made deceptively soft noises: "I'm going to miss you, George."

His son was home when she died, and a comfort. But many days he does not remember, days of friends and sympathy and caring. He does remember the burial, on a warm, cloudless afternoon, an Irish wake. He has no anger.

He wonders if dead people can miss the living, hanging on to Agnes' final words. He holds the words close, tries to trust them, but cannot. He has seen too much death in his life.

He gets out of the car, careful not to swing the Mercedes' heavy door into her BMW. "I miss you. Missus McKlane." He always calls her that, in public and in private: "Missus McKlane."

At first, she hates it, tells him it sounds like ownership. He answers that it always reminds him that it is a miracle, her being his wife.

He never stops calling Agnes "Missus McKlane," not even when they make love.

Agnes grows to accept it, even laughs at it in very private moments, but she never cares for it.

She spends a lot of time in the 1970s and 1980s trying to explain George's endearment to the women she meets. Most of them do not buy it, figuring George McKlane is just a stubborn ex-Marine, and a hard-nosed business person, set in his moronic ways. Some women, who know Agnes, try to argue with him about it at cocktail parties. He never discusses it with them. He listens, quietly, attentively, and then smiles. George has terrific teeth.

In the garage, George touches the hood of Agnes' BMW, recognizing a lot of similar fingerprints in the area. He puts a key in the garage door that leads to the laundry room, turns it, and hears the security bolt close. George has forgotten to lock it. He turns the key again and opens the door., and a woman stares at him.

"Don't forget to put down the garage door," she says.

George fumbles for the close button on the garage wall, and it slides shut. "Sharonda," he says.

"You gotta wear more clothes," she says. "I'm doing a week's worth of laundry, and it doesn't look like you've worn more than three different shirts. At least you're changing your socks and underwear." She bends and tosses a small pile of clothes into the dryer, turning it on as George walks into the laundry room.

"Thank you, Sharonda," he says. "I always change my socks. If you know anyone who wants to buy a BMW, let me know." He starts to walk out of the laundry room.

"How many times have I told you I only know people who want to steal one, George?"

She calls him by his first name because they are friends, and he likes it.

He stops, turns around, and looks at the woman who comes every day to take care of him and his home. "Twenty grand," he says, smiling at her. "And it's only been driven by a little old lady."

Sharonda shakes her head. She also smiles, but not as much. She took care of his wife, Agnes, for over a year before she died. She is a registered nurse with a Master's Degree in Nursing, a Nurse Practitioner, an NP who can easily make well over $100,000 a year doing it. After almost ten years in two different Florida hospitals, she burns out.

She starts a caretaker service for wealthy people. She continues to keep her Advanced Practice Registered Nurse (APRN) license current.

After Agnes dies, she stays on to take care of George, at his son's request. George becomes her only client, probably her path to early retirement. She cooks, cleans, and professionally cares for him. It is the most money she has ever made in her life.

Sharonda knows that George and Agnes McKlane loved each other deeply, and she worries that he hardly ever talks about her, except as a tough guy.

George walks down the hallway into a kitchen filled with marble, granite, and stainless steel. He moves through the living room, with its centerpiece collage of original paintings, including a Turner, a van Gogh, and a Velázquez.

A black Steinway Grand Piano stands to the side of a series of evenly-spaced, two-story, hurricane-proof windows. Sharonda can play the piano reasonably well, mostly jazz, but not like Agnes.

George McKlane's wife could have been a concert pianist. She played once, at a charity event, with George Szell, the famous composer and conductor who visited Florida with his world-famous Cleveland Orchestra. The talent of Agnes surprised the conductor, and he said so in a short speech following the symphony.

The vast living room's slightly-tinted hurricane windows overlook a wide canal connected to Florida's Intracoastal Waterway. A narrow, 50-foot pool separates George's estate home from the water. A gardener putters around the edges of a one hundred and twenty-foot, wooden boat dock, replacing flowers that probably do not need replacement. George does not own a boat, never did. The boat dock is empty.

George walks into his office and sits down at a large mahogany desk. A bank of computer screens, now rarely used, are behind him. Mahogany shelves fill three of the four walls of the room, loaded with books, most of them on business. Very few of the books deal with military matters.

George has read every book that lines the shelves. They are not decoration, not always neatly stacked, not even the leather-bound editions. Many of them contain personal messages on their title pages from authors.

Once, George had been an active and well-connected trader of financial derivatives. He understood markets, and he valued intelligent people. He appreciated the fear, and the greed, and the hope of other traders, and he used that knowledge to build a fortune.

Framed photographs cover the one wall that has no bookshelves. George and Agnes had many friends, some of them famous.

His large, polished, mahogany desk, slightly darker than the shelves, has almost nothing on it: a yellow legal pad, a pen, and pencil, a reading lamp, nothing else.

He looks at the pad, recognizes the scribbles. "I used to have nice handwriting," he tells the empty room. The yellow pad has a nervous, almost unreadable message, and a phone number. Call Accelerated Realty Sales.

He swivels his leather chair around to face the computer screens, fumbles a portable phone off its charging stand, turns back to the desk, and dials the number. It rings once, and he hangs up immediately. He needs to organize his thoughts.

Never phone without understanding the outcome you want. Discipline always counts. Don't ask questions unless you know two or three likely answers beforehand. George makes a fortune understanding this, and it saves his life more than once. He reaches into a desk drawer and pulls out a family-sized chocolate bar with almonds in it.

He starts eating the small squares, one after another.

He gets through about three-quarters of the chocolate bar before the remaining quarter, still wrapped in tin foil, falls to the floor as he blacks out again.

<u>North Korea, The Chosin Reservoir, Nov. 27, 1950</u>

On a moonlit night, a young Marine jerks around in his foxhole, challenging the shadow approaching him from inside the perimeter. He lowers his rifle when he hears the right password. the young Marine knows the voice. "Sweet Jesus," he says. "I danged near pulled the trigger and shot you, Socks, I mean Captain McKlane ... sir."

"Good ears, son."

Captain George McKlane is only two years older than the Marine that he talks to, but the word "son" seems natural to both men.

"Don't worry about anything behind you," he says. "Nothing but Marines. Worry about China out there." He motions towards the dark, menacing outline of North Ridge beyond the Yudam-Ni perimeter.

"No, sir. Yes, sir, Captain Socks."

It is a nickname that Captain George McKlane accepts from his men.

He and the staff sergeant commandeered boxes of socks early in the campaign, and they regularly hand them out to the men to fight off the sub-zero temperatures that endanger all of them. Frostbite claims more casualties than bullets.

In the moonlight, Captain McKlane sees the young Marine kicking at the sleeping bag in his two-person foxhole.

"Let him sleep," the captain says. "He'll be awake soon enough." One man sleeps. One man watches. That's how it works. The entire perimeter is on fifty percent alert.

They dig their foxhole waist-deep, with a horseshoe of sandbags and rocks surrounding it, piled towards the valley below. China will come from that direction. A Browning Automatic Rifle (BAR) rests on the sandbags on a portable tripod, and two M-1s lean against open boxes of ammunition. The BARs keep freezing up in sub-zero temperatures. When it happens, the machine gunner grabs the extra M1, or a Tommy Gun if he has one. The Tommy Guns often freeze up as well.

The captain tosses two pairs of thick, green socks into the foxhole. "Put 'em on when you have a chance. Give the other pair to Smartass when he wakes up."

Captain McKlane fades into the darkness, crouching along the foxhole perimeter, whispering, throwing socks to his men. His parka, the shape of a balloon when he starts, returns to average size as he meets Staff Sergeant Raymond Chapman coming from the other direction. They move back towards a black tent that is his Command Post, built on a hardwood platform.

November 27th, 1950, is one of the coldest nights on record in North Korea, touching forty degrees below zero. Wind sweeps across the Chosin Reservoir whipping around the North Ridge and relentlessly lashing at the Marines dug into hillsides around Yudam-ni.

In the distance, they can hear the groaning whine of Allied convoys rumbling through Toktong Pass. The sound changes when the trucks move over the summit. Their rumbling turns into a roar as transport drivers race downhill on the treacherous, twisting mountain road over which they will eventually retreat.

About an hour before midnight, the last trucks make it over the top. Their sound lifts the spirits of the Marines. They need fresh supplies, including rations, bullets, hand grenades, and ammunition for their 81mm mortars as well as the 75mm recoilless guns.

They need plasma and bandages.

The previous two days have seen massive action. For safety, they have had to move their frontline medical aid stations to the southwest of Yudam-ni.

The North Ridge battle has pushed the triage units to the edge of their capabilities.

Their tents, easy to spot with large red crosses, are riddled with holes from enemy small-arms fire. It is so cold that the plasma won't liquefy. Ice particles clog life-saving delivery tubes hanging uselessly on medicine poles.

Doctors have to work with thick gloves to keep their hands from freezing. They can't change dressings.

If they cut off a Marines' clothing to get at a wound, the Marine freezes to death.

They stuff a lot of the wounded into sleeping bags, waiting for helicopter airlifts to larger MASH units, safe from the frontline fighting.

Surprisingly, because war improves the speed of medical care, very few of the sleeping bags become body bags.

In Captain George McKlane's command center, Staff Sergeant Raymond Chapman says: "It's quiet, Socks; it's too damned quiet."

The captain smiles and looks at his watch: 0200. "That's the kiss of death, sergeant."

"This is going to be our third sleepless night," the sergeant says. "Boys haven't had a warm meal for well over a month." Captain McKlane says nothing. He knows it's not a complaint, just a hard fact.

Across the valley, they watch several five-gallon gasoline booby traps explode into a river of fire that runs down the hillside. They cannot see human shapes because it's too far away. Machine gun chatter drifts across the valley as the gasoline burns out.

An hour later, some of their perimeter tripwires, far in front of their position, cause hand grenade explosions. None of the Marines fire their weapons, but every foxhole immediately goes to one hundred percent alert.

Voices drift out of the darkness, American voices, but they are not Americans.

"I am First Lieutenant Rogers of the United States Marines. They have you surrounded," a voice says, sending slightly metallic tones through frozen loudspeakers. "The Chinese will give you warm clothes, warm women, good treatment. Surrender Marines. You will be free!"

"Light up China, sergeant," Captain George McKlane says quietly.

The staff sergeant speaks into a phone. Almost immediately, 81mm illumination shells streak into the sky.

They reveal wave after wave of Chinese communist forces advancing across the valley from the south, washing up on the hillside, an ocean of undulating, pale green parkas.

Marine Corps machine guns open up. Mortars thud. The Chinese reply, lobbing mortars into the Marines' perimeter. Incendiary rounds explode, white phosphorous spiders, burning fiercely.

The Chinese keep coming, pushing into barrage after barrage of artillery and gunfire. A mat of corpses on blood-soaked snow surrounds the Marine Corps' perimeter.

Box after box of ammunition, artillery shells, and hand grenades are opened, emptied, chambered, locked, fired, thrown, used in the destruction of China.

It goes on for hours. Whistles blow. Loudspeakers blare out messages, all drowned in gunfire.

As the horizon slowly lightens, Marine Corps Corsairs roar into the valley.

The propeller-driven fighter-bombers lay down carpets of napalm. The CCL starts running as soon as they hear the first Corsair. Marine air support destroys an enemy in full retreat. The tension, drawn increasingly tighter for days, finally vanishes. No laughter. No shouting. Most sleep. Some never wake.

"You feel it?" Captain McKlane asks.

"I feel tired," the sergeant says. "I don't think I've ever been this tired."

"It's turning," Captain George McLane says. "The tide is finally turning."

For three days and nights, they have been on the defensive, protecting their foxholes, holding their positions.

Now the Marines will start to move.

13752 Coconut Palm Court
Boca Raton, Thursday

At first, George thinks he might be wounded again, on a hospital ship or in a MASH unit in Japan, being gently prodded back to consciousness by one of the nurses.

"Why do you insist on waking us up to give us sleeping pills?" he asks Sharonda Nelson.

The nurse practitioner says: "Excuse me, George?"

"Oh," George says. "Sharonda." She has a stethoscope around her neck. A black doctor's bag is sitting on the desk. George smiles. "Doctor Sharonda," he says.

"George, you slumped down in that chair. I thought maybe you had a heart attack or a stroke. I almost dialed 911. How do you feel? I'm going to take your blood pressure."

She leans down, picks up the uneaten chocolate bar, and drops it on his desk.

George's large hands press against his eyes, squeeze his forehead, pushing away memories. "I'm fine."

His blood pressure is low but not dangerously so. Sharonda sits down in a chair next to the desk, watching him, asking him medical questions, listening to his answers, watching his eyes, the slight trembling in his right hand.

Finally, satisfied that he just fell asleep, she says: "I put your dinner in the refrigerator, George."

She looks at her watch. She is leaving a bit early, but this is her night out with her husband, who's a police officer in Boca Raton. They will start their evening together at the pistol range in Delray Beach, firing their handguns, and whoever is the worst shot, buys dinner. The winner chooses the restaurant. The winner also pays for the movie that follows, which the loser gets to pick. Sharonda hasn't paid for a meal for several months, but she is getting tired of action, thriller, and science fiction films. What happened to romance?

"You have fish sticks, lima beans, and mashed potatoes," she tells Captain George McKlane. "And also vanilla custard, your absolute favorite."

"My favorite," George says.

"And some of that horrible beer you like," Sharonda says. "I don't know why you won't let me chill it a bit in the refrigerator. Don't know why anyone would drink warm beer. It's not civilized."

She shakes her head.

"Guinness," he says. "In Ireland, it's officially referred to as the Fifth Food Group, Sharonda."

She pats him on the shoulder. There's still some muscle there, not boney like most men his age, and, Lord, did George McKlane have a smile.

"See you tomorrow," she says.

"Twenty thousand for the BMW," George says.

She laughs on the way out.

George looks down at the yellow pad on his desk, checks the time of the grandfather clock standing eight feet tall in the corner.

He watches the huge brass pendulum swing silently back and forth through the glass in its cherry wood encasement. His grandfather in Sandusky, Ohio, built the clock from scratch out of a dying cherry tree growing next to the family farmhouse — an actual grandfather clock, with imported workings from Germany, one minute slow every two months.

George looks back at the pad on his desk: Accelerated Realty Sales. He decides to put off the call to the real estate company until first thing in the morning.

Chapter 3

The History Of Anthony Silberg

The Schuylkill Correction Institution, Pennsylvania

In 1990, there are 66 federal prison facilities in America, and they hold-well over 65,000 inmates. The prisoners include Anthony Silberg, a hardened criminal from Newark, New Jersey, who grows up using his fists, and, on rare occasions, his brains.

He boxes in the Golden Gloves but never makes it to the finals.

Local bookies thought he might win. They did not know he would take a swing at a federal agent two days before the championship, winding up in jail.

Silberg and two of his associates break into a warehouse and steal over $60,000 worth of brass ingots. The Feds have him and his buddies on a watch list of criminals, the result of added surveillance powers created six years earlier by the Comprehensive Crime Control Act of 1984.

As the crooks drive away from the warehouse in a stolen truck heavy with brass, the Feds move in. The only gunfire comes from the agents, shooting out the tires on the truck. All three crooks are carrying guns.

They arrest the trio on a conspiracy charge and felonies for carrying weapons. Silberg slugs one of the FBI agents, pulling his punch without doing too much damage.

It results in nothing worse than a bloody nose for the agent, but an added assault charge for all three of the crooks.

Only Silberg throws a punch.

All of the defendants are found guilty.

During the trial, evidence of Silberg's bad character creeps into the proceedings.

For example, the assistant district attorney points out, "Mister Silberg got tossed out of the United States Marine Corps before graduating from basic training at Parris Island, South Carolina."

The Marines determined that he was crazy, but not in a way that might prove useful on a battlefield.

The federal attorney does not mention this medical judgment, fearing a possible insanity defense. He just points out that Silberg leaves the Marine Corps with less than an honorable discharge.

All three defendants appeal their guilty verdict. Their lawyer is a heavyweight, the result of one of the defendants being the nephew of a high-ranking member of organized crime, who launders mob money through commercial real estate in Atlantic City.

The appeal points to what the defendants call a bogus search warrant used by the government to seize the brass ingots that they temporarily and innocently are transporting in a borrowed truck.

The owner of the truck admits under oath that he loaned the vehicle to the defendants, something that slipped his mind in his original transcript and testimony.

The government agrees to a judgment of acquittal on one of the four charges against the crooks. Three of the charges survive the appeal process. They include the charge against Silberg for assaulting, opposing, impeding, and interfering with an agent of The Department of Justice, the Federal Bureau of Investigation (the United States Code 18, paragraph 111).

The defendants all go to prison, serving four-and-a-half-year terms in different federal correction facilities. In jail, Silberg is called "Pop," not based on his age, but because of the sound of his punches.

He becomes the warden's favorite in organized inmate boxing matches.

He never loses a fight in the ring at the medium-security Federal Correction Institution in Schuylkill, Pennsylvania. However, he does falter in one battle outside the ring when he gets shanked by a black inmate.

After his release, Anthony Silberg moves to Palm Beach County in Florida. He applies for a real estate license, admitting his prior felonies.

Some local real estate developers and contractors vouch for his redeemed and outstanding character. Foremost among them is the largest developer in Palm Beach County, Angelo Rossellini, who has plans for Silberg. The Department of Business and Professional Regulation issues Silberg a sales license. Two years later, he gets a broker's license. Less than a decade after he arrives in Florida, ten percent of the members of Boca Raton's Board of Realtors® work for him. His company is called Accelerated Realty Sales, the name that George McKlane has scratched on the yellow legal pad lying on his desk.

Accelerated Realty Sales
Boca Raton: Friday AM

George dials the number on the yellow pad and asks to speak directly to Anthony Silberg. The girl on the phone says Mr. Silberg is very busy, and without skipping a beat, she asks. "How can I help you?" She's on the front desk, a sales agent, looking to intercept business before it gets transferred to an agent on the floor.

"You cannot help me," George McKlane says, pushing his voice lower.

"I'm sure I can help you, uh ... I'm sorry, sir, but I did not get your name." Her pen hovers above a pad next to the telephone. She has already written down the phone number on her computer screen, but it shows no name.

"I am a friend of Mister Silberg," George says. "My name is George McKlane, and we live in the same development. Please put me through to him."

The agent on the desk understands. She's reasonably sure the caller is a seller, but she also knows that any friend of Anthony Silberg is probably way above her pay grade.

Although nearing middle-age, she is new to the business and new to this office. It's her first job in real estate. Silberg will assign the listing to one of his seasoned pros.

"I'll put you right through," she says. She transfers the call, makes sure the connection to Silberg's executive secretary occurs, and hangs up the phone. She writes the name George McKlane next to the phone number on her pad, sighs because of its familiarity, and goes back to reading an expired listings printout.

Every time the door to Accelerated Realty Sales opens, she looks up with a bright smile.

It might be a walk-in customer looking for a home. It's usually another agent, which quickly flatlines her welcoming expression.

Anthony Silberg comes on the line. He knows George McKlane by sight, but they've never actually had a conversation together.

"George McKlane," Silberg says.

"Mister Silberg," George says.

"How can I help you, Mister McKlane," he asks, replacing the cheerful tone of his voice with an octave lower, indicating more serious attention.

"I'm thinking of selling my house," George says. "You are the first person I am calling."

Anthony Silberg speaks quietly, measured. "I am very honored." He pauses, almost whispers: "Semper Fi."

George reacts, holds the phone away from his face, stares at it, brings it back, says: "What did you say?"

"I was also in the Marine Corps, sir."

Everyone who lives in The Royal Coconut Yacht and Country Club knows the story of Captain George McKlane.

"I did not know that," George says.

The conversation pauses. "Anyway, you're the first real estate agent I am calling because I know your company sells more homes in this development than anyone else. Doctor Gunther Klein told me that."

"Yes, sir," the broker says. "I sold Doctor Klein his magnificent home personally, over a decade ago."

"Well, I would like you to sell my home personally," George McKlane says. "But I don't want it to take a decade."

"I would be honored to do so, sir." Anthony Silberg puts a slight smile in his voice. They arrange a meeting for that afternoon, at two o'clock.

Before he hangs up, George says, "Semper Fi, and please call me George."

In his office, Anthony Silberg smiles. The Royal Coconut Yacht and Country Club consists of 637 privately-built estate homes.

They surround the finger canals that branch into southern Florida's Intracoastal waterway. A lot of luxury yachts line the canals.

The timing could not be better. McKlane's home will be his first solo foray into laundering money for the mob. He has spent 18 years in the shadow of Angelo Rossellini's operation, and now he has decided to go into business for himself.

He will use the sale of high-end homes to legitimize drug money coming out of Miami.

He will not launder money using commercial property or raw land. Those bailiwicks belong to Angelo. He will do it with George McKlane's home, as his initial test.

Once that succeeds, and he knows it will, he will renegotiate his terms with the Rossellini organization.

His company lists and sells more high-end homes in Boca Raton than the next three brokerages combined.

The financial gains from money laundering will make the six percent commissions earned on luxury homes look like chump change.

To legitimize his involvement in this first deal, he will use it as a training exercise with a new agent who has just joined the company.

Brokers do not typically handle listings. They do not want to compete against the agents working for them. A training exercise with a new agent will take the edge off of his involvement. He'll be a good boss, helping a new agent.

Silberg cannot remember what the girl looks like, just that she is cute.

He does remember her last name: Rossellini. It will give his money-laundering plan an ironic twist, keeping it in the family, so-to-speak; he steps out of his office.

"What's the first name of that new girl, Rossellini, who just joined us?" he asks his executive secretary, Sarah Golden.

She taps her computer screen, finds it, and remembers a conversation she had with the woman. "Barbara Rossellini," his executive secretary says.

"How is she related to Angelo?" he asks.

"I asked her that, and she says she isn't."

Silberg seems disappointed. He asks: "Is she married?"

"Divorced. Barbara might change back to her maiden name, but she hasn't done it yet. She told me that."

"Barbara Rossellini," Anthony Silberg says. He smiles and steps back into his office. His executive secretary shakes her head, rolls her eyes. Maybe she should warn Barbara Rossellini about Anthony Silberg's reputation for womanizing. Not worth it. Sarah Golden is just a few months away from retirement.

Barbara Rossellini was quite small, she remembers.

"She can take care of herself," Sarah Golden says out loud, to nobody.

13752 Coconut Palm Ct., Boca Raton, FL: Friday

At his almost empty mahogany desk, George McKlane glances at the yellow legal pad. He has scribbled another name and phone number on it. He phones a small real estate firm in the area, one suggested by Judge Ralph Broadslate, the retired attorney, and a former federal judge.

George arranges a meeting with a broker associate named Martha Krumble. She will come to his home an hour before Anthony Silberg. The agents will cross paths if George times it correctly. He thinks Martha Krumble has an unusual name for someone who works with clients who frequently tear down the homes that they buy, replacing them with modern mansions.

George gets up and goes into the kitchen, where he finds Sharonda. "Are you making those delicious egg sandwiches for lunch?" he asks.

"Bologna," she says.

"Are you discussing the menu?"

Sharonda laughs and opens the refrigerator.

"Well, we have plenty of eggs to make them with, if that's what you want, George."

"Can you make a lot more than usual and cut them up into little squares? I'm going to have a couple of meetings with real estate agents, starting at one o'clock."

Sharonda closes the refrigerator and cocks her head to the side. She stares at George, saying nothing.

"Yes, I'm going to sell my home," George finally says.

Sharonda sighs. She asks: "How long have I got?"

"It will be months," George says. "Probably a half a year, maybe even more."

"Maybe you'll change your mind," Sharonda says.

"You better hope not."

"Why's that?"

"Because you're going to get the biggest bonus you've ever had in your life when it's over," George says.

She grins and says: "Provided that the egg sandwiches are good."

"You're a smart lady, Doctor Sharonda."

She thinks George McKlane may have the best smile she has ever seen on a white man.

Martha Krumble arrives five minutes early. She parks her car and steps out to admire the custom-built home. She makes a show of studying it: five bedrooms, six and a half baths, two stories, three attached structures, on an oversized lot. It's a magnificent home, perhaps a bit dated, located in what many consider the best location in Boca Raton, Florida. It's a 50-minute drive from Miami, outside of rush hour.

Prices at The Royal Coconut Yacht and Country Club start at close to a million dollars for an interior tear down with no canal frontage.

The highest-priced home is a $23,000,000 behemoth with 19,000 square feet of air-conditioned living space on a semi-circular corner lot curving into the Intracoastal Waterway. All of the houses at the club are custom built.

Martha Krumble knows some sellers will peek out the window and start forming an opinion of her before she ever punches the doorbell. That's why she arrives early and spends several minutes admiring the home.

She is the top producer for her broker, year after year. Her customers appreciate her honesty, her integrity, and her willingness to tackle whatever problems they encounter selling their home.

She works almost exclusively with sellers, not buyers. She's a listing agent.

A large, smiling woman opens the door, introduces herself as Sharonda, and says that George is waiting for her in the Birdroom. She follows the woman and says, "Thank you, Sharonda," as she walks into an extended sunroom that parallels a crystal blue swimming pool. There are no live birds in the Birdroom. Twenty original Audubon prints in thin, wooden frames line the interior wall. At the far end, an elderly gentleman with an extraordinary smile stands up and introduces himself as George McKlane.

Martha Krumble has looked him up on the Internet. She walks up to him, shakes his hand, and says, simply, "Thank you for your service, Captain McKlane."

He seems surprised, oddly humbled.

"That was a long time ago," he says.

"And you're still here," she says, smiling.

He laughs, sounding younger than he is. Martha Krumble thinks he must have been handsome and commanding once. He still looks pretty good.

"Please," he says. "Sit."

George McKlane motions to some small and neatly squared sandwiches on a silver tray on an antique glass table between them. "Sharonda makes the best egg sandwiches in the world."

The agent looks at Sharonda, smiling in the entryway. Again, she says: "Thank you, Sharonda." She nibbles on one, then pops it into her mouth and gulps it down. "You're right," she says to George McKlane. She grabs another, and he grabs a few himself. Sharonda disappears into the interior of the house.

"In New Orleans, I once stayed at the Audubon Apartments near Burgundy Street," Martha Krumble says, admiring the prints along the wall. "These are all originals, aren't they?"

"Yes, they are. Agnes collected them." She sees his eyes start to water. "She died a year ago."

"I'm sorry." So his wife has died, and he wants out. And he loved her very much.

"Is that why you're selling?" she asks.

"No," he says. Martha's forehead wrinkles because she wants to know why he's selling.

"My son wants me to sell," he tells her.

They spend time talking about selling his home. Martha Krumble knows how much George and Agnes McKlane paid for it fifteen years earlier before the housing bubble blew prices through the roof. They bought it for just under three million dollars.

The housing bubble led to a housing bust, which sent prices tumbling, producing foreclosures throughout the United States.

Homes owned by the wealthy fell, but not as much as they had risen.

She knew the home had no mortgage. She knew the real estate taxes paid and the carrying costs, including mandatory club membership. She can tell George McKlane the final selling price of his home, within a few percentage points. She does not do so.

"Can I get a tour of your castle?" she asks. He does not smile, and she realizes that she may have stepped over an invisible boundary of familiarity.

Sharonda magically appears.

Martha understands that they have planned this, rehearsed it. She thinks Sharonda may be a significant influence on George McKlane.

"Sharonda will give you the full tour," George says. "I'm going to stay here and eat all her egg sandwiches." He smiles. She feels oddly forgiven for her "castle" remark.

The tour takes over 40 minutes. It's not a huge house, but everything is well cared for, expensive, quality, from the crown molding to the Burberry carpets and Brazilian hardwood flooring. George and Agnes built the house, using a famous contractor and a costly designer. The house does not feel 15 years old. It feels like a show house. Nothing in the home seems out of place, and it does not require staging.

Sharonda asks if Martha Krumble wants to take the sweeping staircase to the second floor, or would she prefer the elevator.

"Please call me Martha. You choose."

Sharonda surprises her, taking the staircase. George's housekeeper is a big woman, but she moves up the 42 steps with surprising speed. She arrives at the top without even breathing heavily.

"I'm going to drop twenty pounds if it kills me," she tells Martha Krumble.

The agent, a little out of breath, says: "What if it kills me?" They move through the bedrooms, look at beautifully-appointed, spacious marble bathrooms with floor-to-ceiling, seemingly invisible showers.

"How long have you been with Captain McKlane," Martha Krumble asks.

"A few years," she says. Martha is surprised. She thought it might have been much longer.

In what appears to be an entryway to the master bedroom, Sharonda opens the double doors of a huge walk-in closet. Martha stands in the doorway and says, "Wow."

Sharonda says: "The War Room."

This closet is George McKlane's museum, the size of a small bedroom in many homes. It includes two comfortable, long-backed leather chairs, a very ornate wooden desk, a large, rectangular safe, and a reading lamp. The room is completely enclosed, with no windows. It's a huge closet. Ambient light casts a warm glow over the entire area, emanating from the crown molding. A mahogany center island, topped with dark granite, is softly spotlighted by an electrical hi-hat in the recessed ceiling. A pyramid of four green socks are on it, nothing else.

George McKlane left the Marine Corps at the end of the Korean War, despite attempts to keep him in its ranks. He had seen enough killing, enough to fill a closet with rows of medals, battle ribbons, neatly pressed uniforms, battle flags, some of them from the enemy, and lots of commendations.

Framed letters line one of the walls, around 50 of them, each with different handwriting.

Some of them are typed, using real typewriters, not word-processed through a digital printer. Martha steps close and reads a few of them. They come from the mothers, fathers, wives, and children of men who served, and died, under Captain George McKlane. They are heartfelt thank you notes, celebrating military ghosts.

Most of them have official, wallet-sized Marine Corps photos in the bottom corner of the frame.

Martha Krumble points at the thick green military socks in the spotlight on the center island. "What does that mean?"

"He gave his men extra socks when they were fighting in North Korea. It saved a lot of them from frostbite," Sharonda says. "I don't ask him a lot of questions about this room. He doesn't talk about it."

She taps on the safe, which is six feet tall, four feet across, and three feet deep.

"This is full of guns," she says. "Machine guns, according to George. Hand grenades and stuff like that. There's something in there called a burp gun, but I don't think it makes people burp." Martha steps further into the closet. Other things catch her attention.

A detective's badge and ribbons from the Cleveland, Ohio police force in one area. A lot of African memorabilia, including a magnificent spear, in another. Martha has noticed a lot of very tasteful African statues and artwork during her tour of the home.

Martha sees a military watch on the floor, almost hidden behind the safe. She picks it up, reads an inscription on the back:

> **To Capt Socks from**
> **the men he saved and**
> **those he could not**

Martha crouches and puts the watch back where it was, although it appears to have gotten there by mistake. They step out of the closet, continue the tour. "We'll take the elevator down," Sharonda says. They do not smile at the irony of walking up and riding down. They have both become more solemn after visiting the War Room.

They walk through a picture-lined hallway that leads to an attached guest house. Two bedrooms, a small kitchen, a luxury bath. "There's an open loft upstairs," Sharonda says. "Got another bathroom. Want to see it?"

"No," Martha says. "I'm losing too much weight." They like each other. They walk across the driveway pavers to another attached structure, the garage.

"That BMW needs some love," Martha says. Dust covers it.

"He won't let anybody touch it," Sharonda says. "But he'll sell it to you for twenty thousand dollars." Martha does not quite understand, but she doesn't say anything. She wants to get down to business.

They move through the laundry room, the kitchen, the living room with its towering windows and Steinway piano, and finally back to the Birdroom.

George is reading a book, glasses perched on his nose. He looks up, closes the volume, stands as the women approach. Martha notices that George has not eaten any of the egg sandwiches on the silver tray. He says: "Thank you, Sharonda," and she starts to leave.

"You are a great guide," Martha Krumble says.

Martha looks at George McKlane, waits as Sharonda to move out of earshot, and says: "She'd make an outstanding real estate agent."

"I think she makes a lot more money as a Nurse Practitioner," George says. "I call her Doctor Sharonda."

They both sit, facing each other.

"How much?" George asks.

That's fast, Martha thinks. Georgen McKlane was probably an outstanding businessman.

"I think you should list your home at five and a half million dollars, and I think you will sell it for slightly less, perhaps two or three hundred thousand dollars less."

Martha pauses, detecting a slight nod from George. She continues: "You should not sell it for under five million dollars. That's unfurnished. If you want to sell paintings or furniture, do it separately. Don't pay a real estate commission on your belongings. And the Turner painting in your living room is probably worth more than your house."

George laughs. He likes Martha Krumble.

The doorbell rings. George stands up. Sharonda has returned to the kitchen, and she does not move to answer the door. "I'll walk you out," George says. "We'll talk more on the phone."

Martha Krumble feels suddenly rushed, pulls a Comparative Market Analysis out of her bag, and looks at it. George takes the CMA and carefully puts it on a chair.

"It's worth reading," she says.

"I know it will be."

Sharonda remains in the kitchen. The women smile at each other, flutter their hands, say goodbye. George and Martha walk towards the front door.

The doorbell rings again. When George opens it, Anthony Silberg smiles. He sees Martha Krumble. His smile flickers off, then back on.

"George," Anthony Silberg says, extending his hand. "My excellent neighbor."

George looks at Martha and says: "We'll talk more. Thank you for coming." He shakes her hand.

"Thank you for your time," Martha says as he lets go of her hand and reaches for Silberg's.

"Martha," Anthony Silberg says.

"Antonio," Martha Krumble says.

She sees his jaw tighten a little, then quickly relax. She knows he hates the name.

Martha moves past him and walks to her car, a brand new KIA. She gets in and waits for the front door to close to George's house.

Then she bangs her fist on the steering wheel before driving away.

Chapter 4

In The Company Of Marines

13752 Coconut Palm Ct., Boca Raton, FL: Friday

Anthony Silberg decides not to bring his newest agent, Barbara Rossellini, to the listing meeting. It will be Marine to Marine. He will return to his office with a signed agreement and then bring her into the deal to do all the hard work of selling George's home.

Silberg smiles as he drives to George's house, thinking about how he will guide Barbara carefully through the entire process. He will help her discover how to become a top producer at his brokerage. If all goes well, he might teach her the rewards of laundering money.

She will earn a huge commission, almost $100,000 after his company's split, twice that if she gets both sides of the deal, which he might give her.

That depends on her willingness to make personal sacrifices. She will have to show a vast amount of passion for succeeding at Accelerated Realty Sales. Silberg smiles.

A woman in a car next to him, at a stoplight, smiles at his vehicle, then glances away.

He pulls the steel-gray Maserati into George's driveway, next to another, much larger car. He wonders why McKlane would let one of his servants park an ordinary vehicle in plain view of all the neighbors: some sort of KIA, big, but still a KIA. Dumb name, Killed In Action.

He rings the doorbell and looks at his Maserati, sees himself driving it. He takes off his sunglasses and puts them in the breast pocket of his personally-tailored jacket. He waits. He begins to feel angry. He cannot stand servants who do not hustle to answer doorbells. He rings it again.

George opens the door himself. When Martha Krumble steps into view, Silberg feels stunned. He recovers quickly. "George," he says. "My excellent neighbor."

He does not lower his extended hand when George does not immediately shake it. The man is a Goy, burdened by Protestant or Catholic manners.

He fawns over Krumble, and then finally shakes Silberg's hand as she brushes past him. She calls him "Antonio" – a name she knows he hates – instead of "Anthony" or, even better, "Mister Silberg, sir."

The brief exchange at the front door changes how Silberg will take this listing. He's sorry that the Rossellini girl is not here to witness his ability to mold events into a completely different sales approach. Perhaps it will make for exciting pillow talk.

As McKlane walks him toward something called the Birdroom, Silberg thinks: This aging hero is shopping for real estate agents; he wants the best, and my company is it.

Silberg knows all about Martha Krumble. She's the top-selling associate broker at The Luxury Partnership, a small real estate boutique on A1A, virtually on the beach. Her company has a sizeable piece of the high-end luxury market, but it has sold very few homes at The Royal Coconut Yacht and Country Club. Silberg intends to keep it that way.

Silberg knows that Krumble does not like him. He tried to recruit her once, a few years earlier. She ended the meeting by calling him a cheap, lecherous crook. He had laughed at her and said that he was not "cheap" as she tried to storm out of his office.

He had locked the door without her knowing it, and he unlocked it standing next to her. He could feel her body heat. He expected her to slap him, but she did not.

Maybe she liked it.

Silberg knows how Krumble works, and he knows he can beat her in any listing competition. She's an honest real estate agent, always tells prospects the truth, trying to list their home at a realistic price. It's a very dumb approach.

Silberg tells homeowners what they want to hear, and they always think their home is worth more than how much for which they will eventually sell it.

Silberg's agency overprices listings, then uses the inflated numbers to sell their inventory that lingers on the market for a half a year, or a year, or longer. Accelerated Realty Sales, competitors joke, always runs out of gas.

Eventually, frustrated sellers slash their prices down to a bargain level. Accelerated Realty Sales agents lament the changing market forces that make price reductions necessary. They sell the bargain. But first, you need the listing. That requires exaggeration.

Anthony Silberg owns the largest, most successful brokerage in Boca Raton. The proof of his approach rests squarely on his company's bottom line.

When they sit down in the Birdroom, George asks Anthony: "Where did you serve?" Anthony almost asks, serve what? Then he realizes George is talking about his military service. He needs to focus.

"Vietnam," Anthony says. "I was a buck sergeant at Khe Sanh during the Tet Offensive, a grunt, infantry. I don't talk about it." The room fills with silence.

"No," George finally says. "We don't talk about it."

Silberg sighs, deeply. He leans forward and looks at George. He turns his voice into a harsh whisper. "I need to ask you something."

"Yes?"

Anthony searches for the right words. Finally, he asks: "Does it ever go away?"

George does not move. "Does what go away?"

"The pain."

George studies him and says, "What pain?"

Silberg leans back. He starts to tug at his silk shirt but stops as a servant puts a plate of miniature egg sandwiches on the table separating the two men.

"Thank you, Sharonda," George says. Silberg does not look at her. She disappears, and he pulls out his shirt, lifts it. An angry scar rips across the left side of Silberg's chest, going towards his right shoulder.

It's the result of a disagreement with a Black inmate at the medium-security Federal Correction Institution in Schuylkill, Pennsylvania, many years earlier.

George McKlane watches Anthony Silberg pulling out his shirt. He wants to tell the man to stop, starts to hold up his hands, and then he just stares at him, shaking his head slowly, saying nothing.

The surgeon that stitched up Anthony did a lousy job. Silberg remembers whiskey on the Doctor's breath. The prison physician did not wear a surgical mask. The reasonably shallow shanking wound became infected. The result looks much worse than the actual injury, but it still kept him out of the Warden's boxing matches for three months.

During his absence from the ring, Silberg lost some privileges. His first two comeback fights opened the wound and had the inmates chanting for more blood.

The Warden restored his privileges after he scored two substantial, but bloody knockouts.

The person who shanked Anthony fell over the second-floor railing of his cellblock, landing headfirst on concrete.

Silberg was in his cell when it happened, an innocent bystander peering through bars as the man dropped two stories into the common area.

Silberg did not see him hit the floor, hidden from view by the cellblock walkway, but he heard the commotion of an apparent suicide.

Anthony lowers his shirt, feigning embarrassment. The silk fabric slides back over the bulge of his belly, and he tucks it into his loosely-fitted, neatly-pressed, $350 Signature Gabardine Pleated dress pants.

George remains silent throughout the display.

"Shrapnel," Silberg says. "I think it probably saved my life because they evacuated me before the VC blew up our ammunition dump a second time." Over the years, Anthony Silberg has built an elaborate story around his chest wound.

George tightens his mouth, then relaxes. "It never goes away," he finally says.

Anthony leans forward and samples a few of the small egg sandwiches. "They're delicious," he says.

"Sharonda makes the best egg sandwiches in the world," George says. "She's going to show you around the house." The woman is standing behind Silberg. It surprises him. He wonders if she was standing there the whole time.

She's a big woman.

During a tour of the first floor, Silberg tells Sharonda he lives a few streets away, on a superior canal. He does not talk to her very much, strangely uneasy as she leads him through the house. They stop at the base of the stairway, next to a softly lit, five-foot-tall golden statue of the Tree of Life, a centerpiece in the stairway alcove.

Sharonda says: "It is a rare work of art from the southern highlands of Tanzania, from the land of my ancestors: the Nyakyusa tribe in the southern highlands."

Silberg looks at Sharonda and says: "I'm not a big fan of anything or anybody from Africa." She looks at him sharply, feeling insulted. He smiles at her, but not nicely.

She looks at Silberg and says: "The elevator doesn't always work." It works perfectly, but Sharonda is angry at the prejudice of the man. "We'll have to take the stairs to see the Master Bedroom and George's secret War Room."

He is about to tell her to forget it, but "secret" catches his interest. Silberg sighs. He weighs fifty-five pounds more than he did when he fought in the ring, the price of wealth and success.

Sharonda moves up the sweeping staircase quickly, and Silberg struggles behind her.

"You need to get the elevator fixed," he groans, out of breath, at the top.

"You need to get in shape," she replies, smiling.

"What did you say?" Silberg widens his eyes, surprised. He seems suddenly angry.

"I'm a Nurse Practitioner, Mister Silberg," she says. "A nurse with a Master's Degree."

Anthony does not know what to say, finally settling on: "What doctor do you work for?"

He tries to make the question sound as threatening as possible. He is surprisingly offended, Sharonda thinks.

"I'm on my own," she says. "Nurse Practitioners go through the same training as doctors. We go to medical school; we just don't have the residency requirement." She smiles, tries to lighten the moment. "Our insurance costs less," she says. The man does not smile.

"I apologize if I offended you, Mister Silberg," Sharonda continues. "Consider the walk up the staircase a personal stress test. You're seriously overweight, and you're going to face a lot of unnecessary medical problems if you don't do something about it."

Sharonda thinks she may have made a terrible decision, letting this obese white man get under her skin, and she hopes it will not affect George McKlane adversely. She moves to the closet and opens the double doors. The lighting turns on automatically. She apologizes again: "I'm sorry, Mr. Silberg."

She moves back, and Silberg stands in the doorway to George McKlanes War Room.

"Sorry for your bad manners or my early death?" he asks without looking at her. His neck, she notices, is bright red. He is an outraged person.

She considers saying both but instead answers: "My poor manners. Your African comment about the statue offended me, Mister Silberg. But I sincerely apologize for talking out of turn, sir."

"This is the secret room?" he asks.

"The War Room," Sharonda answers. She notices the redness disappear quickly from his neck.

Silberg moves into the room, looks at the letters on the wall without reading them, notices the commendations, sees the uniforms, including a blue one with Cleveland Police on the shoulder patches.

He did not know George was an ex-cop. Silberg looks at an ornate African spear. He flips some red feathers on it with his fingers.

"This yours?" he asks Sharonda.

"You're very funny, Mister Silberg," Sharonda says.

"You bet I am, Chanda."

"Sharonda," she says. She realizes he does not like people of color. She has no way of knowing that its foundation lies in America's prison system.

Silberg moves around the back of the dark granite island in the closet, looks down, and there it is. It's in a simple, clear plastic case, hung almost as an afterthought among the closet's furnishings. A shiny blue ribbon, thirteen stars on its centerpiece, the original American colonies, with a five-pointed bronze star hanging from a Navy anchor: the Medal of Honor.

Why in the world, Silberg wonders, would anyone hide something like this in the back of a closet?

If he had the medal, he'd wear it around his neck every day. It would be great for business.

He notices a watch on the floor, next to a giant safe. He bends down, picks it up, reads the inscription on the back to Captain Socks. He looks at the pyramid of green military socks spotlighted on the granite center island. Sharonda is looking at him. He puts the watch back where he found it, but he almost puts it in his pocket, probably would have if the woman hadn't been there.

Anthony Silberg has a long-standing history of taking things that do not belong to him.

He steps back out of the room and follows Sharonda through the bedrooms and baths on the second floor. They finally arrive back at the staircase.

"We can take the elevator down," Sharonda says, opening the tinted glass door and pulling back the collapsible metal hatching.

She steps into the spacious cab and holds the hatching open. Silberg steps in.

"I thought you said it wasn't working," he says.

"It'll work fine," she says. "Especially with all the extra weight." She smiles at him. He does not smile back.

On the ground floor, she starts to move toward the connecting hallway that leads to the guest house, but Silberg walks instead back towards the Birdroom. "Excuse me," Sharonda says.

Anthony Silberg stops, turns around, and stares at her. "I've seen enough, Chanda." He turns and continues back to the Birdroom. George is reading the extensive, 23-page Comparative Market Analysis that Martha Krumble has left with him.

He smiles at Anthony Silberg, puts down the CMA, and motions to a chair.

"I saw the Congressional Medal of Honor, sir," Silberg says. "Extraordinary, sir."

"Medal of Honor," George McKlane says.

Silberg does not understand McKlane's echo. "Yes, sir," he says, "that's what ..."

"It's called the Medal of Honor," George says. "Not the Congressional Medal of Honor."

Silberg says nothing.

"It goes through military bureaucrats, the chief of staff, service secretary, and the secretary of defense. Then the President of the United States approves it and hangs it around your neck.

Congress has nothing to do with it."

Silberg realizes he needs to be careful.

George looks at him, a fellow Marine. He smiles. "We don't talk about it," George says.

"Right, we don't talk about it," Anthony repeats, congratulating himself on the strategy of silence that surrounds his washed-out military history — a flash of genuine Silberg genius.

George says: "I was reading Martha's report." He leaves the sentence hanging.

Silberg says: "She's terrific, George. One of the best. I thought about hiring her myself a few years back."

"Why didn't you?"

Anthony Silberg pinches his mouth, looks down, measures his words. "She lowballs customers." He puts air between each word for emphasis.

"I don't understand what that means," George says.

"She tells people their home is worth less than it is. It makes it easier for her to sell.

At Accelerated Realty Sales, we set a higher price and work a lot harder for sellers."

It is the best excuse anyone has ever figured out for overpricing homes and getting away with it.

"How did you know she 'lowballed' customers before you hired her?" George asks. Silberg thinks: Pretty quick for an old guy.

"I had already hired some people from The Luxury Partnership before she asked for the job," Anthony says. "All of them contributed to my decision not to have Martha Krumble come aboard at Accelerated Realty Sales."

George thinks about it. Nods. It sounds like a valid Marine Corps answer.

"So, what do you think of our home?" He still says, "our" after almost a year.

"It's beautiful. George. It's a showcase. I wish my own looked as nice. If I had any brains, I would probably buy your home myself."

George says nothing, and his face shows nothing. He is not impressed by bullshit.

"What can you sell this house for?" George asks.

The speed with which George arrives at the edge of a listing agreement, or no listing at all surprises Silberg. This old hero, Silberg thinks, makes decisions, and he will probably stick by them.

Silberg also knows that George might brush him off, give his listing to a woman like Krumble. She's attractive. Anthony Silberg remembers brushing up against her and trying to fondle her during their only interview.

Silberg needs to give George an inflated price, and he needs to make George believe it's a certainty.

Silberg does not know what price Martha Krumble arrived at in her Comparative Market Analysis.

However, he does know what range a "normal" CMA would suggest. His office ran several versions for him a few hours earlier.

Silberg also knows that Krumble's office is having a hard time making ends meet right now. Some of Anthony's silent partners have even suggested a takeover. However, that is not immediately likely because his partners prefer buying floundering, broken remnants, and not enterprises that still make money.

Silberg knows that the managing broker at The Luxury Partnership has started to inflate prices, the only proven way to get more listings.

All of this passes through Silberg's mind in a matter of seconds, a fast-forward movie, as he leans back and stares at George, looking him directly in the eyes.

"I think Martha suggested that you list your home for around five million seven hundred and fifty thousand dollars," Anthony says. He knows that it was probably less, but his suggestion substantiates her reputation as a lowballing real estate agent.

George McKlane shows nothing. Anthony leans forward, studies the tiles on the floor of the Birdroom. He looks up.

"George," he says, "I have a buyer for your home who I believe will pay six million dollars."

Nothing.

"He's flying in tonight from Brazil. I don't know if you speak Portuguese, but ...."

"I do not," George says.

"I can show him this home tomorrow, or the next day, whenever it's convenient. This guy speaks almost no English, but his money is real. And it's clean. He's a businessman. And I think he's going to love your Brazilian hardwood floors."

George smiles and asks: "How do you know him?"

"I know a lot of people, George. It's my business."

George says nothing.

"We don't talk about it," Anthony says.

George smiles. Anthony Silberg decides, once again, that Anthony Silberg is a genius.

They spend fifteen minutes eating Sharonda's egg sandwiches and reviewing the listing agreement, which George says he will sign, but not yet. He tells Silberg he has to run it past his lawyer, and Silberg agrees that this is a good idea. It's a simple FAR/BAR contract, approved by the Florida Association of Realtors and the Florida Bar. No gimmicks. No tricks. It should be no problem.

Before leaving, Silberg stands up and snaps a Marine Corps salute at the winner of the Medal of Honor.

George waves it off, a little embarrassed.

Chapter 5

The Breakfast Club

13752 Coconut Palm Ct.
Boca Raton, FL: Saturday

George McKlane hosts a small breakfast every Saturday at ten o'clock. They gather at his home, usually under a lanai near the pool, occasionally in The Birdroom. It depends on the weather, and the same people typically attend if they can.

This Saturday, five settings, with silverware on colorful table mats, are evenly spaced on the heavy wrought-iron and glass table under the lanai.

George sits at the head of the table.

Doctor Gunther Klein and his wife, Rachel, sit opposite one another at the far end.

Judge Ralph Broadslate sits to the left of George. The seat on George's right remains empty.

Sharonda Nelson rolls out an extensive service trolley from the entry to the pantry on the far side of the blue pool.

The trolley moves smoothly and quickly across the patio. It contains four-minute eggs in small egg-holders, bacon, sausage, toast under linen napkins, cereals in plastic containers, orange juice, grapefruit juice, muffins, jam, fresh bagels, and pastry.

Everyone is smiling as Sharonda approaches with the cart. She positions the trolley at the bottom of the table. Chairs scrape backward, and the guests surround the trolley, filling their plates, except for George. Sharonda knows that he's just going to eat the pastry, so she fills a plate and brings it to him.

"Really," Rachel says. "He took his shirt off? I've seen Silberg at Temple on Friday nights. That could not possibly be a pretty sight."

"A walrus," George says. "Maybe a beached whale."

"You know," Doctor Gunther Klein says, "It's not true that real estate agents emerged, full-grown and covered with slime, from under rocks in swampy areas." They wait. They know a punch line will come. "They come out of dark caves in mountainous regions, dragging nail-studded clubs along the ground behind them."

They become serious when George says: "It was a pretty ugly shrapnel wound."

He marks on his chest where it went, tracing his finger from the bottom of his ribs up to the right shoulder. "It happened in Vietnam during the Tet Offensive."

"Great MASH units in Vietnam," Doctor Gunther Klein says. He was an Army Surgeon during the Korean War, but he never knew George in those days. "You know, he probably would have lost a limb in our war, George."

"Probably," George admits. "Although they did a good job on me."

George suffered four bullets wounds and a bayonet strike down his back. He almost bled out. "Thank God I didn't have an Army Surgeon working on me." He smiles, and Doctor Gunther Klein does as well.

Sharonda puts two eggs and some toast on a plate and walks behind George.

She puts the plate down on the fifth setting and takes her place at the table.

"I don't think Mister Anthony Silberg likes black people," she tells the gathering.

"Why do you say that?" Judge Broadslate asks.

"Just a feeling I get," she says. "We know when you white people don't like us."

They smile. The entire group likes Sharonda.

"Well, he's going to have to learn to like you," George says, "because he's getting the listing, and you're going to keep an eye on him for me."

"Yes, sir, George. Eyes on the walrus."

They all laugh.

"Ralph?" George asks.

The retired judge has been skimming through the Listing Agreement and sees nothing wrong with it.

"But you might ask him to cut the listing to six months instead of a year. If he doesn't sell it in six months, then give your listing to my friend, Martha."

"I liked her," George says. "But her company hasn't sold anything in the Club this year. Not one single home. Silberg says he already has a buyer for more than Martha Krumble was willing to list it."

"That's a no-brainer," Rachel Klein says.

Doctor Jokester almost quips, "You should know," but he holds his tongue.

He winks at her instead, and she smiles back, wondering what he's planning now.

The Saturday Breakfast Club breaks up around eleven-thirty. Doctor Klein asks Judge Broadslate to give his wife, Rachel, a ride back home.

"I have to talk to George about a private medical matter," he explains.

They leave, and Sharonda starts to clear the table. Doctor Klein holds up his hand. She stops and looks at him. "Sit down, Sharonda."

"Doctor," she says, sitting back in her seat to the right of Captain George McKlane. Doctor Klein moves to the chair on the left of George.

"Medical profession going to gang up on me?" George asks. "You know, this won't be the first time people surround me, and I escape."

"How do you feel, George?" the retired neurosurgeon asks his old friend.

George looks at him, breathes deeply, says: "I'm tired. I'm always tired."

"I watched you eat five Danish pastries for breakfast," the Doctor says. "If I ate like that, Rachel would probably kill me before the sugar did."

George looks at his Nurse Practitioner and says: "They were exceptional, Sharonda."

"Yeah, well, I want you to eat another one, George," Doctor Gunther Klein says.

"You're my kind of Doctor, Jokester." He eats the pastry in five bites. Then they talk about nothing for a few minutes. George smiles at them, enjoying the game.

"Have another," Doctor Klein says. He is not smiling.

George takes one bite. The rest of it falls into his lap.

"I'll get my bag," Sharonda says. She scrapes back her chair to run for it.

"No STAT," Doctor Klein says. "Get it. But he'll be fine. He's got the heart of an Ox. And Sharonda, please bring me his latest blood work as well."

"Yes, Doctor," Sharonda says.

"Bring the last four or five of them." She starts to leave. "And his list of medications, too." George is back in Korea.

"On it," says the Nurse Practitioner.

The Battle of Northwest Ridge, November 29, 1950

The Marines hold most of the high ground around Yudam-ni and Hagaru. They identify the snow-covered, jagged terrain in meters. Hill 1276, Hill 1426, Hill 1294, Hill 1240, Hill 1282, Hill 1403 – all bristle with Marines and their weapons of war. They have no tanks, but roughly four hundred Marines possess three-fourths of the firepower available to the 1st and 4th Battalions: howitzers, mortars, recoilless rifles.

They are all slowly freezing to death, not just the men, but also their weapons.

"Sergeant," Captain McKlane says, "tell them to test-fire the BARs. Twenty-minute, rotating intervals. We have to make sure they don't freeze up."

"The supply dumps are pretty low, Socks."

"I know. Short bursts. I don't want to see more than one tracer round when they do it."

Staff Sergeant Chapman passes the word.

"How about illumination shells," Captain McKlane asks. "Can we light China up when they attack?"

"No, sir. We're out of stars. Trucks never got through. No airdrops after dark. We're blind."

Sporadic gunfire echoes across the ridges every twenty minutes as rotating squad leaders test-fire the Browning Automatic Rifles in their platoons, keeping them ready.

As soon as a tracer round streaks through the air, the gun falls silent. They don't test fire their M-1 rifles. They simply oil them more than usual.

The M-1 remains the Marine's most reliable weapon. The Corps has a long-standing legend. If your M-1 fails, just slap it hard a couple of times against a tree or a boulder. Then it will work correctly.

While the Marines curse the cold, the hills around them begin to swarm with thousands of Chinese troops.

Disguised in darkness, endless columns of quilted green parkas move through the valleys and over the mountain trails leading towards Northwest Ridge.

Red China's Ninth Army Group, led by Sung Shin-lun, one of the CCF's best field commanders, has only one objective: obliterate the 1st Marine Division, at whatever cost becomes necessary.

Although the Marines do not know it, the odds are over 13 to one against them. Just under 14,000 Red Chinese regulars are about to launch an attack against 1,152 Marines.

Three Chinese divisions will try to swallow two Marine Corps regiments.

"How many do I need to kill?" a squad member asks his platoon leader as the sun falls behind Sakkat Mountain. In the valley below, Yudam-ni turns pitch black.

"You'll know when you run out of bullets," Captain McKlane says, coming up behind them.

The captain tosses thick, green socks to both men, moving down the line.

Frozen moisture encrusts everyone's parka hoods. Even with extra socks, their cumbersome shoepacs fill with sweat; their feet turn into lumps of frozen pain.

The Red Chinese have numbers, mobility, and the element of surprise on their side.

They have learned to hide during the day, avoiding UN spotter planes as well as the inevitable death of Marine Corps air support. When they hear the roar of the Corsairs, they scatter quickly into hiding places. Most of them survive.

The CCF moves at night. They do not suffer the burden of heavy equipment that the retreating columns of Marines drag towards the port of Hungnam.

A few hours before midnight, Northwest Ridge crawls with Chinese only a few hundred yards from the Marines. The CCF pad softly in rubber sneakers, giving no hint of their presence. The Chinese commander sends false signals with diversionary attacks on roadblocks on either side of Northwest Ridge. It lets infiltrators, heavily ladened with grenades and Shpagin burp guns, sneak between two companies of Marines.

"Time to test the BAR," one Marine whispers to his foxhole mate. Metal clicks.

The young Marine's frozen finger aches on the trigger, even wearing thick gloves. He pulls the trigger — the tracer round from the BAR slams into a green Chinese parka. The enemy looms up five yards in front of the Marine. The CCN tries but fails to throw a hand grenade.

The BAR chatter becomes constant as Chinese Bugles blare. Up and down the line, machines guns open up.

M-1s puncture the high-pitched sounds of the Soviet Shpagin submachine guns used by the Chinese.

A mortar bombardment from the CCF pounds the perimeter of the Marines' front line.

The first Chinese assault waves wash against the outer perimeter, breaking through the line.

Captain McKlane sends a light machine-gun section and a squad from his 3rd Platoon to reinforce another Platoon where the break occurs.

Staff Sergeant Chapman lays down mortar barrages on the center of the breach.

"Set that hut on fire," Captain McKlane shouts to his machine gunners. They send a steady flow of tracer rounds into a native hut, which finally starts to burn.

The illumination exposes the CCF troops in a narrow corridor, trapped, and it turns into a turkey shoot that ends just after midnight with the complete annihilation of the enemy's main force.

As the fighting dies down in his sector, Captain McKlane watches it erupt in other areas all down the breadth of Northwest Ridge.

The assault by the 89th CCF Division partially succeeds.

The Marines on Hill 1403 face a brutal frontal assault as well as attacks on both flanks, but initially, they hold.

Two hours of ruthless fighting, much of it face-to-face combat, turns into two hours of almost total silence.

The Marines withdraw quietly from an untenable position, and the CCF troops occupy Hill 1403.

When the sun rises, it will give them a bird's eye view of almost two thousand Marines dug in below, waiting to be slaughtered by the Chinese.

13752 Coconut Palm Ct.,
Boca Raton Saturday AM

"Command gave away the heights, for no reason," Captain George McKlane says to Doctor Gunther Klein. He looks over at Sharonda, then back to the retired neurosurgeon, trying to place them in his mind. "Oh," he says.

"What heights are you talking about, George?" Doctor Gunther Klein asks.

"Korea, Hill fourteen-oh-three, nothing," he says, shaking his head back to the present. "I seem to daydream a lot since I had that hernia operation."

"George," the Doctor says, "We're going to get you back in shape. We're going to figure out how to improve your body, and your memory, too."

"I'm not sure that I want to improve my memory," George says.

Doctor Klein smiles, and he understands. They've been friends for a long time, with Korea still touching their lives.

"When you wake up in the morning, you're going to feel like you're in your mid-eighties, " the Doctor says. "By lunchtime, you'll feel like sixty-five." George can feel another joke coming. "By dinner, forty-five. And by bedtime ...."

"If you tell me I'm going to feel like a teenager, I'm going to ask you to leave my house," George says, beating him to the punch line. Sharonda laughs.

Doctor Klein shuffles through the medical reports Sharonda has given him. "Your blood work looks better than I thought it would. You don't have any anemia. Your lymph, uh, your red and white blood cell counts are okay. You have a slightly higher count of white cells, so you may have a little infection wandering around your body. Just about everyone our age does. But overall, everything looks okay."

"Okay," George repeats.

"Only every time you raise your blood sugar levels, your brain takes a vacation," Doctor Klein adds.

"I wouldn't call it a vacation, Gunther. Tell me, why does it happen?"

"You're stuffing too many sweet things in your mouth, too much sugar. You do not have diabetes, at least not yet. But that's not the cause. That's just a symptom. I think Sharonda found the cause." He looks down at one of the sheets she has shown him, the one with medications on it. She has circled one of them.

"How long have you been dropping off like this?"

"Since the hernia operation," George says. "But usually at night. Then I just go to sleep. And I wake up a lot. It doesn't usually happen during the day, but it's happened more in the last few days. Twice yesterday. I wake up a lot at night. It makes me tired all the time during the day."

George remembers something.

"I stopped my car at a light coming off the Glades exit on the Interstate three days ago, and all of a sudden, everyone is honking at me. I fell sound asleep, foot on the brake. Don't know what would have happened if the horn-honking hadn't woken me."

George looks at Sharonda and Doctor Klein. He watches them nod at one other.

"I don't for the life of me know why a doctor would put you on a steroid like Prednisone because of a hernia operation," Doctor Klein says. "And it's a huge dose. Eighty milligrams. Do you have kidney problems, George?"

"Not that I know of."

"His creatinine level is normal," Sharonda says, shuffling pages. "And so is his BUN."

"Watch your mouth," George says.

Sharonda laughs. "It's an acronym for Blood Urea Nitrogen, George."

Doctor Klein says: "George, you're coming off the Prednisone. It's hurting, not helping."

"I'll stop taking it today."

"No, you won't," Doctor Klein says. "You're going to wean yourself off of it, lowering the dose ten milligrams every couple of days for starters, then five, then two and a half. Then none. If you stop taking it all at once, at your age, you'll probably drop dead. It's going to take a month. Sharonda will make sure you do it right."

George looks at Sharonda and says: "Well, I guess that makes you the doctor."

"No," she says. "Doctor Klein is the MD. I'm the NP."

"And I'm the patient," George says. "So, my cognitive powers are getting better already."

He smiles. He feels silly.

"Dietician," Sharonda says.

"Yes, George, you're going to hire a dietician, and I just happen to know a great one."

"I'll bet you do," George says.

"She was a dietician for over fifty years." They are talking about Rachel Klein, the Doctor's wife. She will plan all of George's meals. They get up from the table. "You're going knock the salt out of your diet, and cut down on sugar," Doctor Klein says.

"I'm still drinking my Guinness."

"I would never dream of taking Guinness away from an Irishman, George."

"That's why you've lived so long," George says.

He feels an unexpected spark of life he has not felt for some time, and he likes it. "This may be the best Saturday breakfast we've had."

Ten minutes later, he goes into his office and phones Anthony Silberg.

He thinks he recognizes the voice of the operator he spoke to the day before.

She puts him through right away.

"Good morning, George," Silberg answers.

"Semper Fi, Anthony. I have signed the listing. I've initialed an amendment that makes it's duration six months rather than a year." He pauses. "I have also put a strike through the one hundred and eighty-day post-listing clause. I have done all of this on the advice of my attorney."

"George," Silberg says, "I have to spend a lot of money marketing your home, and ...."

"You said you had a six million dollar buyer," George says. "It doesn't sound like you're going to have any marketing expenses at all."

Silberg smiles. George does not know how to act his age; he talks 30 years younger than he is.

"I agree," Silberg says, not entirely giving up. "I would like to show him your home tomorrow morning if that's convenient. But he has to decide to buy it. If he does not, then I must immediately spend a great deal of money on marketing: brochures, social media, YouTube, Facebook, Twitter, Pinterest, a dedicated website, newspaper and magazine advertising, direct mail ...."

"I'm certain you will earn a substantial commission within six months," George says.

Silberg smiles at the quickness of George McKlane. "I am going to give in to you on this one because I think you're right," he says. "I'd like to send someone over later today to get the signed agreement. She'll be handling the day-to-day work on your sale. Of course, I will show your home to buyers, and so will she. Her name is Barbara Rossellini."

"Fine," George says. "If I'm not here, have her speak to Sharonda, who speaks for me."

Silberg raises his eyebrows at the apparent power of Sharonda. He should not have called her Chanda or made the "spear" joke.

Rossellini will smooth that over for him.

"When do you want to show the home to your Brazilian buyer?" George asks.

"I was thinking about tomorrow at 10:30. Would that work all right?"

They agree and hang up.

Silberg steps out of his office and looks at his executive secretary. "Get Rossellini up here. Now."

He steps back into his office, goes to his private bathroom, brushes his teeth, puts on some aftershave, and unbuttons his shirt one more notch.

Opening his shirt makes his scar slightly visible. When he steps out of the bathroom, Barbara Rossellini is standing at the door. She's a little older than Silberg thought, but she's a very nice looking person.

"You wanted to see me, Mr. Silberg?"

"Come in, shut the door, have a seat," Anthony says. He watches her walk to one of the chairs in front of his desk, sit down, and slowly cross her legs. Anthony Silberg walks over to the door and locks it. He does not try to conceal the move. She arches her eyebrows at him, but with a slight smile on her face. He's not sure what it means.

George phones Martha Krumble, where she works. He tells her how much he enjoyed meeting her and how highly former Judge Ralph Broadslate recommends her.

"But I have decided to list with Accelerated Realty Sales," he tells her.

"Of course you have," Martha says.

George feels he has to explain his decision further. He likes Martha Krumble. The flat, lifeless sound of her voice surprises him.

"Anthony Silberg already has a buyer for the home at six million dollars."

"Of course he does," Martha says. Same dead voice.

"Well, thank you," George says. He starts to hang up but hears her say something, catching the end of it as he brings the phone back to his ear.

"... and I will certainly show your wonderful home, especially if Mister Silberg's buyer turns into a ghost. I very much enjoyed meeting you, Captain George McKlane."

That's the voice he remembers.

"And I liked meeting you, Martha Krumble. I'm sure we'll meet again." He hangs up the phone and stares at it.

He almost calls her back because of her "ghost" comment but decides not to.

Chapter 6
The History Of Barbara Rossellini

Barbara Rossellini needs to start a new life. Born in the late 1970s, her father is an older man of 67 when she draws her first breath. She never connects with her father. Too many generations and events separate their lives.

Her mother walks out of her father's life a little over five years after Barbara enters it. Her mother leaves Barbara behind with her father.

Barbara turns into a difficult child, a rough teenager, and an uncontrolled young adult. She marries four times, first to a drummer in a band that never makes it out of the lead singer's basement. Her second husband works as an electrical engineer on oil rigs. He goes to Alaska and writes her a letter saying he will never return. The divorce is uncontested. He sends her alimony payments for about a year, with the final one postmarked from the Arabian Peninsula.

Her third husband is pretty nice, very handsome, a funny drunk who never gets violent, just kinky. He teaches her things about sex that she never knew. She's a quick and willing learner. Her husband dies in a terrible car wreck, and her best friend dies in the same wreck. Analyzing the almost total lack of tire marks left at the scene, the accident investigator estimates they were having sex at around seventy miles an hour when they hit a well-cemented support rail on a metal bridge over an almost dry river.

Her third husband has a $250,000 life insurance policy. The insurance company tries to get out of paying it by calling her husband's death a suicide. She finally gets a tax-free check from her lawyer for a hundred and eighty-five thousand dollars, a year and a half after the deadly accident.

She threatens to sue her lawyer for excessive and largely unsubstantiated legal charges. He puts another twenty thousand dollars into her settlement after four months of wrangling, much relieved to see her name disappear from his list of clients.

That money is half gone when she meets Roberto Rossellini, a good-looking barfly at the watering hole where she works as a bartender.

They get married on the weekend during a two-day trip to Las Vegas. Within three months, Barbara realizes that Roberto has neither the ability nor the ambition to follow in the footsteps of his wealthy father, Angelo Rossellini. The father is a developer of condo conversions in the Palm Beaches and hi-rise condos in Miami.

Angelo Rossellini washes a lot of mob money through the construction lines-of-credit that he gets and then pays back to different banks.

He does this mostly on commercial property and large plots of raw land. He also occasionally builds ghost houses that only exist on paper. He has a few bought-and-paid-for inspectors who approve the final construction of his imaginary projects.

Barbara Rossellini does not know of any of this.

Her marriage to Roberto Rossellini ends in a civil annulment after six months.

Technically, Barbara marries only three times.

"But it feels like four," she tells friends, who sometimes smile at the way she says it.

She decides to become a real estate agent, but she has no high school diploma. She gets her GED online in less than three weeks. She enrolls at the Platinum Realty Institute in Boca Raton to get her sales license.

The real estate school's classroom is on the second floor of an aging building off Camino Real. On her first day, hopeful, largely-unemployed faces wait for a real estate instructor to show up.

Most of the students are women. Real estate is one of the few industries in America, where they have real equality and power. They earn it, deserve it, and prove their value with every sale that they make.

In the classroom, Barbara sits next to a man much younger than her.

She whispers: "How much money do you think you'll earn in the first year?" Because she has a slight cold, her voice cracks in the middle of the question. She sounds nervous. The young man thinks she might have the bitterness of foreclosure in her throat, or maybe a recent divorce.

"I'm going for triple digits," he answers, dropping his voice deeper than necessary.

His parents taught him that a deep voice was a sign of confidence, along with a bone-crushing handshake. "I think $150,000 would be a good start."

"I like it," she says.

She thinks about Roberto Rossellini, her fourth attempt at marital bliss, who gave up looking for honest work after finally landing a permanent position in front of a 72-inch, flat-screen TV.

"Time to start a new life," she says.

"You bet," the young man says.

The classroom goes quiet as a real estate instructor walks through a side door.

The teacher turns his back to the class.

Suddenly he throws his arms against the black, slate chalkboard covering most of the front wall. He flutters his hands in a series of spastic, bug-like moves. Mouths drop in every corner of the room.

A few students hover on the edge of their seats, focused on the red "EXIT" signs. The instructor turns to the class, smiles, suddenly calm. He's middle-aged, a little overweight, but seemingly sane. He's not carrying a gun.

"That's the butterfly of greed as the financial expectations of new real estate agents consume it," he says. He has taught this class for over a decade, and for the last four years, he has always started it the same way. "Reality has a price tag."

Fingers start to tap this phrase into portable notepads and tablets.

"Stop writing," the instructor says. "Start listening."

Fingers freeze.

"Most real estate agents earn between $25,000 and forty$45,000 a year in commissions," he says.

Barbara glances at Mr. Triple Digit, whose face has lost some of its summer tanning.

"They sell between four and six homes a year. After splits with their brokers, after taxes, overheads and expenses, they might net as little as $18,000." The instructor pauses. "It's usually less in the first year or two."

The classroom is quiet. The instructor smiles and raises his eyebrows. "But, hey, you get to be your very own boss."

Some people laugh. Most don't.

Rossellini's class has thirty-seven students. A few, like Mr. Triple Digit, will drop out during the two months, three-times-a-week course. Students study real estate practice, from brokerage relationships to fair housing, escrow accounts, finance, and property inspections.

They study real estate law on both the state and federal level, from listings to contracts to closings. Thirty-one of the thirty-seven original students take the Florida State exam. Twenty-nine pass it on their first try.

Barbara Rossellini gets exceptionally high marks in the classroom and on the state test. She joins Accelerated Realty Sales, the largest broker in Boca Raton.

She gets a listing on a home from a friend on her first day at work. She gets a contract on the house three days later. When it closes, she'll make a net commission of just under eight thousand dollars. If I can do this once a month, she thinks, I'll make $96,000 in my first year.

At her initial weekly office meeting, the manager, Bill Brownstone, introduces her by joking: "Meet Barbara, folks. She has already sold her entire inventory! Yes, yes."

Behind his back, the agents at Accelerated Realty Sales call him Tony Silberg's "Ultimate Yes Man" because of his stuttered "Yes."

Bill Brownstone breaks into applause but stops quickly when only a few of the other agents participate. Barbara feels, and immediately understands, the resentment from overly-competitive colleagues towards a quick sale by a "newbie" in her mid-thirties.

Brownstone tells her, after the meeting: "People joke that the Real Estate Industry eats its young, but it's not a joke. It's true. Yes, yes."

"I'm not young," Barbara says. She moves closer to him. "I am very experienced."

The manager is a college-educated, former real estate agent who prefers working for a salary rather than a commission. His wife believes strongly in financial stability.

The manager says to Barbara: "Scientists who have studied cannibalism suggest that many of nature's filial dieters commit the act, not for nutritional purposes, but because it exerts an evolutionary pressure on the species: the ultimate survival of the fittest."

Barbara hooks a finger in his shirt, pulling him closer: "I want you to assign me to the front desk," she says. After just a week, she knows where the power lies.

If you work at the front desk, you can answer the phones, direct floor traffic, and you can grab occasional walk-ins off the street who are looking for a new home. Bill Brownstone, a bit flustered by her closeness, says he'll see what he can do. Barbara tickles his chest with her finger.

"If you don't get me desk time," Barbara Rossellini says, "I'm going to eat you alive."

She winks at him and smiles.

The next day, she gets desk time.

The second call on her first shift comes from George McKlane, whom she finally puts through to the executive secretary of Anthony Silberg, who owns the brokerage.

She has never met the big boss until now.

After Anthony Silberg locks his door, he looks at Barbara. Perhaps her arched eyebrows and slight smile are a good sign.

He returns to his high back leather chair behind the desk and swivels it slowly back and forth. With each turn, he says Barbara's last name, thoughtfully.

"Rossellini. Rossellini. Rossellini."

Barbara slowly raises her hand, smiles, and says: "I'm right here, Mister Silberg."

"Tony," he says.

"Tony."

Silberg thinks it sounds nice coming out of her tight, thin-lipped little mouth.

Silberg leans forward and looks at her. "Are you related to Angelo Rossellini?" he asks.

"No, sir."

Technically, she's telling the truth.

She married his lazy, worthless son for a few months, but she is not a blood relative.

She wants to see where this is going before she makes any connection to the Rossellini family. Barbara understands the control of not revealing too much. She understands the power of secrets.

"You know who Angelo Rossellini is?"

"Yes, sir. Big condo developer. He built the Rhondo Homes community up on the border of Boca-Delray. That's where I live."

"Really?"

"Really."

"But, you're not related to him?"

"No, sir. If I were related to Angelo Rossellini, I wouldn't be living in a crummy place like Rhondo Homes, would I?"

Anthony Silberg smiles. "No, I guess you wouldn't."

Barbara sits in her chair, and she fidgets with her hands. It's an act. She wants to appear nervous, but not much has ever scared her in her life, except maybe her father. He always frightened her, although Gunnery Sergeant Raymond Chapman never abused her.

The man behind the desk, the owner of Accelerated Realty Sales, certainly does not frighten her. To Barbara, Tony Silberg has opportunity written all over his chubby body.

And he's not bad looking.

"You probably won't have to stay in a Rhondo condo much longer, Barbara."

"Why's that?" she asks.

"Because I'm about to give you a six million dollar listing at The Royal Coconut Yacht and Country Club," he says. "I'm putting you on a 50/50 split, so your commission, if you do both sides of the deal, will be around $216,000, half that if you only get the sell-side."

Barbara feels her heart pumping.

She feels the heat of excitement rushing into her face.

She's pretty sure she understands the rules of getting ahead at Accelerated Realty Sales.

She immediately understands the opportunity of Silberg locking his office door.

"Your face is very red," Anthony says, smiling.

"And my nipples are as hard as rocks," she says.

For a second, Anthony doesn't think he hears her correctly. Barbara holds up her hand and puts about an inch between her thumb and forefinger. "My hard rock nipples extend about this much when I have sex." Suddenly, Anthony Silberg can hear his heart beating in his ears. He feels what she says in his groin. "But I have small breasts," she says.

Anthony says nothing. "Everything about me is small and tight. Very tight."

Her third husband gave her lessons in suggestive conversations. He liked it when she talked that way.

"I don't believe this," Anthony says.

"Believe," Barbara says, smiling. "Just one thing. We're not going to have sex here, not in your office."

Her third husband taught her how to make a man beg a little. She learned her lessons well.

"Now. Here," Anthony says. He's breathing heavily. He starts to rise from the leather chair.

She can see he's excited.

Rossellini holds out the palm of her hand. "I want you to come to my condo Sunday night."

"Not here? Not in the office?" Silberg asks. He's feeling his high blood pressure.

He hears his heart in his ears.

He falls back into his leather chair.

"We'll need more recreational space," Barbara says. "And I love my hard bed. I like hard things." She smiles.

Silberg watches Barbara stand up slowly. She comes around his desk. "Let me give you a preview," Barbara says. She unbuckles his expensive alligator belt, deftly shifts his boxer shorts. "Oh, my goodness.," she says.

Anthony Silberg is quite a bit larger than any of her former husbands. The thought interests her.

"Lean back, close your eyes, think about tomorrow night, Tony." Silberg does not know what she does or how she does it. She never removes any of her clothes. Her hands press hard between his legs. Silberg arches his back, feels his lower abdomen tighten. It all happens in a matter of seconds.

He shudders, then slumps into the leather chair with a grunt, feeling a little embarrassed.

Barbara smiles sweetly at him and sways across his office, into his bathroom.

He hears water running. Barbara returns with a warm washcloth and cleans him up, then daintily drops the rag into a fancy mahogany wastepaper basket.

She sits back down in the chair in front of his desk.

"You're amazing," Anthony Silberg says. "I mean, that was really, truly amazing."

"Thank you very much, Tony. Now let's talk about this six million dollar listing."

13752 Coconut Palm Ct., Boca Raton: Saturday PM

Sharonda answers the door. "You must be Barbara," she says to the smiling, small woman on the doorstep.

Barbara Rossellini hands Sharonda an invitation-sized envelope, a handwritten note from Anthony Silberg. In the letter, Anthony apologizes to Sharonda, for his bad behavior and hopes that they can all work well together.

"That's very nice of him," Sharonda says. "Tell him we'll start over. Let me show you the house."

After three-quarters of an hour, they end up in George's office. The listing agreement is on the desk.

Sharonda picks it up and watches Barbara move down the photo wall, looking at famous people with whom George and Agnes McKlane spent time.

"They knew the President?" she asks.

"Three of them," Sharonda says.

George played golf with someone named Bobby Jones at a course in Erie, Pennsylvania, at a place called the Chautauqua Club.

George and Agnes stand with crossed golf clubs on the first hole of The Homestead in Hot Springs, Virginia, with a famous golfer named Sam Snead.

"They were a lovely couple," Barbara says.

"In every possible way," Sharonda says.

A portion of the walls has military photos. George knew a lot of generals and full-bird colonels, although he was only a captain.

"He looks like a movie star," Barbara says. "He looks outstanding in a uniform."

Sharonda smiles. "Yes, he does."

Barbara stops at a photo at the end of the military section. She leans close to it, steps back.

She draws, as silently as possible, an intense breath.

Sharonda walks over to her with the listing agreement, gives it to her, looks at the photo.

"Captain George and a sergeant who I know had a lot of stripes and hash marks when he got cleaned up," Sharonda says. "I think he and George went through Korea together.

The picture shows the two men in full combat gear, dirty, standing in mud and snow.

George holds a machine gun. The staff sergeant has a heavy Browning Automatic Rifle slung over his shoulders like a cross. His hands hang over the weapon's handle stock on one side, and the barrel on the other. Neither man smiles, nor do they look brave. They look exhausted.

"Can't recall the sergeant's name," Sharonda says.

Barbara says nothing. She knows the power of secrets. She knows their strength can vanish, once revealed.

A slight cough draws their attention to the double-door entry to the office. George McKlane stands there, looking at Barbara Rossellini.

"George," Sharonda says, "This is Barbara Rossellini. She's helping Mister Silberg sell your home."

"You look familiar," George says. Something about the eyes, the sharp nose, the solid chin line.

Barbara moves to where he is standing. She shakes his hand, and he does not let it go. Barbara does not try to withdraw. She is a tiny woman, almost a foot and a half shorter than him, with a tight smile.

"I don't believe we've ever met, sir. But I certainly look forward to working with you, Mister McKlane."

"Yes, of course," he says. "Good. Will you be here for the showing to the Brazilian buyer tomorrow?"

Barbara Rossellini does not know about a meeting with a buyer the following day.

"If Mister Silberg asks, of course, I will be here, Mister McKlane," she says.

George walks over to the photo of himself and Staff Sergeant Raymond Chapman, which he saw the two women examining earlier. He touches the frame.

"He saved my life. He would never admit it."

He looks back at the women. "Gunnery Sergeant Raymond Garfield Chapman. He was a Staff Sergeant, and we fought together in Korea."

Barbara Rossellini says nothing, shows nothing.

Much later, after Sharonda leaves for the day, George McKlane takes his prepared meal up to his bedroom on a silver tray and sets it on a small table in a nook overlooking the pool. He can look down the canal and see the sun slowly dropping behind the horizon, flattening out at the edges, turning red on another cloudless Florida evening.

"I'll miss this view when I sell our home, Missus McKlane," he says to a gold-framed oil painting on the wall.

It is a beautiful portrait of his wife when she is in her early Forties. George McKlane raised his glass of Guinness, first to the setting sun, then to the picture of Agnes. He smiles at Agnes, pops two small white Prednisone tablets in his mouth, and drains the glass. He stands up, goes over, and gets into bed. He picks up the selection device for a 48-inch flat-screen television that slowly rises out of a recessed slot at the foot of the king-sized bed.

"What should we watch tonight, Missus McKlane?" he asks. The television channel selector falls on the bedspread before the TV can answer the question. He's back in Korea

Hell Fire Valley, November 30, 1950

The Marines are on the move along a war-torn road running parallel to the Changjin River. A frozen, tree-lined creek meanders through a plain a few hundred yards wide, with rolling

wooded hills on the left side of the road and jagged peaks on the right. Captain George McKlane and his men are part of a massive convoy of tanks, machinery, trucks, artillery, and personnel, all moving towards the eastern coast and the embarkation area of Hamhung.

Parts of the long convoy grind to a halt as small arms fire rips into it from the woods and sharp peaks. Marines jump out, take cover, return fire.

Air support swoops into the valley and silences enemy gunfire with strafing runs and napalm.

Twenty-nine tanks swivel from side to side, finding targets, rocking back as they fire into the woods. Mortars search and destroy the enemy's hiding places in the steep peaks bordering the road. Stop. Go. Stop. Go. The convoy of men and machines moves forward, broken continuously, and then rebuilding itself into a stable formation after each attack. On the last night of November, the convoy has fallen apart in three significant areas. And the fractures themselves have been splintered into smaller groups.

"We're going to be in trouble as soon as it gets dark," Sergeant Chapman radios to Captain McKlane. He's in a truck fifty yards behind the captain.

"Koto-ri," Captain McKlane radios back. He watches a string of Corsairs sweep into the valley and lay down a carpet of fire. Darkness will put an end to the Marine airstrikes. The trucks turn around and race back towards the safety of the well-protected Koto-ri perimeter.

Captain George McKlane is now at the rear of the formation instead of the point. As they scramble to safety, he sees the Chinese attacking the convoy still heading south. The road is severed, first by explosions and then by swarms of green parkas descending on the trucks and machinery. In the approaching darkness, the captain knows the outcome will be a disaster.

"Koto-ri," he radios again.

"Koto-ri," Staff Sergeant Chapman confirms.

They make it back with all their men and no casualties. News of what they left behind trickles in during the night. They call it the fight in Hell Fire Valley.

When the Chinese initially overrun a portion of the convoy, they settle on looting rather than fighting. Quite a few of the Marines escape and set up a perimeter. They are headquarters and service troops: clerks, truck drivers, cooks, and military police officers. A few of the Marines are World War II vets, and they become the backbone of the battle against overwhelming odds.

By 02:00, the Marines are out of grenades. An Army crew, with a 77mm recoilless rifle, fires at enemy flashes, driving the Chinese briefly from their mortars. Eventually, the Army crew falls silent, out of ammunition, all dead or wounded. A group of Marine Commandos sneaks out of the perimeter in an attempt to reach Koto-ri. Three of them try to break through enemy lines in a jeep. The enemy captures all of them.

At 04:30, the Chinese send their prisoners to the perimeter with a surrender demand. The Marine commander, a major, demands that the CCF surrender, pointing out that his men can now fire in any direction and hit the enemy. The Chinese threaten an all-out attack. They give him ten minutes to discuss surrender with his officers. The Marine commander has only 42 non-disabled men left, most of them entirely out of ammunition, one man with seven rounds. As he speaks to them, he tells them to try to escape if they can. He then returns to the surrender negotiations and wants to discuss how the CCL will treat the seriously wounded. He tries to stretch out the negotiations as much as possible as his men slip away in the darkness.

All night long, Marines struggle back into the safety of Koto-ri. At sunrise, the CCL moves back into the hills for the day. But over 300 Marines and Army warriors have been killed or wounded.

"You saved a lot of men last night, turning around when you did," Sergeant Chapman says to Captain McKlane. "It was the right thing to do."

"I think we might have made a difference if we'd stayed," the captain says.

"Only in the number of casualties we would have suffered," the sergeant replies. "You did the right thing, Captain McKlane."

Chapter 7
Welcome To Rhondo Homes

Rhondo Homes, Boca-Delray, Sunday Night

In her Rhondo condo's only bathroom, Barbara Rossellini prepares for Anthony Silberg with a complex combination of Eucalyptus Oil, Rosemary Oil, Montana Flower

Tincture, and various pain-relieving salves. It's a mixture that her third, sexually experimental, dead husband developed. It prevents or at least disguises pain when more substantial than ordinary objects enter the sexual arena.

Within five minutes of opening the door to her condo, Anthony Silberg proves he qualifies as a larger-than-normal object. He wonders how she can accommodate him.

She's a small person. Standing behind her, with her on the bed, she slowly accepts all of him. He cannot believe it. Her tightness takes his breath away. He begins to breathe hard, holding Barbara's hips with both hands.

Barbara is not breathing hard. She does, however, make fake sounds of passion and joy, timed to Silberg's movements, but she closes her eyes tight. Despite the painkilling salve, his size *does* hurt her. She effectively hides her pain. She thinks about her commission.

She squeezes her legs together as much as she can without screaming, although she thinks Anthony Silberg might enjoy hearing her give voice to her pain. She knows he cannot last much longer.

"You're great, you're great, you're great," he says.

Suddenly he thrusts painfully into her.

He explodes, holding her in a tight grip that reveals much more strength then she thought he had. He collapses on top of her. She feels the pain quickly shrink away. He rolls away, and she catches her breath. It is not as much fun as she thought it would be. She goes into the bathroom, applies more of her third husband's topical pain reliever, and returns to Tony with a warm washrag and towel.

"You're a magician," he says. "I never met a woman your size who could take all of me like that."

She's bleeding a little, and he notices it.

"Oh, hell, I didn't mean to hurt you," he says.

She uses his washcloth.

"I forgot to tell you I was a virgin," she says, smiling.

He stares at her.

"I used that line on every one of my husbands," she says. "But you're the only one who let me prove it."

He smiles, but cautiously. Barbara kisses him lightly, hoping he doesn't require any more attention.

"You haven't told me about the Brazilian buyer, Tony," she says. He stares at her.

She suddenly realizes she might have made a mistake. This moment could go very wrong for her.

"Mister McKlane asked me if I would be showing a Brazilian buyer his home tomorrow."

Silberg's eyes soften, but only slightly.

"I'll handle it alone," he says. "He's an old business contact. I've known him for years."

Barbara says nothing, thinks about pouting, but does not. She feels her heart beating, and she feels oddly and unexpectedly cautious. Silberg takes her hand.

"You have the sell-side no matter what happens, Barbara," he says quietly. "The name Barbara Rossellini is on the listing contract. Don't worry about it."

Barbara traces her finger over the angry scar that rips across the left side of Silberg's chest, fading into his right shoulder. Anthony says: "I was at Khe Sanh during the Tet Offensive. I don't talk about it." She kisses the scar.

He smiles at her, starts getting dressed.

"Shrapnel when our ammunition dump took a direct hit," Silberg says. "Probably saved my life, because they got moe out of there before the VC blew our ammunition dump a second time inside the perimeter, a week later. That wiped out my whole platoon, every last one of them. I survived, truly by accident." Silberg thinks it's a good story.

She puts back on the black silk robe she greeted him with at the door when Silberg arrived. "I need to tell you something," she says. She wants to solidify her position and importance to Silberg and Accelerated Realty Sales.

"I know," Silberg says. "You're a virgin." He laughs at the joke again. His friends will enjoy the story. He hitches his alligator belt loosely and starts buttoning the rest of his shirt.

"My father was an important friend of Captain George McKlane," Barbara says.

Silberg stops buttoning his shirt. He sits down.

"What are you talking about?"

"My father fought with him in Korea."

"What are you talking about?" Silberg repeats.

It is not the reaction Barbara expects. She sits on the edge of the bed, and she cannot reclaim the secret. She says nothing. Silberg finishes buttoning his shirt, very slowly.

"Your father would be much too young to fight in Korea," he says to Barbara.

"My father was sixty-seven when I was born," she says. "His picture is on the wall in George McKlane's office."

"Are you sure?" Silberg says. It is not the reaction Barbara Rossellini expects.

Of course, she is sure. It's a very dumb question. She does not point this out to Silberg.

"Gunnery Sergeant Raymond Garfield Chapman," she says. "When I was born, he named me Georgette Barbara Chapman."

Silberg says nothing.

"I think the 'Georgette' was in honor of Captain George McKlane," Barbara says.

"Get me a drink," Anthony says. "Whiskey."

He moves out of the bedroom and into the small dining area. He sits down at the table.

He needs to think. Can he trust Barbara?

He does not want his first attempt at big-time money laundering to blow up in his face.

"Jameson Black Barrel," Barbara says, putting a glass in front of him. Her third husband's favorite, and never served with ice. "You want ice?" she asks.

"Yeah, put a few cubes in it," Anthony says. She goes back to the kitchen, puts ice and Jameson in a second glass, returns and sits down at the small dining table across from him. She trades whiskey glasses with him.

Husband number three flashes through her mind. Drink it as God intended. He always said that, and always too often. Still, he remains the only man she ever loved.

Anthony Silberg opens and closes his fist.

"I was a good boxer when I was a kid," he says, looking at his fist, then at her.

"I'll bet you were," Barbara says.

What's he trying to prove?

"So George McKlane thinks the world of you, right?"

Barbara does not know where this is going, but it alarms her unexpectedly.

Silberg seems dangerous but without reason.

"McKlane doesn't know," she says.

"What do you mean he doesn't know?"

Barbara understands that she's missing some essential pieces in a completely unknown, conceivably rewarding, and possibly dangerous puzzle.

"He does not know," she repeats. "He has no idea that I am his namesake. He knows nothing." She almost adds more, at this stage, but instinctively holds it back. She needs to put herself on Silberg's side, although she does not yet understand why it is necessary.

"You sure?" Silberg asks.

"Yes."

Silberg leans back, but he does not relax. "Tell me why you're so damned sure."

"My father died fourteen years ago. I left home when I was seventeen, three years before he croaked. I never even knew he died until a year later when some lawyer named Adams sent me a bunch of medals and a copy of his will. My father didn't like me, and I didn't like him. He gave everything he had to some stupid charity for Korean Marine Corps vets. I got only medals. Sorry. Didn't mean to insult the Marine Corps. *Semper Fidelis*."

Anthony Silberg does not seem insulted.

"You never met Captain George McKlane when you were a kid?" he asks.

"Never. I think McKlane went to my father's funeral. I didn't. I never even knew about it."

"Why didn't you tell him when you met him today?"

Barbara thinks this whole conversation is strange, disjointed, unexpected, and dangerous.

She has no right answer to Silberg's question, but she recognizes that there might be some very wrong answers. She did not enlighten McKlane because it was her instinct to protect her secrets.

She always does this. Now she must use the instinct to her advantage.

"When McKlane asked me about showing his home to the Brazilian, and you had not told me about it, I knew I should keep my mouth shut until I spoke to you."

She smiles at him and lets her robe drop open a little, reaching for her glass of Irish Whiskey. "You weren't much interested in chit-chat when you got here tonight."

Silberg laughs, but not enough to make her comfortable. "Barbara, I don't want you to say anything about being the daughter of Captain George McLane's war buddy, do you understand me?"

"Yes, sir."

"Not to him, not to anybody."

"Yes, sir."

She wonders why. She does not ask.

"One more thing," Silberg says. "And I don't want to hear bullshit coming out of your mouth."

"Okay." Tough guy. Marines always play the tough guy.

"You said you weren't related to Angelo Rossellini."

Now she knows she has fallen into a trap, and she is standing on dangerous ground.

"I didn't lie," she says, but she feels the heat on her face. Silberg stares at her. Of course, he would know Rossellini. He has probably spoken to the developer.

"I met Mister Rossellini twice," Barbara says. "I married his son, Roberto, in Las Vegas one weekend. So I'm not related to him by blood. Plus, the marriage never happened after a few months, annulment."

Silberg nods. She thinks maybe he knows all this.

"Tell me why your marriage to Roberto Rossellini never happened," Tony says, taking a mouthful of whiskey.

"Because Roberto had a dick the size of titmouse, only with a lot less imagination." She says it immediately because she had said it often, but, before this, only to girlfriends that she worked with at the bar.

Anthony Silberg sprays a fine mist of Jameson Black Barrel Whiskey across the dining room table. Barbara smiles and takes his mostly-empty glass. She says: "Let me freshen that for you. It's on the house."

As she does this, she flashes back to her days as a bartender, filling the tips jar with wisecracks.

She returns to a relaxed smile from Silberg. She wipes down the table with a dishcloth.

"You've got a lot of spunk," Silberg says.

She tries to remember the last time she heard the word "spunk," but it's lost in the cobwebs of her life.

"You know about the Goldfish Bowl?" Silberg asks.

She decides there are no straight lines in his conversation, perhaps not in his life, either.

"I know where it is," she says.

The Goldfish Bowl is on the main floor of Accelerated Realty Sales. It's a series of floor-to-ceiling glass enclosures where the brokerage's heavy hitters have their offices. On her first day at the agency, the manager, Bill Brownstone, tells her it is her goal to move into one of these offices. It might take years, but that is the gold ring to grasp. As he walks her past the Goldfish Bowl offices, he says: "Location, location, location, yes, yes."

"I spoke to Bill Brownstone late today," Silberg says. "You'll move into the Goldfish Bowl tomorrow."

Barbara jumps up, twirls around, and gives him a huge hug. Her silk robe drops to her waist.

"See?" she says. "Rock hard."

Silberg laughs. Everyone relaxes.

Barbara goes to the kitchen and refreshes her drink. She comes back, sits down, and says: "I think some of your best agents might get a little pissed off tomorrow."

"They're always pissed off," Anthony Silberg says. "They're all on eighty percent splits. They'll get over being pissed off when they get their next commission checks on Tuesday afternoon."

He does not tell her that most of the women in the Goldfish Bowl made it there in a similar fashion to her journey, just not as quickly.

Every last one of them, subsequently, did become a top producer. Only three men work in the Goldfish Bowl.

"Eighty percent splits?" Barbara says.

Silberg laughs and shakes his head. "You're unbelievable," he says. She smiles at him, puts her chin in her hand, and makes her eyebrows arch up and down.

"You're not getting an eighty percent split," he says. "You'll get sixty. Anything over ten million in sales annually gets eighty percent. Calendar year."

"You're my favorite Broker," Barbara says.

"I'm your only Broker."

"That, too," she says, laughing. Silberg watches her. She turns her laughter into a smile, knowing this is some sort of test. She waits. Her silence might teach her something.

"Three guys work in the Goldfish Bowl," Silberg says. "One of them went to Harvard Business School, and he's an arrogant prick. But he also does twenty-five to thirty million a year with overeducated customers. The other two guys rarely show up. They're licensed, but they don't sell much. That's for your ears only."

He watches her. He likes what he sees as she registers something given to her in confidence. She will make sure it remains there.

"Why are they in the Goldfish Bowl?" Barbara asks.

"They work for Angelo Rossellini."

Barbara says nothing. She does not know how to interpret this information, but she knows a secret when she hears one. Barbara is smart enough not to ask about it. She knows she will eventually figure it out. She nods to him, and he nods back. He drains his glass and places it carefully on the cheap dining room table.

"Another?" she says.

"No."

"A little more exercise?"

"You gotta be joking."

She smiles, relieved at the safety of temporary abstinence. She lets her robe slip back to her waist.

"Hell," he says. "I gotta go, Barbara. I think you're going to kill me."

"Not a chance," she says. "If you can make it through 'Nam, you can sure as hell make it through me, and as often as you like. *Semper Fi.*"

He stands up, gives her a look she does not understand, then pulls her to him. "You're an interesting girl, Barbara Rossellini. Make sure you keep your mouth shut. Don't ever cross me."

"I will never bite the hand that feeds me, Tony. Although I may put it into all of my body's secret places."

Tony shakes his head, smiles, and says: "I'll let you know how it goes with the Brazilian buyer."

She closes the front door after him, leans up against it, and exhales until her lungs start to hurt.

Then she walks back into the bathroom and applies some more painkilling salve. She looks in the mirror. She does not smile.

"Marines," she says. She thinks about an old saying that her third husband's father, a draft dodger from the Vietnam era, taught her.

He was the sort of man she wishes her father had been.

She repeated his anti-war chant to her father, at the end of a phone conversation when she tried to get some money out of him.

It was after her second husband had died, but long before the insurance company ever coughed up the policy money for which she had to sue them.

What she said to her estranged father enraged him. She was glad she was two and a half thousand miles away at the time. He slammed the phone down on her.

"Eat the apple," she says to the face in the bathroom mirror of her Rhondo Homes condo. "Fuck the Corps."

It was an often-chanted anti-war slogan that started in Chicago before she was born.

The Goldfish Bowl at ARS, Monday Morning

William Brownstone, the Manager of Accelerated Realty Sales, understands the Digital Age. He's a computer geek.

He joins Silberg's company in 2005, after years of struggling as an agent in much smaller real estate firms in the Boca Raton area.

He continues his record of mediocrity at Accelerated Realty Sales, registering consistently in the bottom quarter of property closings. He manages to survive on rentals, an area with which few real estate agents bother.

Then one day, Silberg has a severe problem with the company's computer network. The crisis pushes Accelerated Realty Sales off the grid, unable to conduct regular business.

William Brownstone fixes everything in about three hours, pulling computers apart and writing a few simple programs.

He has a better network at home than Accelerated Realty Sales has as a business.

Over the next few weeks, he installs state-of-the-art networking protocols and transmission controls at Anthony Silberg's company.

He improves security with hardware, firmware, and software. He carefully explains everything he does to Anthony Silberg, who understands about ten percent of what Brownstone tells him.

Brownstone continues to refine and organize the systems at Accelerated Realty Sales, and he becomes the digital handyman of anyone at the company who has a problem with computers, tablets, notebooks, or cell phones. His rental returns suffer. He does not sell a single home.

"Bill," Silberg says when they meet in the elevator one morning, "you're one of the worst real estate agents I have ever known."

Brownstone's lack of confidence, a primary cause of his poor salesmanship, leads him to say immediately: "I'll clean out my cubicle, Mister Silberg."

Silberg laughs, which William Brownstone interprets as extremely rude, and quite cruel. His head fills with images of his angry wife overpowering him with physical and verbal abuse as soon as he gets home.

She outweighs him by over 120 pounds, and she is Irish.

Brownstone's life appears to be taking a dramatic and dangerous spin into unemployment. Silberg grabbed his hand and started pumping it up and down. "Well, uh, yes, thank you, sir, and goodbye," Bill Brownstone says to Silberg.

"Hello," Silberg says, hanging on to Brownstone's hand. "Bill, I am going to make you the Manager of Accelerated Realty Sales. You will be my right-hand man, my eyes and ears, and your salary will start at three times what you made in commissions during the last two years. Triple. You may be one of the most valuable resources I have. If you ever sell another house, I will fire you."

Bill Brownstone bursts into tears, embarrassing both himself and Anthony Silberg.

From that day forward, anything that Anthony Silberg does enjoys the unquestioned support and obedient approval of both Bill Brownstone and Brownstone's wife. In her neighborhood, his wife grows both in stature and in girth, and she becomes increasingly devoted to the man she starts calling "My Billy Boy."

On Monday morning, Bill Brownstone is waiting in the lobby of Accelerated Realty Sales when Barbara Rossellini arrives at work.

"Hello, Barbara," he chirps. "Are you all right? You're walking a little funny."

"Hi, Bill," she says. "I think I pulled a muscle in my groin. Jogging too much." Brownstone's face reddens just a bit when she says groin.

"Well, congratulations," he says. "Yes, yes."

"For pulling my groin?"

"Oh, no ... no, no. You must be more careful, Barbara." His face reddens further. "You have become a great asset to Accelerated Realty Sales. Goodness. Six million dollars worth of listings in just a few weeks. Oh, my. Extraordinary. Mister Silberg wants me to show you to your new office."

"In the Goldfish Bowl."

"Yes, yes. The Goldfish Bowl," he says. "Please, Barbara, follow me."

They make their way through the maze of cubicles where real estate agents sit, phone, and analyze their computer screens. It's called the Bull Pen.

"The term originated in the seventeenth century," Bill Brownstone explains. "It is what they called the holding room for criminals before they went before the judge and were sentenced to prison: the Bull Pen."

As they make their way towards the Goldfish Bowl, some people greet her. None of them even knew she was alive the day before. She smiles and says, "hello" to all her new friends, prisoners in the Bull Pen.

The Goldfish Bowl takes up twenty-five percent of the office space on the ground floor of Accelerated Realty Sales, although it only consists of ten, glassed-in offices. Each one could comfortably accommodate four bullpen cubicles.

All of the Goldfish Bowl offices look the same, personalized only with different plants and pictures on the wall. All the images are the same size, in similar frames, showing several black and white landscapes or historical scenes. Nothing hangs on the glass walls; they have no distractions breaking their uninterrupted view in and out.

"So this is how a goldfish feels," she says.

"Yes, yes," he says. He cannot think of anything else to say. In Barbara's office, three computer monitors attached to a single computer, hidden out of sight.

The monitors are horseshoed together on an L-shaped black walnut desk. It looks like a traders' station in a financial company's television commercial.

A sleek telephone console with six buttons on it fits into a corner of the desk. A neat stack of leather-bound real estate books lines a double shelf sitting on legal-sized filing cabinets. They fill one of three floor-to-ceiling glass walls.

Two comfortable guest chairs face her desk. A small window looks out on a manicured "take a break" garden that nobody ever uses. Barabara's work area holds some neatly stacked papers next to a pile of legal-sized pads and a leather pen and pencil holder. The documents are the contract on George McKlane's home.

The phone rings on her desk.

She picks it up, says her name, punches a blinking button, repeats her name. Somebody is looking for a home, but nothing more than two million dollars, preferably close to the ocean, and it doesn't have to be right on the beach.

She takes their name, phone number, desired bedrooms and baths, garage requirements, school requirements, and club membership needs. She listens to them for a while, jotting things on a pad next to George McKlane's contract.

She assures the buyers that she has precisely the property they want, in fact, three homes that might interest them. She promises to call them back within the hour. She thanks them for calling. She hears the person on the other end say: "Well, our friends say you are the best."

Barbara says: "I am, and I'll call you back quickly. We're going to have a lot of fun finding you the perfect home." She hangs up and smiles at Bill Brownstone.

"Every eighth call will go to your desk," he says. He hands Barbara a list of names. They all have percentages in brackets, followed by an extension number.

Barbara looks at the list and then at Bill Brownstone.

"I think you may need an assistant," he says. "These are all young agents who work here, and I've ranked them according to my opinion of their abilities. They can learn a lot about selling homes by interning with someone like you. I can see that just listening to you on the phone."

"Thank you, Bill. I guess I need to get to work."

"Yes, yes," He says. "Anything I can do for you, Barbara, just give me a call."

"I will."

She sits down in her comfortable leather desk chair, set at just the right height for her. She realizes that someone has thought of adjusting it correctly. She twirls around a few times, stopping as a woman suddenly appears and leans against her door.

"Hello, Barbara."

"Hello, uh ...."

"Alice," she says. "Alice Koenig."

"Hello, Alice."

"You've been a busy little girl," Alice Koenig says. No smile. Barbara studies her. Mid-forties. Attractive, but a little overweight. A tough face. Barbara remembers her from the first official meeting when Bill Brownstone said she had sold her entire inventory. This woman had glanced at Barbara, crossed her arms, and snorted something to the person next to her, who snickered something back.

"Yes, I am busy," Barbara Rossellini says. "And I am getting busier every minute." She picks up her phone, although she has no intention of calling anyone.

"Yes, well ...."

"Yes," Barbara says, without smiling. "Do you need help with something, uh, Alice?"

"We'll talk sometime," Alice Koenig says. "Once you get a little more settled."

"That would be nice," Barbara says.

"Perhaps," says Alice Koenig. It seems a strange response. "At least we could compare notes. Welcome to the Goldfish Harem."

Then she is gone.

Chapter 8

The Buyer From Brazil

13752 Coconut Palm Ct.
Boca Raton: Monday AM

Anthony Silberg introduces Gustavo Oliveira to George McKlane at exactly ten-thirty, their agreed time to meet at his home. Silberg opens the door with a key that George McKlane has given to the brokerage for pre-arranged home showings. George is standing in the foyer. He glances at his watch, smiles, and says: "Good, the new key works."

Mr. Oliveira seems very well-mannered and quite well-fed. He likes expensive clothes and watches, but he speaks very little English. "I talk *muito pouco Inglês*," he says to George.

"I speak even less Portuguese," George says with a friendly smile. "Although I learned a few words in Mozambique many years ago." He speaks too quickly. The Brazilian turns to Silberg with a confused look, and Silberg himself seems a bit surprised.

George says: "*Bem-vindo à minha casa, talvez o seu novo lar.*" He has practiced this phrase since breakfast, but he thinks his pronunciation needs a lot of work.

The Brazilian buyer gives George and then Silberg a blank stare. Anthony Silberg, looking at George, remaining completely silent.

"Oh, well, so much for my Portuguese," George McKlane finally says. "Welcome to my home, perhaps your new home."

Silberg laughs, turns, and quietly whispers something to the Brazilian.

"*Ah, claro. Claro*," the Brazilian smiles, grabbing George's hand and pumping it as he smiles wide enough to reveal a few gold teeth in the back of his mouth.

"Anthony," George says, looking at Silberg during this overly enthusiastic handshake, "I'm going to let you show Mister Oliveira around. Please take as much time as you need. Sharonda has some snacks for you if you want. I have a workout scheduled at the clubhouse."

Sharonda steps out of the kitchen and says: "Food and beverages are on the patio, Mister Silberg, whenever you and Mister Oliveira want them."

Silberg smiles at her and says: "Call me Tony, please, and thank you, Sharonda."

George heads for the front door. "I'm off. Very nice meeting you, Mister Oliveira."

"Gustavo," the Portuguese Buyer says, giving his name a slow roll with his right hand.

"Gustavo," George says, without using his hands.

Anthony Silberg leads the Portuguese buyer through the first floor of the house, making small gestures as they go. Gustavo Oliveira mimics many of these gestures, but on a far grander scale. Sharonda watches from the kitchen, and it seems quite comical. The man likes the house a lot. She might retire sooner than expected.

The two men move through the Birdroom and onto the patio. Sharonda watches them walk down to the dock and sit in the comfortable chairs on its western edge. They seem to talk more outside. They both use their hands a lot. She wonders where Silberg learned to speak Portuguese.

She wheels out the trolley filled with pastries and lemonade, parking it under the lanai. "If you want anything stronger than lemonade, let me know," she shouts to them. Both men wave to her. She returns to the kitchen.

The broker and the Brazilian eat pastries and drink freshly-squeezed lemonade. Then they return to the house and spend a lot of time in George's office, mostly looking at photographs on the wall. Sharonda thinks she hears them speaking English softly, whispering to one another.

From the office, Silberg and the Brazilian move to the second floor, taking the elevator.

Sharonda immediately goes into the office, opens a cabinet to the right of the desk, and pulls out a sliding drawer. She throws a switch, and a lot of lights start blinking. She puts on a headset and makes some adjustments to a recording device called the Magic Wand.

The men upstairs spend less than ten minutes in the War Room. Silberg once again picks up and examines the watch that has fallen on the floor. This time, he slips the engraved timepiece into his pocket.

Silberg and Oliveira return to the first floor and move to the guest house. They do not walk up the flight of stairs to the loft. Oliveira is in worse shape than Silberg. After that, they walk across the driveway and re-enter the house through the garage.

"Sharonda?" Anthony Silberg calls as they walk into the main room. She appears from George's office.

Silberg thinks she probably fell asleep. She acts as if she has just woken up from a nap.

"He loves the house," Silberg tells her. "Tell George we probably have a sale."

"I'll do that," Sharonda says. She does not smile, and Silberg wonders briefly if she still carries a grudge from the previous day.

"Thanks for the lemonade and pastry," Anthony says.

"You bet," Sharonda says.

They turn and leave. Sharonda goes back into George's office. She phones the manager at the club for the third time and asks if anyone has been able to find Mr. McKlane.

The manager says they're looking for him. After he hangs up the phone, the manager looks at his assistant and says: "Mister McKlane said he did not want to be disturbed, and I'm not going to go against his wishes." He's asleep and in Korea again.

North Korea and The Breakout from Koto-ri: December 1-4, 1950

Planning for the breakout from Koto-ri begins in early December. Several companies, making up a composite battalion of about 700 Marines, start down the winding road, but they fail to clear a sustainable escape route. The problem is the wounded, the broken, and the dying men.

Their evacuation slows down everything. It remains the weakest link in a deadly chain.

"How many Marines have we lost, sergeant?" Captain McKlane asks.

"Less than we lost going from Yudam-ni to Hagaru," the sergeant answers. "You know when we came here four months ago, when we poked our mighty stick into this stinking hornet's nest, the temperature was over one hundred degrees. Can you remember sweat when it didn't freeze? Every time we sweat now, it turns into icicles."

"How many, sergeant."

"Less than we lost going from Hagaru to Koto-ri," Staff Sergeant Chapman tells Captain McKlane. He's looking left and right, trying to find an exit sign in the conversation.

"How many?"

Finally, facing the tired, unblinking stare of the captain, he comes up with numbers.

"We had 236 when we left Yudam-ni. We fought our way into Hagaru with 195. We had 160 at Koto-ri, but we picked up ten new men there. We've got 154 right now, but 12 of them are among the walking wounded."

"We've lost 92 men."

"Yes, 92, if you count the walking wounded as ready to fight, which they are," Sergeant Chapman says. "But we need to rest, captain. Our men need to sleep. Perkins is in a straitjacket because he cracked up after five days with no sleep, not because he's nuts."

"I know," the captain says.

The NATO forces, mostly United States Marines, start at Yudam-ni, on the edge of a frozen finger pointing west from the Chosin Reservoir.

From there, the Marines fight their way through 12 Chinese divisions sweeping down from the north.

It is not a Korean War. It is a Chinese versus the 1st Marine Division War.

"We could have airlifted ourselves out of here, right at the start," the captain says. "We could have blown up all of our equipment, destroyed it, and flown out of here."

"Probably," the sergeant says.

In the darkness outside their tent, the horizon flashes, not with lightning, but with death. The low rumble of explosives takes a long time to reach them.

"Why didn't we do that?" Captain McKlane asks.

"Because command said we needed to take a seventy-two-mile hike and drag all our equipment with us," Sergeant Chapman says. He's observing the captain. He has never seen him like this. "Plus, they had a lot of green socks they needed to get rid of."

The captain looks up at him. He knows he is being studied by Sergeant Chapman, watched. He takes a deep breath, smiles slightly.

"I'm all right, sergeant. I'm okay."

"I know you are, sir."

"I'm going to try to get some sleep."

"Good idea, sir. It's going to be a bright, new day in about four more hours."

"I doubt that," Captain McKlane says. "It's going to be another day to kill China."

13752 Coconut Palm Ct., The Magic Wand: Monday

The masseuse is holding George McKlane's right wrist in the health club nook attached to the Men's Locker Room at The Royal Coconut Yacht and Country Club.

"Are you okay, Mister McKlane?" the masseuse asks. "You dropped off the end of the earth. I had to check to see if you had a pulse. Are you all right, sir?"

"No," George tells him. "It's the damned steroids I'm taking every day."

He pulls his hand away from the masseuse.

"Gotta watch the steroids, Mister McKlane." The masseuse is over-muscled, has a round face, and almost no neck. He has a great deal of experience with steroids.

"Doctor Klein will get me off them in the next few weeks," George says, sitting up on the massage table.

The masseuse makes a mental note to discuss steroids with the retired neurosurgeon the next time he gets Doctor Klein on the table.

The masseuse is a young man. Erectile dysfunction should not be part of his vocabulary.

He helps George McKlane off the massage table, once again telling him he's in great shape for someone his age.

"Manager gave me a message, Mister McKlane, the masseuse tells him. "Your Nurse Practitioner wants you to give her a call."

As he's leaving the club, George sees the manager and tells him to call Sharonda, tell her that he's on his way home. She's standing in the driveway when he pulls through the gates, with her arms crossed. She looks angry. For a moment, he wonders what he's done wrong.

"George," she says as he gets out of his Mercedes, "we have a serious problem."

"How serious? What is it?"

"Come and listen for yourself," she says. They walk together into George's office. One of the cabinets is still open, below the bookshelves. It's to the left of the three computer monitors, within easy reach from George's desk.

A machine randomly blinks a lot of green, yellow, and blue lights on a pullout drawer. She throws several switches, and a very slight buzz comes out of some speakers set into the bookshelves.

The surveillance system is initially installed by George McKlane when he and Agnes build their home. George has a similar setup in the home he leaves, which he removes before closing the sale on that house. George trades it in on a newer system. What he gets is called The Magic Wand, which is also the name of the security company that installs it.

George uses it to record financial discussions in his home. He hosts gatherings of critical people, many of them The Wizards of Wall Street and The Captains of Industry. His recording system documents a lot of secrets, much of it inside information. The Securities and Exchange Commission would question the legality of such electronic eavesdropping.

Magic Wand instructions stress that it's designed solely for personal protection, and under no circumstances for eavesdropping. One crucial lesson George learns from the Magic Wand is that what people say to your face, and what they plan and believe, often differ. More than a dozen seemingly meaningful friendships cool off after George listens to the truth of the Magic Wand. But the associations do not end. Knowing a lie possesses as much value as knowing the truth, sometimes more.

What George does is illegal, and he knows it. He could go to jail for it. He has also seen good, brave men die for no reason, and the legality of gaming the system with insider information pales in comparison to his life's journey.

The Magic Wand helps turn George McKlane into a wealthy man, even if its legality remains doubtful. Few people know about George's surveillance system, although Sharonda does. George wants a record of everything involving the failing health of his wife, Agnes, and he teaches Sharonda how to use it.

He also wants Sharonda to know that it is there for her protection as a caretaker and Nurse Practitioner and because he trusts her.

In his office, Sharonda says: "This comes from The War Room." She pushes a button, and laughter suddenly fills George's office.

"*Claro, claro, claro.*"

It is not the Brazilian buyer's deep voice. It sounds a lot more like Anthony Silberg. A low rattling sound filters into the recording.

"*Claro*, my ass," someone says, but not Silberg's voice. "I thought we were dead, Pop." The Brazilian buyer is speaking.

"Maybe I should use African buyers instead of Portuguese," Silberg says. "*Claro, claro.* What do they speak? Zulu? Swahoosie?" The rattling sound occurs again.

"Swahili," the Portuguese buyer says. "Stop shaking that frigging spear at me, Pop."

The man speaks with a Midwestern accent, flat with almost no fluctuation in his voice. "When the old geezer started speaking Portuguese, I was ready to give it up, man. You got to be careful."

"I know," Silberg says.

For a while, they say nothing to each other, although the sound of the spear continues. Then Silberg says: "Look at this. The Congressional Medal of Honor."

"Holy shit, Pop. I've never seen one before. Why the hell does he hide it there?"

"It's a Goy thing. Most people got to drop dead to get one of these," Silberg says. "Stop juggling the socks, Snake."

"Why doesn't he keep them in a drawer like everyone else? Why the spotlight on a bunch of thick green socks?"

"Put them back. Put the socks back just like they were."

"I need some socks."

"Put them back."

"Then you put the watch back. I saw you pocket it."

"You don't want to screw around with me, Snake."

"All right, Pop, all right."

Gregory 'Snake' Richards has personal knowledge of how Silberg acquires his nickname, Pop, at the Federal Correction Institution in Schuylkill, Pennsylvania. Richards is in the ring for forty-six seconds when he experiences it. He doesn't remember getting hit, but he feels it for a week.

"You want to get paid, don't you?" Silberg says. The man called Snake puts the socks back.

"Shit, this guy was a Cleveland cop?"

"Looks like it."

"Remember Shivers up at Shitkill, Pop?"

"Yes, I do," Silberg says.

"He killed a cop in Cleveland."

"Yes, he did," Silberg says. "He killed him three times." They laugh. "Okay, enough of the hero's museum. I have to show you the guest house. I haven't seen it myself, and then the garage. Then we have to get you out of here. You have a plane to catch."

"You know, it's been nice working again with you, Pop. It's been a long time."

"I like to stay in touch with good friends, Snake," Anthony Silberg says.

The closet door closes.

Sharonda flicks a switch on the recorder.

The slight hiss from the speakers fades slowly into complete silence.

"There's more from the guest house and laundry room," Sharonda finally says, "but I think you get the gist of it, Captain George."

"Jesus Christ," George says.

"I have to tell you that, in my professional opinion, Anthony Silberg is a dangerous man. He has a terrible temper. I saw it in the redness of his neck when he felt insulted by me during the tour I gave him the day before yesterday. I saw his anger disappear as fast as it developed. It's a classic indicator. He has a very short fuse, and my best guess, without wiring him up, is that he's a genuine psychopath."

George McKlane says nothing.

"Anthony Silberg also has a set of keys to this house," Sharonda points out.

He looks up at her, nods. "And my watch."

Sharonda repeats, "And your watch."

She sees him thinking and waits.

Finally, George McKlane says: "But he has no knowledge that we know anything, right?"

"None," Sharonda says. He continues thinking.

"Okay, I don't want to get security here now, but we might need them. Don't phone security yet." He keeps thinking. "I think I need to call the colonel."

"Say hello to him for me," Sharonda says.

"I will," George says.

He leans back in his chair. He asks Sharonda: "So what do we have for lunch?"

"Whatever you want, George."

"Vanilla custard and Guinness," he says.

"Except for that," she says. "Your dietician, Rachel Klein, has suggested a nice tomato, spinach, and lettuce salad, with a light olive oil and low-salt vinaigrette dressing."

"She's going to kill me," George McKlane says. "I don't know how Gunther has lived as long as he has."

As Sharonda goes to get the salad, but with diet Russian dressing instead of Rachel's suggestion, George makes a phone call.

He knows the number by heart, but it takes quite a while to get through.

The hierarchal maze of the Pentagon phone system reflects the military traditions it serves.

"Colonel McKlane," a deep voice says, George's old sound, before his last trip to the hospital.

"Captain McKlane," George says.

"Dad," Colonel George McKlane, Jr. says. "Sir!"

"Cut it out," George says, smiling in his office. "You outrank me." They enjoy going through this customary greeting of respect and camaraderie.

It never seems to get old.

"Never going to outrank you, Dad. Never going to happen." George's son is a full colonel in the 2nd Marine Aircraft Wing out of Cherry Point, North Carolina, assigned to the Pentagon, just one step away from his first star as a brigadier general.

"What's up, Dad?"

"I need a favor."

His son says nothing. He always waits to hear what the favor requires before committing to it. He even does this when he's dealing with his father.

"There's a Marine down here that I am doing some business with, and I need to know how his record looks. Vietnam. Wounded pretty badly at Khe Sanh in Huong Hoa during the Tet Offensive."

"Do you have a name, rank, and serial number?"

"Don't have the last, but he was three stripes up, none down at Khe Sanh. His name is Anthony Silberg. He's a big real estate broker down here. His company sells more homes at the Club than anyone else in the area, by a wide margin."

"I'll get back to you in about twenty minutes, Dad, a half an hour tops. Semper Fi."

Forty-five minutes later, George is staring at an empty salad bowl. He opens his desk drawers, looking for chocolate bars. Sharonda comes in to take away his lunch tray.

"I hid them all," she says. The phone finally rings.

"Well, sir," Colonel McKlane says to his father. "That took a lot longer than expected, Dad."

"What did you find."

"Medical discharge."

"Guess he got hurt pretty bad," his father says.

"I suppose carrying buckets of sand around the track in the special PT punishment unit at Parris Island might stretch a recruit's arms a bit," the colonel says. "But I don't think it creates any serious physical wounds."

"What?"

"They threw him out of the Corps, Dad, after four weeks of basic training and three weeks in the psych unit. He was a certified, full-fledged whacko."

"Jesus Christ," George says. He rarely swears. "He's got a huge scar across his chest, an ugly one."

"He didn't get that working for us, Dad. What are you doing with this person?"

"I just signed a contract with him to sell the house, and he brought over someone who supposedly couldn't speak any English, a Brazilian who might buy it for six million dollars."

His son says nothing.

"Only the guy wasn't Brazilian, and he spoke English perfectly. Sharonda recorded him on the Magic Wand. It's some sort of scam. Or worse," George says. "They were joking about a police officer in Cleveland that one of their friends killed. Some inmate named Shivers up in Shitkill. I think that's the nickname that inmates have for the Schuylkill Correction Prison in Pennsylvania."

George pauses to see if his son has anything to say, but he remains silent. "You know, this broker is running the biggest real estate company in Boca Raton. He lives here at the Club. His house is bigger than ours."

Colonel George McKlane finally says: "You want me to come down there, Dad?"

"I might," he says. "But not yet. I've got Sharonda here. She sends greetings."

"Tough lady," Colonel McKlane says. "Give her my best. Look, Dad, I'm there in less than three hours if you need me. I'll fly myself. I can get military clearance into the Boca Airport in a minute, although they might get a little excited when I set a Hornet down on their runway."

George knows his son is smiling.

He remembers standing on the bridge of "the big stick," the Nimitz-class Fleet Carrier USS Theodore Roosevelt, in the Spring of 1990. It is just before the ship, with the call sign "Rough Rider," deploys to the Persian Gulf. He watches his newly-commissioned son touch and go with other Navy and Marine Corps pilots, qualifying for aircraft landings off the coast of California.

George, in his office in Boca, says: "Thank you, Son. I'll let you know. We're going to do a little more research on this guy first."

"I'm there if you need me, Dad. *Semper Fi.*"

"I love you," George says. "*Semper Fidelis.*"

He hangs up. He says, loud: "Sharonda." She appears from the kitchen and walks into his office.

George looks at her and asks: "Do you have a carry permit for your gun yet?"

She looks at him and says: "What the hell."

George stares at her.

"I've had it for six months now," she says, "but I didn't sign on for combat, sir."

She does not usually call him, "sir.". He notices it.

"What happened to George?" he asks.

"Well, I'm not sure," she says. "I think he might have just declared war."

A Dangerous Snake In The Grass: Monday

Gregory 'Snake' Richards takes a stretch limo to the Miami Airport, paid for by Anthony Silberg. He tips the driver generously, walks into the American Airlines terminal, and makes a phone call. Through the tinted glass, he watches the limousine as it drives away.

Less than 20 minutes later, he walks out of the terminal and gets into a black Lincoln Navigator. It takes him to North Miami Beach, to a construction site on which a new, multi-building condo complex has just broken ground.

The sign outside the site announces, in large gold letters: "Coming Soon! Rossellini Towers."

Gregory Richards steps into a construction trailer on the site. Angelo Rossellini greets him and motions him into a chair, getting up from behind a large metal desk and taking a seat opposite him.

Angelo asks several men to leave the trailer. He doesn't say anything. He simply points to the door, and they exit.

"So why do you think my friend Tony is going into business for himself?" Angelo asks.

"I'm not sure he is," Snake says. "I may be way out of line here, Mister Rossellini."

"Talk to me as a friend," Angelo says. Snake knows this is not possible. It scares him.

"I just bought a house in Boca Raton for six million dollars," Snake says. "I never signed the contract. I never agreed to the price. I never escrowed any money. And no company name was on the contract, Mister Rossellini. I barely had a chance to look at the paperwork. Silberg signed everything, initialed every page."

Gregory Richards has made many real estate purchases before, but always for Angelo Rossellini and one of his companies, usually for commercial property or a large tract of raw land. Putting $6,000,000 into a luxury home seems unusual, unexpected, and careless. It is not something that Angelo Rossellini would do.

"I am delighted you have come to talk to me about this," Angelo says. A sigh of relief passes through Snake, although he does not show it.

"Tell me how my good friend Anthony Silberg did all this. I want to hear everything."

Gregory Richards tells him how he pretended to be Brazilian. He ends the story by saying he felt uneasy when he left the house because a person named Sharonda, some sort of medical assistant to McKlane, appeared uncomfortable about him and Anthony.

"Silberg did not seem to notice, but I felt that something was wrong," Snake says.

"And what do you think this means, Gregory?"

"I don't know, Mister Rossellini. I've worked with you for a long time, sir. And with Tony Silberg. But this seems, well, unusual. It doesn't feel right. It feels like something the Feds could sink their teeth into pretty easily."

Angelo Rossellini says nothing.

Gregory Richards feels a trickle of sweat running down his side, even though the air conditioning in the construction trailer blows cold air directly at him.

"Perhaps Tony wants to buy and sell a house for himself," Angelo says. "Make a little extra money."

Gregory Richards knows that this makes no sense. What was the point of him pretending to be a Brazilian buyer?

He says nothing.

"I thank you very much for coming," Angelo says. "I appreciate your concern. One of my men will take you back to the airport."

Gregory Richards steps out of the trailer and gets into the front passenger's side of the Lincoln Navigator. He does not relax until he's sitting in the First Class Lounge at Miami International, having his second drink.

Angelo Rossellini, sitting in a construction trailer 15 miles from the Miami airport, has always known that Anthony Silberg would make a mistake.

He did not think he would also be stupid.

Chapter 9

Thank God It's Tuesday

Accelerated Realty Sales,
Boca Raton, Tuesday PM

Once a week, on Tuesday afternoons, at precisely two o'clock, Anthony Silberg starts his walk through the Bull Pen, eventually ending up at the Goldfish Bowl. Most of the real estate agents brighten up and react with exaggerated good humor to whatever he says to them. Some of the agents quietly disappear, knowing that he will not stop by their desks. The company's agents handle almost 35% of all home sales in the greater Boca Raton area.

In the past 12 months, 5,508 homes successfully close. Over 28% of the time, Accelerated Realty Sales agents handle both sides of the deal, representing both the buyer and the seller as transaction brokers.

Although the average home in Boca sells for just under $400,000, the average sale at Accelerated Realty Sales closes at over $600,000. Silberg's company focuses on the high-end residential real estate market.

Excluding commercial sales, which operates as a separate entity, the men and women working at the company sell over a billion dollars worth of homes every year.

This level of sales generates over 54 million dollars worth of commissions. An average of 40% goes to the brokerage, and 60% goes to the agents. Heavy-hitters earn a higher split while newcomers get as little as 20%.

Every Tuesday afternoon, Anthony Silberg passes out white envelopes containing lime-green commission checks or electronic deposit notices, depending on how his agents want to get paid. They are all treated as contractors to avoid corporate healthcare insurance costs and social security payments. They are not employees. Each of them pays a nominal fee for desk space.

The value of the checks that Silberg puts in the hands of his agents every week amounts to over $625,000. The Spring selling season raises the total amount, while the Fall doldrums shrink it.

Tuesday is a happy day at Accelerated Realty Sales.

Barbara Rossellini watches Anthony work his way through the maze of smiling agents in their cubicles. The man, she thinks, is genuinely made of money.

He makes his last stop at her office, standing in the doorway, looking at a sign Barbara has taped to her glass door, facing towards the Bull Pen. The poster shows a severely overweight goldfish in a bowl, with an underlined caption: *Goldfish Never Drown*. Silberg smiles and peels it off the door, putting it carefully on her desk.

"Cute," he says, "but nothing gets put on the glass in your office. No sticky notes. No photos of your new boyfriend." He smiles. "Company rules. Tape it to one of your filing cabinets. I like it."

"You jarheads have far too many regulations," she says, using a common nickname given to the men and women of the United States Marine Corps.

He hands her an envelope. Before she can ask what it is, he says: "Look happy. It's important to get an envelope on your first Tuesday in the Goldfish Bowl."

She flashes an exaggerated smile, mimicking all the ones she has seen as he walked through the Bull Pen. She looks in the envelope. It's a certified check.

Silberg says: "An advance against the house you sold the first week you arrived, even though it hasn't closed yet. Seven thousand and something dollars."

"Thank you, Tony. You're still my favorite broker."

He smiles and sits down in one of her guest chairs.

"It gets even better. The showing with the Portuguese buyer went very well," he says. "We were there for over an hour and a half. Oliveira has made a full-price offer, subject only to inspection. There are no contingencies other than that. There will be no mortgage. It's a cash deal. It's official."

"All right!" she says. She jumps out of her chair and gives a double fist pump.

Silberg takes a purchase agreement out of another envelope. Gustavo Oliveira signs the contract for six million dollars.

"The Buyer must complete the inspection within forty-eight hours."

The agreement shows that $600,000, ten percent of the contract, has been escrowed at Accelerated Realty Sales.

"Congratulations," Silberg says. "You get both sides of the deal, Barbara. That will be a little over two hundred thousand dollars."

He waves the contract towards the Bull Pen. Some people are clapping their hands, and a few stand up. A lot of them smile at Barbara Rossellini in the Gold Fish Bowl.

"They knew?" Barbara asks.

"They don't know anything," Anthony Silberg says. "But they smell success."

She turns to the crowd and gives them two thumbs up, getting more applause.

It might be the happiest day of her entire life: a commission of $216,000. She wrote that number on a piece of paper, imagining it, earlier that morning.

"So," Tony says. "I want you to phone Mister McKlane and tell him what you just learned and what you now have in your hands." He gives her McKlane's sales contract.

"Will do," she says.

"Now," Tony says.

She gets George McKlane's number from the listing contract and taps it into the phone.

"Sharonda," she says, "I have some great news. Can I speak to Mister McKlane?" She waits.

"Hello, Mister McKlane? Barbara Rossellini here. The Brazilian buyer fell in love with your wonderful home. He was there for an hour and a half and ...."

He interrupts her.

She puts the call on speakerphone, catching the last part of his statement: " ... and I'm enormously curious about how much he liked the home. I am a good deal more than just curious, Barbara Rossellini."

"Well, sir, he liked it enough to make a full-price offer. The only contingency is an inspection within forty-eight hours. There's no financial contingency of any kind. Six million dollars ...."

"I'm not sure I believe what you're telling me," George McKlane says.

Accelerated Realty Sales has an excellent telephone system, an upgrade by Manager Bill Brownstone. It sounds as if George McKlane is in Barbara Rossellini's office.

"I have an offer in front of me, Mister McKlane. I'm looking at it. Mister Silberg just gave it to me."

"Hello, George," Silberg says. "You're on the speakerphone. Gustavo loved your home. You can't do better than a full-price offer on the first showing on the second day of a listing. I think we're going to want a glowing testimonial from you, sir."

"I don't believe it," George says.

"It is hard to believe," Silberg admits. "But Mister Oliveira officially escrowed $600,000 and signed the offer just two hours after viewing your home, before I had him driven to the airport in a stretch limousine. That's a cost we'll cover on this end, George, the marketing costs we were discussing on the phone when you gave us the listing. The $600,000 is in our escrow account, and the deposit was a cashier's check, so we know it's real money."

"I don't believe it," George repeats.

"All we're missing is your signature on the contract," Silberg says.

There's a long pause.

George McKlane finally says: "I want both of you over here at five o'clock today, and I would like to see this contract for myself."

"I'll be there," Barbara Rossellini says.

Anthony Silberg detects something in the tone of George McKlane's voice that bothers him.

"Would it be all right if Barbara came alone?" Anthony Silberg asks.

Barbara gives him a big smile. The boss trusts her.

"No, that would not be all right," George says. "I want you here as well, Mister Silberg."

Anthony recognizes that something has happened: Mister Silberg. Something has gone wrong.

The silence in the room stretches into discomfort. Barbara Rossellini rolls her chair away from the telephone. She looks at Silberg, holds open her hands, arms outstretched.

Barbara widens her eyes in a silent, universal expression of, "What's going on?"

"I'll be there with pleasure, George," Anthony Silberg says. "Congratulations on selling your home."

"I look forward to seeing you," George McKlane says.

The phone clicks. A dial tone fills Barbara Rossellini's office. Silberg leans forward and punches a button on her phone, turning it off.

Barbara watches him, says nothing, waits.

Silberg suddenly stands up and says:

"We're going to take this listing and mark it as a Pending Sale immediately. I'll have Sarah Golden, my secretary, enter it that way in the Multiple Listing Service upstairs. You don't have to worry about it."

"Yes, sir," she says. "What's wrong with McKlane?"

"With no contingencies. The buyer waives the inspection clause," Silberg says.

"How do you do that?" Barbara asks.

"With a pen," he says.

Anthony Silberg takes Gustavo Oliveira's Contract for Sale and draws a circle around the inspection contingency, which he then puts a large "X" across.

He then initials it. He seems angry as he does this, and the pressure of his pen rips through a page of the contract. His jaw tightens, then relaxes.

He crumples the page.

"I'll bring an updated contract with me to the meeting."

He starts to walk out of her office, stops at the door, and says: "Quarter to five, out front, a gray Maserati."

Barbara looks at another copy of the contract. Initials are at the bottom of every page. All of the initials are identical to the one that Anthony Silberg put next to the inspection contingency that he just crossed out.

She flips to the final page. Gustavo Oliveira's signature scrawls across the Buyer's line. It might be from the same person who initialed each page.

She looks at the bottom of the page, which the manager, Bill Brownstone, has signed for Accelerated Realty Sales. His signature is small and precise.

Barbara Rossellini's name appears on both sides of the deal, representing the buyer as well as the seller.

The closing date is 60 days away. The contract awards a net commission to Barbara, after splits, of $216,000. She decides she has some important things to learn that they do not teach people in the real estate school she attended.

13752 Coconut Palm Ct., Boca Raton: Tuesday PM

For the first time in many months, the bank of computer monitors behind George McKlane's desk comes to life. Sharonda works the keyboard and mouse, and George sits in a chair next to her, watching her skip through programs, searching. George McKlane understands computers very well, but Sharonda amazes him with her knowledge, skill, and speed. She has a credit card of George's next to the keyboard because a lot of what she is doing costs money. As she moves through one program after another, he keeps asking: "How'd you do that?"

Finally, she looks at him and says: "Captain, you've got to let the troops do their thing. I'm working a tight deadline, and I will never make it if I have to teach you what I'm doing. You've got to let me work."

A .40 caliber Glock 35 is in its holster on her waist.

"Sorry," George says. Less than thirty seconds later, he repeats: "How'd you do that?"

She takes her hands off the mouse and keyboard and stares at him. Suddenly, the doorbell rings.

"Get the door," she says, smiling at their role reversal. George nods and goes to the front door.

Doctor Gunther Klein and Judge Ralph Broadslate appear, and a huge man named Samuel Nelson, who is Sharonda's husband.

"Doctor, judge, Sergeant Nelson," George McKlane says. "Thanks for coming on short notice. Good to see you again, sergeant."

Samuel Nelson was a Marine Corps MP in Iraq during the April 2004 assault on Fallujah, which was his final tour of duty. He is now a sergeant in the Honor Guard of the Boca Raton Police Department.

Because he is in uniform, Samuel Nelson snaps a salute at Captain McKlane, a Medal of Honor obligation, and George snaps a salute back.

After that, they shake hands as friends.

They all head towards George's office, but Sharonda redirects them to the Birdroom. "Eat some sandwiches," she says. "I'll be there in five more minutes."

She's on the phone trying to talk to someone at the Realtors® Association of the Palm Beaches.

She has been shuffled back and forth from reception to membership to general information and back to the reception desk with no luck.

She has had a similar experience with the Department of Business and Professional Regulation in Orlando, although she does manage to get some useful information off their website. She can leave messages with either organization, but she cannot find a way to speak to a human being.

She leaves no messages. Finally, she gives up and walks into the Birdroom.

"Okay," she says to the gathering, "Mister Silberg is the Broker of Record at Accelerated Realty Sales, which is a Limited Liability Company. He a broker and the owner, but he has licensed partners."

"He probably has quite a few silent partners as well," Judge Broadstreet says.

"No record of that," Sharonda says. "The Department of Business and Professional Regulation will have that information, but I need more time to get through the roadblock of their telephone system. I have to talk to a real person. Silberg is properly licensed and has been the Broker of Record at Accelerated Realty Sales since it started business seventeen years ago."

"It's the biggest real estate company in Boca," Doctor Klein says. "Sold us our home."

"Silberg has a criminal record," Sharonda continues. "I have copies of the original arrest record and U.S. Code violations. The FBI arrested him for assaulting an agent of the Federal Bureau of Investigation during a warehouse heist with two other men. All three of them were arrested in New Jersey in 1990."

"How about that? That's when I was a sitting Judge," Ralph Broadstreet says. "His name does not ring a bell, but I can get more information if we need it."

"He served every day of a four-and-a-half-year term at the medium-security Federal Correction Institution in Schuylkill, Pennsylvania," Sharonda continues. "He received no time off for good behavior."

"I'm not sure that was possible on a Federal charge in the 1990s," Judge Broadslate says.

"How the hell did he get a real estate license?" George McKlane asks.

"No idea," Sharonda says. "He served his time and moved to Boca Raton in 1995. I Googled Silberg and, in one story back in 1998, when he started Accelerated Realty Sales, the writer mentions his past police record. So it was something that the licensing authorities had known about and had accepted."

"They're all a bunch of crooks," Doctor Klein says. Nobody in the room laughs.

Sergeant Samuel Nelson, Sharonda's husband, has been working on his computer tablet, and he says: "Clean slate in Boca. A model citizen. A big contributor to the Police Athletic League."

"A lot of the information I got off the internet confirms his generosity and the charitable nature of his company," Sharonda says. "I think they have a very effective public relations company working for them."

George McKlane says: "He told me an hour ago that he has sold this home for six million dollars," George says. "He has a signed sales contract, full-price, and when he gets here at five o'clock, he expects me to sign it. The only contingency is a home inspection within forty-eight hours."

"Take the deal," Doctor Klein says. "That's a big number, a good price." George shakes his head, no.

"Rossellini," Sharonda says.

"The big developer?" Judge Broadslate asks.

"No," George says. "She's a tiny little woman who works for Silberg as an agent. Can't be more than four foot eleven." He looks at Sharonda. "What about her?" he asks.

"Well, her last name – Rossellini – is a mystery. She was married three times, never to anyone by that name. And it's also not her maiden name. She has a few arrests for shoplifting in Texas, but no record of guilt. So she either settled out of court or beat the rap. She has no children."

"When I first saw her," George says, "I thought I knew her." The room is silent for a moment.

Sharonda says: "You did." Everyone looks at her. "Her maiden name is Georgette Barbara Chapman."

"I'll be damned," George says. He feels his heartbeat in his chest. "Of course. Gunnery Sergeant Chapman and his wife had a daughter when he was sixty-seven years old. I held her in my arms when she was just six months old." He looks at the gathering. "Sergeant Raymond Garfield Chapman saved my life in Korea. He would never admit it."

Nobody says anything.

"She broke his heart," George says. "She was a real problem child. The wife left Gunny, left both of them when Georgette was just a kid. A wild kid. I only saw her that one time, at her christening. I used to send her money on her birthday until Gunny told me not to. She's my godchild, for

Heaven's sake. I'm her godfather. She's named after me. I'll be damned."

"This is getting a little weird," Doctor Klein says.

"Complicated," Judge Broadslate says.

The room grows silent again. George stands up. The muscles in his jaw tighten. "Let's get back to basics," George says. "Let's go into the office and listen to the reason that I asked all of you to come over here this morning."

Sharonda plays two different recordings. First, the conversation between George and Anthony Silberg in the Birdroom when he reveals his chest wound.

Then she plays the recording of Silberg and the Brazilian Buyer in the War Room.

Sharonda shuts off the Magic Wand, and the sound fades into silence. Judge Broadslate clears his throat louder than necessary. Everyone gives him their attention. He looks first at Sergeant Samuel Nelson and then at George McKlane.

"George," he says, "that's a very nice recording system you have there. And I am sure some people would view it as eavesdropping or a bugging device. But I know that you have installed it to protect yourself and your family from dangerous consequences, some of which might, in your opinion, be life-threatening."

George looks at him.

"Say, 'Yes' George," the Judge says.

"Yes."

"Fine," the Judge says. He looks at Sharonda's husband. "Anything you heard on that recording device is now legal in the State of Florida. It is admissible in a court of law."

Sergeant Samuel Nelson of the Boca Raton Police Department laughs, and everyone else in the room smiles.

George puts an arm around Judge Broadslate and says: "Thank you, Counselor."

The Judge smiles and says: "Wait until you see my retainer fee." Then he adds: "Excuse me for a few minutes, folks. I want to call Martha Krumble, my former Broker, and ask her a few questions. Where can I go, George, and not be spied on?"

George points out that the Magic Wand only works if it's turned on. He also says that he only turns it on for business purposes, adding "for protection" with a glance at the Judge. "I have never recorded any of our breakfast meetings on Saturday morning," he says to Doctor Klein. Sharonda confirms this.

Judge Broadslate goes into the Birdroom to make the call. He comes back around five minutes later and says: "Apparently everyone in the industry knows that Silberg is a reformed felon. As long as you admit it and have done your time, you can still get a real estate license in Florida. It is a state of great opportunity for rehabilitated crooks. Martha was very reluctant to say anything bad about Silberg because it's against their Code of Ethics."

"They have a Code of Ethics?" Doctor Gunther Klein asks. "That's a joke. 'Real estate agent' and 'Code of Ethics' definitely qualifies for entry into the International Oxymoron Hall of Fame."

"Let's not get into that," Judge Broadslate says. "Martha Krumble also says Silberg has a bad habit of making unwanted advances on women, herself included. She interviewed for a job at Accelerated Realty Sales a few years ago, in his office, and he locked the door and grabbed her inappropriately, trying to force himself on her. Martha walked out. She also told me that over ten percent of the real estate agents in the area work for him.

"He's a powerful force in the Chamber of Commerce. He has a lot of significant friends. She says his agents like and support him because he sticks up for them in any real estate dispute. I found it interesting that her exact words about this included, even if they're lying."

"Good information," George says. "I have him on tape saying that the reason he did not hire Martha Krumble was that she, what was the term, lowballed customers. He said she priced homes so that it would make for an easy sale. It was a flat-out lie."

"Is that why you didn't use her?" the Judge asks.

"Partially. But mostly, I bought into the magic of a six million dollar Brazilian."

"How are we going to handle this, Captain?" Sharonda asks. "In about twenty minutes, Silberg and Rossellini will be here, probably in this room."

Judge Broadslate holds up his hand. "Before you answer that, George, I want to caution you against telling any of us that you will record these proceedings. Because if you tell us that, then you are also going to have to tell Mister Silberg that you are doing it before he says a word. So I want you to assure all of us that you have no intention, whatsoever, of doing any such thing."

George wrinkled his forehead, finally saying: "I have no intention, whatsoever, of doing any such thing."

"Good," the Judge says, adding, with a sweep of his hand: "Of course any one or all of us can always become a first-hand witness in a court of law."

They appreciate the intelligence of the Judge.

"One more thing," he adds. "Sergeant Nelson, I think you should not be here. Sharonda can fill you in on any details. But for your own sake, I think you and your police car out front should disappear. I think Mister Silberg may have some significant friends in the city of Boca Raton, and there's no reason for you to jeopardize either your position or your career over this."

"Thank you, Judge," the police officer says, visibly relieved. Everyone shakes his hand. George McKlane and Samuel Nelson snap salutes at one another again.

Then Officer Nelson looks at his wife, Sharonda. He puts his hands on her shoulders and looks deeply into her eyes. He says: "Try not to shoot anyone, sweetheart."

Everyone laughs, but perhaps not as hard as they wish they could.

Chapter 10

Staying Alive

<u>**13752 Coconut Palm Ct.,**</u>
<u>**Boca Raton: Tuesday PM**</u>

During the ride from the office, Barbara Rossellini asks Tony Silberg what role she should play in the meeting with Captain George McKlane.

Silberg says she should simply present the contract to George for his signature, first pointing out to McKlane that the Brazilian buyer, Gustavo Oliveira, called from Miami International and was willing to cancel the inspection contingency.

Silberg says: "Tell McKlane that the buyer did so on the advice of his broker."

"Did Mister Oliveira do that?" Barbara asks.

"I have personally guaranteed the status of the home to Oliveira. If anything does not satisfy him, Accelerated Realty Sales promises to make it right."

"Really?" she asks.

"Did you hear what I just said?"

"Yes, sir."

She knows that he has not answered her about whether or not the buyer called from the Miami airport and canceled the inspection contingency.

She also realizes that she is a pawn in a game she neither understands nor controls.

"This is a beautiful car," she says.

"Yes, it is," Anthony Silberg says. The ride continues in uncomfortable silence until they turn into George McKlane's drive. The gates are already open.

"Someone is having a party," Barbara says. "He must be celebrating the sale of his house." Silberg remains silent. Several cars are in the drive. As they get out of the Maserati, Barbara notices the metal entry gates slowly close and lock into place. She stands motionless as they swing shut. Then she walks quickly to the front door. Silberg has already rung the bell. She stands behind him.

"Please come in," Sharonda says, opening the door. "Hi, Barbara. Hi, Tony." She sounds quite happy.

Barbara starts to move forward, but she runs into the wall of Anthony Silberg, who has not moved to enter the house. She bounces off him, backs up.

"Hello, Sharonda," Silberg says. "If I'm not mistaken, that's a Glock?" He points at her waist.

Barbara notices the gun on Sharonda's hip.

"Oh," Sharonda says with a smile. "I forgot it was there. I'm going to the range up in Delray after our meeting to shoot with my husband. I hope our meeting doesn't take more than a minute or two. I'm already in a rush. I may have to leave early." She backs into the house and looks at Barbara. "Hubby's a policeman here in Boca. He was telling me earlier today about how generous Mister Silberg is with the Boca Police Department."

Silberg steps over the threshold, and Barbara follows him into George McKlane's home.

"We're going to meet in Captain, uh, George's office. I'm just about to wheel in the snack tray. Please, you know where the office is." She heads towards the kitchen.

As Silberg and Barbara enter the office, Barbara sees two men that she has never seen before. George McKlane says: "Welcome." He certainly does have a great smile, Barbara Rossellini thinks.

One of the other men says: "Hello, Anthony Silberg. It's good to see you."

"Doctor Gunther Klein," Anthony says. "How's your wife, Rachel?" They see each other every week at Temple but rarely exchange greetings.

George introduces Ralph Broadslate, and Anthony says: "We've met at the Club a few times, Judge."

"Yes, we have," Ralph Broadslate says.

"George claps his hands together and says: "Well, naturally, I wanted to have my legal advisor here, Tony. I hope you don't mind."

"Not at all," Anthony says. He does not sit down. "And why are you here, Doctor Klein?"

After a moment of silence, Doctor Gunther Klein deadpans: "Well, Anthony, I understand you have sold my best friend's home for six million dollars. I'm here to make sure he doesn't suffer a serious heart attack because of it."

Sharonda's snack cart rolls into the sounds of polite laughter that follows.

Silberg sits down in one of the chairs arranged in front of McKlane's desk.

"Barbara?" he says, "The floor is yours."

Everyone sits, except for Sharonda, who closes the door to the office and remains there, eyes on Silberg. Barbara Rossellini takes the sales contract out of a folder and says: "One thing has changed, Mister McKlane."

"I see," he says.

"Yes, sir. The buyer, Mister Oliveira, phoned from Miami International after we spoke to you earlier."

"I see," George repeats.

"Yes, and he has removed the inspection contingency on the advice of Mister Silberg."

No one says anything for a moment.

"What does that mean?" George asks.

"It means that the only thing left to make this contract valid and binding is your signature, sir."

She leans forward and slides the contract onto his desk. "You need to initial each page."

George McKlane looks at Judge Broadslate, who says: "Let me take a look at it."

It's a standard Far-Bar contract, with no addendums, and with no contingencies. It appears to be a legitimate sales contract that lacks only the seller's signature and page initials.

The clauses that George asks to strike out, the changes he asks for, have all been made, with $600,000 escrowed at Accelerated Realty Sales.

"Mister Oliveira understands that his entire six hundred thousand dollars are at risk as soon as this contract goes live, as soon as it's signed?" the Judge asks.

"Of course," Anthony Silberg says.

"He loves the house," Barbara says.

The Judge keeps reading the contract and then passes it back to George.

Nobody gets up and goes to the snack cart for a pastry. Nobody asks for a cup of coffee.

"I do not see any problem with it, George."

Silberg says: "Better check his pulse, Doc." He and Barbara laugh. Nobody else does.

George picks up the document and studies it. He flips a few pages, puts it down again.

Without looking at anyone, George says: "Where does it say you return the watch that you stole from me?"

Standing at the closed door to the office, behind Anthony Silberg, Sharonda watches as a slight redness creeps into the broker's neck. Then, just as quickly, the coloring fades away.

Sharonda realizes that Anthony Silberg can turn his anger on and off.

"I'm sorry," Anthony Silberg says. "Gustavo Oliveira found your watch on the floor of the closet upstairs. He was going to give it to Sharonda, but then he forgot about it in all the excitement of falling in love with his new home. He promised me when I spoke to him on the phone that he would airmail it to my office as soon as he gets back to Brazil. I trust him. He'll do that."

"Really?" George asks.

"Absolutely." More silence follows.

"Why would you trust someone called 'Snake'?" George McKlane asks.

Sharonda sees some redness reappear on Silberg's neck. She wonders if he carries a concealed weapon.

She quietly unlatches her Glock, but she keeps it in the holster on her waist.

"I have no idea what the Hell you're talking about, George," Anthony Silberg says.

George leans back, opens the cabinet, slides out the drawer, and throws a switch.

For a moment, nothing but silence, then laughter suddenly fills the office, followed by voices.

"Claro, claro, claro

"Claro, my ass. "I thought we were dead, Pop."

It takes less than four minutes for the entire conversation to finish. While the recording plays, Sharonda watches Silberg's neck blush slightly.

She is surprised when it returns to its standard color as the recording fades into the stillness of the office.

Everyone focuses on Anthony Silberg.

Sharonda widens her stance, her hand on her holster, expecting him to stand up, perhaps make some sort of threatening move. He remains seated.

Silberg's face starts to redden with anger as George continues to speak.

"You were thrown out of the Marine Corps on a medical discharge, Mr. Silberg. You never even made it through basic training on Parris Island. You were arrested in New Jersey by the FBI and sent to prison for four and a half years in a facility in Pennsylvania. The wound on your chest has nothing to do with the United States Marine Corps. I'd be very interested to know where you got it. And it's the Medal of Honor, not the Congressional Medal of Honor. Congress has nothing to do with it. I explained that to you before."

Nobody in the room moves. No one says anything. Silberg turns around in his chair and looks at Sharonda standing in front of the closed office door.

He says: "Not going to do any target practice with hubby, huh?" Sharonda stares at him, hard.

He turns back to George, who asks, "Why did the fake Brazilian call you, *Pop,* Silberg?". The creep you called Snake seems a little old to be your son.

"I boxed Golden Gloves," Silberg answers. "It was the sound that my fist made when I crushed the face of one of my opponents."

"So, where did you get the scare on your chest?" George asks. "Did you miss a punch?" George is smiling.

"I got shanked at Shitkill," Silberg says. "You ever heard of Shitkill, McKlane?"

"The Federal Correction Institution in Schuylkill, Pennsylvania," George answers. "You were there for four and a half years."

"Do you want to know what happened to the Black guy who shanked me?"

"Silberg, are you threatening Mister McKlane?" Judge Broadslate asks.

"He committed suicide," Silberg says.

"Mister Silberg," Judge Broadslate says, "I think it's necessary to advise you .. "

"I don't need your advice, Judge. No disrespect, but I've bought better judges than you. I know all about you, Judge. I know things about you that you don't know."

"Mister Silberg, I have no idea what the Hell you ... "

Silberg finally stands up, and Sharonda braces herself against the closed door.

"You have six million dollars sitting in front of you, Mister McKlane. Six million. You can take it and shut the fuck up, or you can keep flapping your aging gums. I don't give a shit. But don't think for one minute that you can hurt my company or me. You bring down my company, you disrespect it, or me, and you destroy this entire city. Do you know what happens if my company gets hurt by you? Do you know how many people will be out of work? People like

Barbara Rossellini here? Shit, you don't even know who she is, do you?"

George leans forward, takes a handkerchief, and wipes off some of the spittle that Silberg has sprayed on his desk. "She's my Goddaughter," George says quietly. "The only child of my staff sergeant, and later Gunnery Sergeant Raymond Garfield Chapman, who saved my life in Korea."

Barbara Rossellini, who has been stunned by everything that has happened so far, somehow manages to open her eyes even wider. Silberg glares at her.

"So you did tell him, huh?"

"No," is the only word that escapes from her mouth, and it barely makes it out as a whisper.

She has nothing else to say.

Silberg turns back to George McKlane.

"Six million dollars," Silberg says. "And McKlane, if you don't sign that contract, my lawyers are going to sue you for performance. It's a full-price offer, with no contingencies. And they're also going to sue your heroic ass for illegally wiretapping my conversations. I will call in the Feds, Mister McKlane, and have your wrinkled ass arrested. I don't care how much of a hero you were in Korea. The headline is going to read 'Hero Turns Chump.' I am not going to be the one who ends up looking like an idiot. You are."

He turns and glares at Barbara. "Let's go, Rossellini." He turns around. "Open the door," he says to Sharonda. "What ... you going to shoot me?" He looks at Judge Broadslate. "Make a note of that, Judge. The Black bitch is threatening my life."

Sharonda drops her hand from her holster and steps aside. "Open it yourself," she says.

He does. "Rossellini!" he shouts. She gets up, barely able to walk, and follows him out the door, into the Maserati. They wait while the front gates slowly swing inward. Silberg drives, surprisingly calmly, through them.

As they start their return to the office, Barbara says: "This was the happiest day of my life three hours ago." Then she starts to cry. Silberg says nothing, flicks a button on the steering wheel. The BeeGees Staying Alive blends into her tears, followed by the extended version of Eric Clapton's Layla. Silberg turns off the music as he drops her at the front entrance of the office. He has not said a word.

She opens the passenger door and steps out, closing it. The window rolls down, and she leans over and looks in at Tony Silberg.

"Listen, Barbara," he says. "I hate to spoil your perfectly rotten day."

"What does that mean?" she says.

"You're fired."

He burns a little rubber leaving.

Accelerated Realty Sales
Boca, Tuesday Evening

Barbara takes out her office key and unlocks the outer door to Accelerated Realty Sales. The office has a time lock on it, which prevents any public access on weekends and holidays, and every workday between five-thirty in the afternoon and seven-thirty in the morning.

Barbara walks through an empty bullpen back to her office in the Goldfish Bowl, turning on the lights. A security guard walks past with a nod and a smile. In just one more day, she realizes he would probably escort her out of the building.

Two other offices have lights on in the Goldfish Bowl: one belonging to a Rossellini man, whom she has never seen before, and the other to Alice Koenig, who is working late.

Barbara slumps into her chair and leans forward onto her desk. She starts to cry again; then, she pounds her fist angrily on the surface. The voice of Alice Koenig, in the doorway, startles her.

"Tough day?" Alice asks.

"Leave me alone," Barbara says.

Alice Koenig walks out. She returns almost immediately with a box of tissues and sits in one of Barbara's guest chairs. "Now might be a perfect time to compare notes," Alice Koenig says.

Barbara blows her nose, takes a deep breath. "Silberg just fired me," she says.

"What did you do?"

"Nothing," Barbara says.

"What happened to the six million dollars McKlane sale?" Alice Koenig asks.

"What do you know about the McKlane sale?" Barbara asks. "How do you know about it?"

"Anthony does not keep very many secrets from me," Alice Koenig says.

Barbara blows her nose again. She leans back in her chair, looks at Alice Koenig, and says: "You want to bet?"

Alice raises her eyebrows, asks her to explain.

Barbara looks at her and says: "Silberg was in prison at someplace called Shitkill for four and a half years."

"Everyone knows that," Alice says. "He paid his dues and became a broker seventeen years ago. He admitted he was a rehabilitated felon on his application. He never lied."

"You ever see the scar on his chest?" Barbara asks.

"More times than I can remember," Alice says. She smiles. "From every possible angle."

"I'll bet you have," Barbara says, but without any bitterness. "You know where he got that scar?"

"Of course I do," Alice says. "Khe Sanh during the Tet Offensive, when he was a buck sergeant in the Marine Corp back in whenever. He almost bled out."

"Wrong," Barbara interrupts. "He never made it through Basic Training in the Marine Corps. They threw him out of the Corps on a Medical Discharge."

Alice says nothing.

"Silberg got shanked by an inmate at Shitkill," Barbara says. "An inmate who then committed suicide, although I'd bet he had some help from Silberg's buddies."

"Where did you get this information?" Alice asks.

"From my Godfather," Barbara says.

"Who is your Godfather?" Alice asks, thinking she's going to say, Rossellini.

"Captain George McKlane," she says. "Winner of the Medal of Honor." She feels an unexpected sense of pride when she says this.

For the next fifteen minutes, Barbara explains what happened at the meeting with George McKlane.

She does not remember everything, nor does she understand all of it.

She recalls the name of the Doctor and the Judge, and she remembers that Sharonda, whose husband she thought was a police officer in Boca Raton, had a gun, a Glock holstered on her waist.

She remembers the almost uncontrolled anger of Silberg, and the foul language he spat at George McKlane.

She does not sensationalize anything about the meeting. She simply outlines what happened accurately, and she ends by saying: "So the best day of my life turned into a piece of shit, and Silberg fired me."

As she reaches the end of the story, the Rossellini man turns off the lights in his office and starts to leave. Alice gets out of her chair, goes to the door, and catches his attention. "Jimmy," she says, "You're going to want to hear what Barbara Rossellini just told me."

The man walks over to Barbara's office, introduces himself as James J. Johnson, and sits down in a guest chair. Alice sits in the other one, looks at Barbara, and says: "Do a rewind of everything, Barbara."

She does. She fleshes it out with a little detail, but still without embellishment.

She remembers George McKlane wiping Silberg's spittle off the desk.

She mentions the recording device, and Barbara remembers Silberg's veiled threat to Judge Broadslate.

Nothing draws any surprise or emotion from James J. Johnson. He asks one question about the recording. Barbara doesn't know much about it, but she remembers that Silberg said he would sue McKlane for eavesdropping.

After Barbara finishes, Alice Koenig looks at him and says: "Jimmy, I do believe the walls of Jericho are about to come tumbling down."

"Explain," he says.

"Our broker has just put this entire agency at risk with one of the most admired and honored men in Boca Raton," Alice says. "I guess that Captain McKlane, winner of the Medal of Honor, will display a good deal of integrity as well as principle. He will not sign the contract. He will dispute it, and he will do it publicly. Even if he does it privately, among his powerful friends, it will be a disaster. This entire organization will collapse because of that dispute. Anthony Silberg will not back down, you know it, and I know it. And he will drag anyone who sides with him and his pack of lies down the drain with him. It will take the agents working here exactly one day, twenty-four hours, to look for jobs at another Brokerage. And I imagine that most of the customers working with Accelerated Realty Sales will immediately demand that their contracts with Anthony Silberg's company are canceled, null, and void."

James J. Johnson's expression never changes. He says: "Stay here. I'll be right back."

He returns to his office, turns on the lights, and calls someone. He has a relatively long conversation, towards the end of which he listens more than he talks.

In Barbara's office, Alice asks: "Explain your last name to me. How did you get to be a Rossellini? I sort of thought that was why you were in the Goldfish Bowl."

"I'm in the Goldfish Bowl because I screwed Silberg," she says.

After a pause, Alice says: "Perhaps you'll have a chance to screw him again, right now."

Alice smiles. Barbara thinks they might become friends.

Barbara talks about her brief marriage to Roberto Rossellini, how they met when she was a bartender, and their

Vegas weekend wedding, followed by an annulment a few months later.

"It was mostly a friendly, mutual agreement," Barbara says. She does not share the titmouse comparison she joked about to Silberg the previous night.

The door opens, and James J. Johnson walks in and sits back down. "You're about to get an important phone call," he says to Barbara. The phone immediately rings.

"Barbara Rossellini," she answers.

A deep and friendly voice says: "Hello, Barbara. It is Angelo Rossellini. How wonderful to hear your voice again. It's been too long since we have spoken. Please, I want you to tell me everything about your six million dollar meeting with Captain George McKlane."

Barbara does not remember mentioning any dollar amount to James J. Johnson, although Alice Koenig seems to know about it.

She tells her story for the third time, occasionally interrupted by a question from Angelo Rossellini.

She ends the story by saying: "This was the happiest day of my life early this afternoon, Mister Rossellini, and it ended in a complete disaster. Mister Silberg fired me. I came into my office to get my belongings and leave." She sniffs, but she does not cry.

She listens for a while, looks genuinely surprised, and then says: "Thank you."

She listens some more and says: "I miss you, too, Mister Rossellini. Say 'hello' to Roberto for me."

She hangs up.

She looks at Alice Koenig and Jimmy Johnson and says: "Apparently, I now work for Mister Rossellini, right here, in this office." Alice points at the poster taped on Barbara's filing cabinet. She repeats its message.

"Goldfish never drown," she says.

Angelo Rossellini sits in a private room at the Palm Beach Kennel Club with four other men, all dressed in expensive clothes, all playing Texas Hold-em, No-Limit Poker. Rossellini rarely loses.

He has spent almost ten minutes away from the card table, talking on an encrypted cell phone to Jimmy J. Johnson, who he calls Triple-J, and then Barbara Rossellini.

He sits back down at the poker table, and the dealer gives everyone three cards, the final one showing face up.

Angelo flips his cards over and lays his hands on the table, showing open palms. The other men slowly mimic this action. The dealer leaves the room quietly and quickly.

"Mister Silberg has put all of us in danger," Angelo says as the door shuts. He explains what has happened. No one interrupts him.

He begins with his meeting with Gregory "Snake" Richards and ends with his conversation with "members of my family, whom I trust." He does not tell them that they are Triple-J and Barbara Rossellini.

"Silberg has always been cancer to our organization," one man says. "For almost twenty years."

"And now he has spread his cancer," Angelo replies. "And his deception has been recorded in a signed sales contract for six million dollars. The Department of Justice will use this to continue their investigation into making our corporate profits legitimate." He does not use the term "money laundering," although all the men understand that this is the meaning of the word legitimate.

"And this McKlane person has a recording as well?" another man asks.

"Yes," Angelo answers.

"So eliminating Silberg will not fix this problem," a third man points out.

"Yes, and no," Angelo says. He says it very slowly. They look at him, but he does not explain. Nor does anyone ask him for details. They understand that Angelo has a solution, and the less they know about it, the safer they will all be.

"There is one regrettable aspect of the cure for this cancer," Angelo says. They all remain silent. "Mister McKlane, who has had a very long and fruitful life, who has served our nation with great distinction, must stop living. And Anthony Silberg must be blamed for his death."

None of the men understand why George McKlane must die, but they all give their permission without question or hesitation.

They all trust the judgment of Angelo Rossellini.

Chapter 11

Killer Computer Games

The Farm In Virginia,
Tuesday Evening

Torbjorn Petersson likes to play gin rummy with his grandmother almost every night. "Don't worry, son," she says to him, not for the first time. They continue the sentence together.

"You'll get it back when I'm dead."

Tonight, it's his turn to add the kicker, which has to be a phrase they've never used before. They spend part of every day working this part out.

Torbjorn Petersson says: "Only I've decided I won't be attending my funeral."

She laughs and slaps the table. She thinks it's one of his better ones. Torbjorn has his back to the computer room.

"It's blinking," she says.

He turns around and looks at a small green light flashing on and off over the doorway.

"I think you better look at it," she says. "You're running out of money, son."

"I reckon you're right, Gammy," he says.

He walks into the computer room. All the modems blink green and blue, some of them pale gray. The UPS units are all solid green.

He sits down at the Brazil computer screen and accesses an encrypted website where a single message waits for him. It gives him an address with a password, a kill date, and the value of the job.

He accepts the assignment, which is marked "immediate." Within less than 20 seconds, half the money, $150,000, is available for placement in any bank account anywhere in the world, with a password that will initiate the transaction and confirm its acceptance.

The contract value is double the standard rate.

Torbjorn rolls his computer chair across the floor to England, where he enters the password and deposits the money in an account in Luxembourg.

He then goes to the Mexico computer and enters the address and a different password. It checks to confirm that the financial code is activated, and the assignment accepted, and then it gives him another address, separate from the first one, with yet another password to use.

He goes to the South African proxy computer and enters the new password. The screen then shows him a photograph of the kill and the person's name and what, if any, additional requirements are attached to the assignment.

Torbjorn is dumbfounded. It shows a recent photograph of an older man: George McKlane. An object to be retrieved is a six million dollar sales contract on his home in Boca Raton, Florida. The kill date is immediate, and another person, a partner, is involved in the job.

Torbjorn has to be in Boca Raton, Florida, and he must confirm the kill within twenty-four hours.

"Gammy," he shouts. She comes into the room.

He has no secrets from his Grandmother, and she has none from him.

She stares at the victim's name. "Look him up," she says.

Torbjorn does a name search. Multiple links point to the same man: George McKlane, a famous Korean War veteran, a Marine Corps captain, and a winner of the Medal of Honor. It shows a picture of him in uniform.

"You cannot kill this man," Ernestine Petersson says.

"I have no choice. I've accepted the assignment."

"We read his letter on Jackson's birthday every year, son. We know it by heart. You cannot kill this man."

"I don't know what to do, Gammy," Torbjorn says. "I have a partner on this assignment."

His grandmother looks at him. After a moment, a smile curls her lips just a bit.

"You cannot kill this man, son."

"I know," he says, feeling lost.

"You must save him by not killing him."

Slowly, he begins to understand what she has said.

"You are the only man who can save him," Ernestine Petersson says. "Just as your grandfather saved him."

"And my partner?" Torbjorn asks.

"I think you must have a terrible, very incompetent partner," she says. "I think he is the one who could not fulfill the contract."

Torbjorn considers what she says, and everything suddenly falls into place. "Thank you, Gammy."

"Now you must go. You have very little time. Go. I will shut everything down here."

"Do you know how?" he asks.

She walks over to the generator switch and shuts it off. All the UPS devices start to beep and blink.

"That's one way to do it," he says, quickly shutting each UPS device off. The monitors go black.

"The whistle pig stew will be here when you get home," she says. "Go and save Captain McKlane, son."

13752 Coconut Palm Court
Boca Raton: Wednesday AM

Sharonda comes to work a little early on Wednesday morning. An hour after she arrives, she greets Doctor Klein and Judge Broadslate at the front door.

"At least Silberg didn't leave any tire marks in the driveway," she says. "He seems to be able to turn his anger on and off. Which is pretty much what a classic psychopath would be capable of doing."

"Mister Silberg might make a good case study in anger management," Doctor Klein says. "I would love to see a CT scan of his brain." They walk into George's office and continue where they left off the previous evening.

"Do you know what mystifies me?" Judge Broadslate says. "That." He points at the contract on George McKlane's desk. "Mister Silberg said a lot of stupid and angry things that he will probably regret, perhaps in a court of law. But that contract looks legitimate. Let me see it again, George."

He scans it, then says: "You have forty-eight hours to sign it."

He slides it back on the desk.

"After that, it's null and void. Right now, from the looks of it, it has a value of six million dollars."

"That may be more than your house is worth, George," Gunther Klein says. "It sounds like a pretty generous offer."

George reaches into a drawer of his mahogany desk and pulls out a report.

"This is the Comparative Market Analysis from Martha Krumble, your friend, Judge." He opens the report to a summary page. "According to her, my home has a top dollar value of less than five and a half million dollars. She recommends a listing price of that amount."

He throws the contract back on the desk.

"In our meeting, if I remember correctly, she said I should be willing to knock a few hundred thousand dollars off the list price to make a deal. I think she said I should not expect to sell for less than five point two million dollars."

George smiles.

"She also told me that the Turner painting in the living room is worth more than the house. She's a smart and sophisticated lady."

"Yes, she is," the Judge says. "Her father was a New York State Supreme Court Judge. The point, George, is that Mister Silberg's buyer has made a very generous offer."

"I don't think ..." George checks the contract "...Mister Gustavo Oliveira is a real person. I do not believe the man who came here with Silberg comes from Brazil. I don't think he even knows how to speak Portuguese."

"Whoever he is," Sharonda says, "he has put six hundred thousand dollars on the line."

"And from what I heard," Doctor Klein says, "that money is yours if the contract does not close in, what, a couple of months? Whoever he is, I seriously doubt if he's going to throw away that kind of money."

"The six hundred thousand will be in escrow at Accelerated Realty Sales," Judge Broadslate says. "Failure to perform puts the money in your pocket, George, less whatever claims the brokerage might have on the funds. Real estate commissions and legitimate expenses might eat up ten percent of the escrowed funds."

"What was Silberg's 'sue for performance' threat about?" George asks the Judge.

"Meaningless," the Judge says. "Unless you sign the contract and then subsequently try to back out of it."

The judge keeps thinking. "There's probably a fraud loophole that Silberg's company could use to renege on the deal. That would be very interesting."

Everyone watches the judge as he thinks.

"They could say that the money Oliveira escrows into their account is not real money, that it is there fraudulently. In which case, Silberg would agree with you that the buyer was not this Oliveira character. You would support his case. The six hundred thousand would disappear into a Federal investigation, and Silberg's company would probably have insurance to cover their losses. You might get nothing in that case. If you tried to get anything, you'd probably be locked up in the court system for years."

"But we can prove that Silberg knew this person was not real with the recording," Sharonda says.

"That's true," Judge Broadslate says. "But Silberg did not know that when and if he created his plan. I have to say that I am not sure that any of what I am suggesting was ever his intention in the first place. I think his company wants to close this deal for six million dollars."

"Why?" Doctor Klein asks.

Judge Ralph Broadslate thinks he might know an explanation of the least resistance.

"When I was a Federal Judge in New Jersey, I benched a lot of RICO cases, the most effective way that the government has to get its hands on Mob money. Crooks like to launder illicit gains through real estate. The Feds like to focus on real estate. The bad guys almost always do it through commercial projects and land development. But they might also do it through expensive luxury homes, although it's riskier." He reaches over and taps the contract on George's desk. "This is a costly luxury home."

"So you think that Silberg is in bed with the mob?" George McKlane asks.

"I did not say that," the Judge says. "But I would be very interested in the names of any silent partners who happen to own a piece of Accelerated Realty Sales."

"I can probably get that information tomorrow," Sharonda says.

George holds up the contract. "What do you recommend I do with this?" he asks.

"Put it in a safe place," the Judge says. "And do NOT sign it. Your forty-eight-hour grace period extends to Friday's close of business."

After everyone but Sharonda leaves, George puts the contract in his gun safe.

He then spends most of the day trying to figure out how to fire Accelerated Realty Sales and cancel the contract, and also what the consequences of revealing the reason for doing so might be.

George considers talking about what has happened to the President of the Homeowners' Association at The Royal Coconut Yacht and Country Club.

He calls Judge Broadslate, who is on the Board, and asks about calling a special meeting to discuss the ramifications of what Anthony Silberg and Accelerated Realty Sales has done.

"I've been thinking about that," the Judge says. "What Silberg said so distastefully and with such extraordinary anger contains a grain of truth."

"What the heck does that mean?" George says.

"It means that you're in a position to destroy his company. It's the largest Real Estate Broker in Boca Raton, and one of the largest in the entire state of Florida. The financial implications of its destruction and the turmoil it will send our housing market into will be enormous. The city of Boca Raton may lose an enormous amount of its tax base."

"Crime has consequences," George says.

"Yes, you can certainly make that argument," the Judge says. "And there will be serious political ramifications, as well, because Silberg definitely has friends in high places in this city as well as in Palm Beach County. It's going to be one hell of a mess, George."

"What are you suggesting?"

"You are going to be part of the mess," Judge Broadslate says. "It will, quite literally, consume the rest of your life, George McKlane."

"That doesn't bother me, Ralph."

"I know it doesn't. But it probably should."

"Does it bother you?"

The Judge takes a breath. George hears it.

"I think it does," the Judge finally says. "I've seen a lot of embarrassing political battles in my life, George, and I've also seen a lot of outstanding people dragged through the mud because they decided to do the right thing."

"I'll take my chances," George says.

"I know you will," the Judge says. "And I believe you will prevail if you live long enough."

"I will," George says.

"I think you probably will, or at least I hope so. I wouldn't mind seeing you in the Guinness Book of Records as the world's oldest whistleblower. But others won't have your stamina, your grit, or your money, George. And many of them, out of work, unable to sell their homes, will suffer enormously. The Sunshine State of Florida will have a dark cloud hanging over it. I guess you call it collateral damage."

George says nothing.

"We have time, George. You have time. Let's wait 24 hours, at least. Let's meet tomorrow and see if we can't come up with a plan that does not destroy a lot of innocent people who don't deserve to be hurt by Anthony Silberg."

"I'm willing to do that," George says.

At five o'clock, Sharonda leaves.

An hour later, George eats a lackluster meal of unsalted wild rice and tasteless chicken, organized by Rachel Klein.

He drinks a Guinness slowly and with great pleasure. Then he starts going through the kitchen and the pantry, looking for the chocolate bars that Sharonda said she hid.

He is about to give up, figuring she has removed them from the house when he hits a chocolate gold mine in the laundry room.

Behind a box of detergent and a jug of Clorox, he finds three king-sized bars.

He takes all of them back up to his War Room, puts two in the safe, does not close it completely, and sits down in a comfortable chair within arm's reach of the chocolate.

He gets through one entire bar and is reaching for another when the magic captures him again.

He slumps into the chair. He travels back to Korea.

After 45 minutes, the ambient light in the closet dims and turns off automatically.

Ten minutes later, the spotlight on the pyramid of socks also flickers off, leaving only darkness.

North Korea: Hill 1081 December 7, 1950

Captain George McKlane looks at Staff Sergeant Raymond Chapman and says a number: "Ten Eighty-One." The orders came down on December 7th, 1950, saying the Marines have to seize the heights overlooking Funchilin Pass on the northern end of Hill 1081.

The razor-like gap of the pass will turn into the most challenging puzzle piece in the breakout of the 1st Marine Division, the bloodiest part of its hellish escape to the Hamhung embarkation area.

The Marines slowly advance from the city of Hagaru to Koto-ri. Men and equipment spill over the perimeter of the overcrowded town.

Almost 14,000 additional troops, 12,000 of them Marines, spill into Koto-ri, assembling for the final push towards Hamhung.

During daylight hours, the Marine Air Wing helps pave their way with strafing runs and napalm. Nevertheless, mistakes happen.

Late starts lead to personnel and equipment losses. The CCF disables Marine Corps M46 Patton tanks at the front of the long, retreating column.

The new tank M46 Patton design has never seen combat before. Korea becomes its baptism of fire, and the tanks will never operate in another theater of war.

The Chinese use Russian-made anti-tank weapons to disable the M-46 Patton tanks effectively. It puts a cork on the bottle of withdrawal.

Marine Command moves the M46 Pattons to the rear, forming the last elements of the motor column, rather than the point.

It's a move that speeds up the retreat and protects the tail end of the long, winding column of men and machines.

In the first week of December 1950, swirling snow cuts visibility down to twenty meters and eliminates any air support as Captain George McKlane leads his men up Hill 1081. Hundreds of tracks in the snow, rapidly disappearing in the howling wind, hint at a large concentration of Chinese communist forces.

A week earlier, a probing attack identifies Hill 1081 as an enemy stronghold.

The Marines come around a bend, and they see a roadblock. Behind it, a bunker is barely visible in the blinding snowstorm.

They approach this objective with caution.

Captain McKlane sends out a patrol that works its way up the hill, carrying 60mm mortars.

The lack of air support unexpectedly turns events in their favor.

Because Corsair bombing runs are impossible, Captain McKlane's men surprise the Chinese troops, who think they are safe from attack because of the weather.

"I guess nobody told them we don't call a 'time out' because of a little snow," Sergeant Chapman says, looking at a kettle of rice still cooking on a hook over hot coals.

The Chinese have fled into the whiteout.

Captain McKlane and his men move towards a larger Command Bunker less than a click down the road, and there the fighting becomes savage.

Captain George McKlane trips over a stool and loses both his balance and his submachine gun during the worst part of the battle.

Hand-to-hand combat surrounds him.

He has fallen on a dead Chinese officer. He rolls the man on top of him, a shield easily punctured by gunfire.

George McKlane grabs the enemy's burp gun, rolls back over, and empties it into the wide-eyed, slow-motion faces of two CCF soldiers lunging at him with bayonets. Their weapons have no bullets left.

Captain McKlane recovers his machine gun as the firefight turns into sporadic gunfire.

The enemy is routed, mostly dead.

Captain McKlane's parka has turned red.

It takes quite a while before he realizes that none of the blood is his.

He loses ten men, and eleven others are wounded. They wrestle control of Hill 1081 from the enemy's deadly grip. The most celebrated retreat in military history can now continue struggling towards Hamhung.

"Sergeant Chapman?" Captain George McKlane says. "Tell Corporal Smartass to get up here. I want to tell him a bedtime story."

The Sergeant leans up against a metal support in the bunker, shaking his head.

"Shit," Captain George McKlane says.

"Yeah, I'm afraid you're going to have to tell that story to his wife, Captain."

"Shit," the twenty-three-year-old captain repeats.

13752 Coconut Palm Court
In the War Room: Thursday 4 AM

In the darkness, George McKlane hears a noise. He thinks for a moment that he is still fighting in the Chinese Communist bunker.

Then 65 years melt away, and he realizes he is in the War Room. He hears someone downstairs pulling out drawers and letting them crash to the floor in his office.

At the same time, he sees a monster, some sort of an alien, move past the open closet door. He thinks he must be in a nightmare, but knows he is awake.

George reaches into the gun safe and pulls out his bulldog, the Colt .45 he carried throughout Korea. The weapon is loaded, oiled, and cleaned, but a bullet is not yet in the chamber.

It will make a distinctive sound when he racks it.

In the bedroom, he hears a single pop. Then the alien is standing at the closet door. He sees George in the dark through his green eyes.

George starts to chamber a bullet.

"Don't," the alien says.

George stops, lowers his gun. The alien steps across the threshold of the closet, and the ambient lights come on. The monster raises its green eyes, snaps them towards the top of its head, with a gun and silencer pointed at George.

"Drop it," he says.

George lets his .45 fall to the closet carpet. He realizes that the alien intruder is a man wearing a ski mask and night-vision goggles, not an alien.

"Don't move," the man says.

With his gun pointed at McKlane, he bends down and picks up the .45. He opens the gun safe all the way, puts the weapon on a small shelf. Then he shouts: "Got it!"

He reaches in the safe and takes the six million dollar sales contract.

Then he closes and locks the safe. A second man, also wearing a ski mask and night-vision goggles, steps into the War Room.

"Keep him covered," the first man says. He looks around and focuses on the letters framed against one wall. He moves down them, stops when he sees what he wants. He takes a framed thank-you note off the wall. He takes five more framed notes off the wall, seemingly at random.

He gives the framed letters to the second man, who puts them in a black bag, along with the sales contract, and then both of them back out of the closet.

The second man heads downstairs. The first man, standing in the doorway, points his silenced gun at George McKlane and says: "Sorry."

He pulls the trigger. George hears the pop.

He also hears the closet door close. He does not know why he is not dead, but his first reaction is to unlock the safe to get his .45 Colt back in his hands.

The Colt .45 used by Marines in Korea is the same one that was used by the U.S. Army during its campaign against the fierce Moro warriors, an indigenous ethnic group of Muslims living in the Southern Philippines. That campaign stretched over three decades, finally ending in 1936. Before the .45 Colt's use in battle, .38 caliber Colt and Smith & Wesson revolvers armed the American soldiers.

The Moro tribesmen wrapped their torsos with vines before charging American positions. Eyewitnesses saw the ferocious Moros continuing to kill Army soldiers with their wavy Kalis blades, even after the Moros suffered half a dozen direct shots.

In 1911, the Army received a shipment of .45 Colt "bulldogs." Legend has it that the first Moro warrior shot got hit in the upper arm. He spun around three times, and the bullet tore off his arm at the shoulder. It was not an exaggerated story.

It takes almost twenty seconds for George to open his safe. His right hand, usually trembling, is surprisingly calm and steady.

With the .45 Colt in his hand, George steps to the door of the War Room and opens it carefully. He sees the two men moving quickly towards the front door. George fires without warning. The sound is enormous.

George hits one of the men in the hand, spinning the intruder around.

The man's hand disintegrates. Both men make it through the door, one leaving a trail of blood. George fires again. The etched window on the right of the door bursts as both men fade into the night.

The wounded man is bleeding badly. As they escape in a car rented at the West Palm Beach Airport, he takes off his belt and wraps it around his lower arm as tightly as possible. The bleeding is reduced, but not stopped.

"Gotta get to a hospital," he says. "It doesn't hurt that much, but I know it's going to."

Torbjorn Petersson is on his cell phone. The wounded man, his attention elsewhere, does not hear what he's saying. Petersson turns off his phone.

"OK," he says. "We got a veterinarian up in Boynton Beach who's going to fix you up. No hospitals."

The man starts to moan.

The excruciating pain arrives. He is buckled over in the front seat as they drive across the border, separating Delray from Boynton Beach.

They're about seventeen miles from the scene of their crime. Torbjorn turns down a small road, following a canal. Only official vehicles of the Boynton Beach Utilities Department use the trail. "Shortcut," he says.

"Jesus it hurts," the wounded man says, leaning forward, hunching his body into the console of the car, trying to curl up. He does not consider how or why an out-of-state driver would be aware of a shortcut to the veterinarian. Torbjorn stops the car. Again, he says, "I'm sorry." This time he does not miss, delivering two shots to his partner's head.

He takes the black bag out of the car, puts the vehicle in drive, turns the wheel to the left, and steps out of the vehicle. Because the car is rolling, he twirls like a dancer as he steps out, falling to his knees.

He watches the car roll forward, tip to the left, and slip almost noiselessly into the canal.

Torbjorn walks up to the main road, and into a shopping center. He uses his cell phone again.

"I think my partner was not very good at his job," he says quietly into the phone. "I don't think he fulfilled the contract. The man was armed. My partner says he missed him in all the gunfire."

Torbjorn knows that Captain McKlane survived because he's the one who missed him.

Go and save Captain McKlane Gammy told him, just as his grandfather had done 65 years earlier.

The failed attempt will throw enough additional protection around Captain McKlane to prevent his murder.

Torbjorn does not know his dead partner's name; that is how the business works. Nobody knows anybody's name.

Perfect murders have no birth certificate, no trail to follow, and no guilt.

The person on the phone line does not yet know that Torbjorn's partner is dead. The voice, digitally altered but seemingly real, suggests that he get rid of the partner he has just shot and rolled into a canal. Torbjorn smiles at the convenience of the voice at the other end, duplicating Torbjorn's actions.

He hangs up. The person on the other end, has asked him to phone back when he has accomplished the task. Torbjorn decides not to do so.

He picked up the phone at the airport when he arrived in Florida late in the afternoon. In the First Class Lounge, a desk clerk gave it to him without question. You have a phone for me, he said, and the attendant looked down at her desk and stretched out her arm, with a thick, white envelope in her hand, but without looking at him.

It's always the same. Only the airports change. It reminds Torbjorn of passing the baton in a deadly race where none of the runners know each other, nor do they want to.

He erases the voicemail message that was on the phone when he arrived in Florida. Now he drops the phone to the ground and crushes it under his heel. They will be tracking him with its GPS. They will see it disappear from the screen of the computer watching him.

He takes a cab to the Fort Lauderdale International Airport, although he arrived at Palm Beach International, and the first leg of his First Class return ticket, which he will not use, was from that airport.

Chapter 12

Making Permanent Vacation Plans

Accelerated Realty Sales,
Boca Raton, Thursday AM

Anthony Silberg is in his office earlier than usual. Bill Brownstone sits in one of the chairs in front of his desk.

Silberg says: "Bill, I had no choice but to ask her to leave the company. She lied to an essential customer, George McKlane, about several things. I will not bother to go into any of the details. I want you to make sure she clears out of the Goldfish Bowl, and I want you to escort her out the front door personally. Use security if needed."

"Yes, sir," Brownstone says. "I'm sorry about this."

"Nobody is more disappointed than I am," Silberg says. "As the trusted manager of this company, I want you to make sure that every single agent in this organization understands that we will not permit any form of culpable negligence in contractual matters."

"Absolutely not," Bill Brownstone says, although he does not clearly understand what Anthony Silberg refers to, or anything about which he's talking.

He does know that "culpable" anything can endanger an agent's license and the legitimacy of the brokerage for which he or she works.

"Now bring me the escrow account report for this month and last month. I have to sign this month's report."

"Yes, yes," Bill says.

"And the escrow checkbook. I need to refund Mister Oliveira's six hundred thousand dollars, and I need to do it immediately. Sign one of the checks, Bill, so I can cosign it and get it in the mail with a personal note immediately. It is the sort of thing that can get the Department of Business and Professional Regulation breathing fire down our neck, not to mention FREC." The latter is a commonly used acronym for the Florida Real Estate Commission.

"Yes, sir," Bill says, "yes, yes," and he rushes out to do the bidding of the man who saved not only his career but also his marriage.

The escrow account of Accelerated Realty Sales is a meticulously monitored financial record, examined not only by the company's bookkeepers but also by the Department of Business and Professional Regulation. "DeBeeper," as the industry nicknames the Department, watches escrow accounts closely. Protecting the public's money remains its primary mission. They regularly send inspectors to Real Estate Brokerages throughout Florida, and the smallest error can grind a company to a temporary halt. Small brokers usually avoid the problem by relegating escrow requirements to title companies and real estate lawyers.

The Accelerated Realty Sales escrow statement contains all funds escrowed by customers who are buying and selling homes through Silberg's brokerage. The account pays no interest, a fact relished by banks.

If a customer demands interest on their frozen funds, a real estate company accomplishes it "off the books" through a corporate checking account. The potential complications and additional bookkeeping requirements of an interest-bearing escrow account make this worthwhile, although it's not legal.

The Accelerated Realty Sales Escrow Account has an average balance that fluctuates between eight and ten million dollars, depending on the season.

Silberg signs the latest corporate escrow report with no more than a cursory glance at its contents. Then, with the corporate checkbook open in front of him, Silberg neatly fills out the check stub.

He dates it and names the recipient as Gustavo Oliveira. He fills in the amount of $600,000.

On the check itself, he neatly writes in a number in the recipient's space, rather than a name. He then fills in the amount of $7,500,000. He leaves well over a million dollars in the account — no point in getting greedy.

He carefully tears it out of the checkbook, folds it, and places it in his shirt pocket.

He walks out of his office, gives the checkbook to his executive secretary, who has just arrived at work and tells her to return it to bookkeeping when she gets a chance.

Anthony Silberg tells her that he has a significant breakfast appointment at The Breakers in Palm Beach.

"See you later, Sarah," he says.

"When will you be back?" Sarah Golden asks.

"Probably after lunch," Silberg says.

He walks out, knowing that he will never see her again in her or his lifetime.

He peeks into the Bull Pen, waves to a few people, and notices that the Goldfish Bowl remains empty. He glances in the conference room, and then he admires the entry into his company. It's a very classy-looking operation.

He steps into the elevator and goes down to his private space in the underground garage. Accelerated Realty Sales is the only Real Estate Brokerage in Boca Raton with its own, private, below-street-level parking.

Silberg knows that his first foray into money laundering has been a dismal failure.

He has about 24 hours to start a new life, and the $27 million he has already tucked away in the Turks & Caicos Islands during the past 12 years makes an excellent golden parachute into anonymity.

He feels comforted by the fact that George KcKlane will take much of the heat for destroying Accelerated Realty Sales, not because he did anything wrong, but because, unlike Silberg, he will be around for the blame game.

Anthony Silberg gets into his Maserati and goes to the Boca Raton Resort & Club for a pleasant breakfast, alone, at the restaurant overlooking the yachts moored on Lake Boca. He enjoys two poached eggs on toast, fresh orange juice, and robust coffee. He signs for it on the corporate account, tipping the waiter three hundred dollars in a moment of largesse that will probably never occur. Accelerated Realty Sales will go belly up in a matter of days, perhaps hours, and its destruction will fall on the shoulders of a war hero who has forced Silberg to resort to illegal activities.

The breakfast waiter thanks Anthony Silberg profusely.

His eyes widen as he looks at the considerable amount written in for his tip.

"We made a tremendous home sale yesterday," Silberg tells the waiter he has known for years. Anthony Silberg still has to look at the man's name tag to remember it. "I'm just living life, Peter."

The waiter smiles and admires his customer as Silberg slowly walks out of the restaurant, greeting some people he knows. Silberg gets in his car, parked in a unique spot right next to the entrance to the Resort & Club, and he drives to the bank.

He enters the main branch of Citibank and asks for his private personal manager.

They have a long-standing arrangement that lets Silberg certify checks, with no questions asked.

He has done it often, and he usually mails the checks to an account in Providenciales on the Turk & Caicos Islands. This time, he will personally deliver the money to the small bank on the sandy streets of Cockburn Town.

Near the end of March in 2015, the Federal government publishes its International Narcotics Control Strategy Report, which names seven Caribbean Islands famous for laundering money. The island nations which make their list are Antigua & Barbuda, The Bahamas, Belize, the British Virgin Islands, the Cayman Islands, the Dominican Republic, and Haiti.

Anthony Silberg's hideaway does not appear on the list. However, his bank has been sending him official letters for several years, suggesting but not yet demanding compliance with new regulations issued by the United States Internal Revenue Service.

Silberg's private bank manager at Citibank takes the $7,500,000 check and vanishes into the bank's inner sanctum as Silberg chews on a complimentary chocolate cookie and sips terrible coffee.

He's in the manager's open office cubicle. When Silberg first opened his accounts at Citibank, his manager has a spacious office all to himself, completely enclosed in glass. It spawned the Goldfish Bowl concept. Now that the bank is cutting costs, private offices no longer exist.

The manager disappears for a long time, annoying Anthony Silberg, and making him vaguely nervous.

People in the bank duck and some scramble for cover when they hear a loud shout: "WHAT!"

One older woman thinks it's a holdup, and she drops to the floor with the speed of someone half her age. Several of the tellers slip below the barrier separating them from their customers, the youngest one trembling.

The bank guard puts his hand on his gun but does not pull it out of the holster. He does bend his knees a little, considering getting down on them. He thinks about his retirement in three weeks.

The personal manager holds the $7,500,000 check out and repeats to Anthony Silberg: "There is no money in the account, Mister Silberg. I'm truly very sorry. I had to check. I did so twice."

"HOW CAN THERE BE NO MONEY IN THE ACCOUNT?" Silberg shouts.

"The account has moved, Mister Silberg. Two hours ago. I don't know who authorized it. It appears to have originated through an overseas office in Luxembourg, a small country in Europe, sir. I am very sorry."

"WHO AUTHORIZED IT?"

"It must have gone through our head office in New York City, in Manhattan, Mister Silberg."

Silberg tries to calm down. "Not on your end, you IDIOT! Who authorized it at MY company?"

The manager says nothing. He holds out his hands, helpless. He is afraid to suggest that Silberg call his office.

Silberg snatches the check, ripping it slightly, and storms out of the bank.

13752 Coconut Palm Ct.,
Boca Raton: Thursday AM

Sharonda Nelson wears her .40 caliber Glock 35 on her waist. She knows most of the Boca Raton police officers walking around the crime scene of Captain George McKlane's home.

The Feds arrive around nine-thirty, and she has to show them her carry and concealment license. Her husband does not show up, although she has spoken to him several times on the phone.

Nobody knows why the Federal Bureau of Investigation takes over the case.

Several of the Boca Raton cops assume that it has something to do with George McKlane's Medal of Honor.

George McKlane is asleep in a spare bedroom in the main house. The police tape off the master bedroom, a crime scene. The War Room also is out of bounds, as well as George's office.

Workers try to repair the broken etched glass to the right of the entryway, but the Feds stop them and suggest that they return the following day.

"Call and check first, just to be sure," they are told.

Judge Broadslate appears just after the Feds arrive, and they treat him with respect, both as a former Federal Judge and also as George McKlane's legal advisor.

They do the same when Doctor Klein appears, saying that he is George McKlane's medical advisor. Both men are in the Birdroom, talking without George. Sharonda joins them.

"In the clubhouse," Doctor Klein says, "half the people say someone tried to murder George McKlane, and the other half say it was a robbery. What was it, Sharonda?"

"I'm not sure," she says. "I spoke to Captain George for about five minutes, and I don't think he knows either. Two men, wearing night-vision goggles and carrying guns with silencers, broke in around four o'clock this morning. He hasn't told me much else. He's asleep, and he needs it. He'll tell us more when he gets up, probably within the hour. I called his son, Colonel McKlane, about forty minutes ago. He's flying in. He should be here around noon."

"I assume the blood on the front entryway belongs to the bad guys," Doctor Klein says.

Sharonda nods.

George has no injuries.

"The police may get a DNA match from the blood of the perpetrators," the judge says.

Thirty minutes later, George walks out of the bedroom into a house filled with local and federal cops.

He takes the elevator to the first floor and discovers that his friends have gathered in the Birdroom.

He explains to the Feds surrounding him that he will answer whatever questions they have, but that Doctor Klein, Judge Broadslate, and his Nurse Practitioner, Sharonda Nelson, will be with him at all times.

He wants to have a private conversation with his advisors first.

He walks over and joins them in the Birdroom. Sharonda stands up as he enters and tells him that his son is flying in around noon.

"Good," George says. "Please sit."

McKlane's group huddles at the far end of the Birdroom while the Feds are watching from the living room door.

The Judge notices one of the Federal Agents fiddling with his ear and a small hand-held device. He gets up and walks to where the man is standing thirty feet away.

Judge Broadslate says, louder than necessary: "There will be no recording of our conversation. None. You should be ashamed of yourself, young man. I speak as a former Federal Judge. We live in the United States of America. It is not the Soviet Union."

The agent disconnects the hand-held device and agrees, but he does not look at all embarrassed.

As the Judge returns to the huddle, another agent looks at the federal recording artist and says, in excellent Russian: "Nice try, comrade."

In the Birdroom, George McKlane says: "First of all, I don't think we should reveal the recording of Silberg and his non-Portuguese pal to anybody at this stage. I think it's my own private business and no one else's. Does that present any problems, Judge?"

"Yes, it certainly does," the Judge says. "Depending on the nature of the federal inquiry, it might be withholding evidence. That could, and in all likelihood, would be construed as a first-degree felony, and a severe one."

George thinks for a while.

"OK," he says. "If you see the recording as withholding evidence, Judge, then you reveal its existence. It will be up to you. If you can avoid revealing it, I would appreciate it."

The Judge thinks about this. He is not at all comfortable with the recording device. "Tell us what happened, and then I'll give you my answer," he says.

"Fair enough." Captain George looks at Sharonda and asks: "What have they found so far?"

"Well, for a start, I don't think they have opened the recording cabinet, but they might have and closed it again. The bad buys pulled out most of the drawers in your desk, and they broke one of them. The police found four bullets and two bullet casings. The casings are from your Colt .45, as are two of the bullets holes, although they have yet to find the bullet that broke the front-door window. They assume all of that was your doing."

"It was," George says. "I told that to the Boca police when they first arrived. They got here quickly."

"The two other bullet holes are upstairs," Sharonda says. "One is in the headboard on your bed, and the other is in a wall of the War Room. They are both .22 caliber, hollow points. Deadly stuff."

After a moment of silence, George McKlane says: "I don't know how he missed me. He wasn't more than eight feet away. I tried to chamber a round, but he stopped me, made me drop the Colt .45. He took it and put it in the gun safe. Then he took out the sales contract and shouted 'Got it!' to his partner."

"So, they were after the real estate contract?" Judge Ralph Broadslate asks.

"Yes."

"Did you sign it?"

"No."

"Keep going," Doctor Klein says.

"So the man backs up to the doorway, and he points his gun at me. I didn't even have time to taste any fear in my mouth. He looks at me and says, 'Sorry.' I remember thinking that's the last words I'll ever hear and how stupid and mundane it seems. Then 'plip.' That cottony sound that quality silencers make. So that's the last sound I will ever hear. Only then I hear the door close. He misses me from eight feet. It doesn't make any sense. I get down on my knees, open the gun safe, get out my Colt, walk out the door and take a couple of shots at them as they're running out of the house. I think I blew the fingers off of one of them. His right hand." Everyone remains silent, watching George McKlane think.

"Anything else?" Sharonda asks.

"No," says George, then, "Yes. The 'Thank You' notes. The guy took a bunch of the letter frames, five or six of them, six, I think."

No one talks.

"The contract and thank you notes," George says, shaking his head, seemingly bewildered.

"I think he might have missed you on purpose," Sharonda says.

"I think you're right," George says. "But why would he do that? And who the hell sent these people here to kill me? And why? It doesn't make any sense."

"Well, it's time to talk to the FBI," Judge Broadslate says without moving, and everyone can feel that he's decided on the recording device in George's office.

The judge says, "I think you better tell them about the recording you have and give them a copy of it. I will make it clear to them that the device is and has been used solely for the legitimate purpose of personal protection. Its necessity is now obvious. I see no point or value in risking a felony charge for withholding information. None."

"You're the judge," George says, but he's not happy.

Accelerated Realty Sales,
Boca, Thursday Lunchtime

Accelerated Realty Sales turns upside down less than 24 hours after everyone gets their latest commission checks. The day starts with a surprising struggle between the office manager, Bill Brownstone, and the newest addition to the Goldfish Bowl, Barbara Rossellini. Brownstone attempts to walk her out the door before she gets to her office, and she sends him through two partitions in the bullpen with a hard shove. She's not a big girl, but she's a tough one.

Bill Brownstone returns for Round Two with three security guards.

Alice Koenig, one of the most respected people at the brokerage, suddenly shouts and curses at Bill Brownstone. She does this at the very top of her vocal range, and Brownstone, and the security guards, pull back to regroup.

One of the Rossellini men intervenes and calls Angelo Rossellini. He hands the phone to Brownstone, who knows that Rossellini is an essential partner in the firm.

Brownstone listens carefully, and then hands the phone back to its owner, takes two steps, and collapses on the floor. His face turns ashen, but he does not pass out.

He stands up and stumbles through the bullpen in an apparent daze, surrounded by security guards who try to make sure he remains on his feet. As he heads for his office, several agents hear him clearly say that Anthony Silberg has cleaned out the escrow account and has disappeared. The story multiplies exponentially.

Most of the real estate agents have already deposited yesterday's commission checks, and those who have not, hurry to their banks to do so. The payments seem to go through, but everyone knows that they might bounce off a frozen account. The money could quickly vanish retroactively.

Almost every agent is on the phone by noon, calling other brokerages and telling them how fabulous they are as real estate agents.

A few of them tell the truth: Silberg has disappeared with the company's escrow funds.

Accelerated Realty Sales has no Broker of Record. It is legally out of business.

At the Forked Reef Title Company, the first of 14 homes, slated to change owners on Friday, stalls at the closing table. In a dimly lit conference area that resembles a private dining room in an upscale restaurant, without place settings, a title agent says: "Reverend Henderson, the bank has not received any escrowed funds from your broker's account."

Reverend Henderson looks at his real estate agent.

She calls her office.

Reverend Henderson watches the blood drain out of his real estate agent's face, making her look like a clown with well-rouged cheeks.

The real estate agent looks at the title agent, who has recently received a law degree from Florida State after being a title agent for 21 years.

The real estate agent says: "Silberg has cleaned out the corporate escrow account and disappeared."

The title agent, who Reverend Henderson considers a quiet, sophisticated, God-fearing lady, a member of his church's choir, says: "Holy shit!"

The real estate agent excuses herself, saying she needs to use the lady's room.

She walks out of the conference area, through the entrance door and runs to her car. She has not yet deposited her commission check from the day before.

Also, with no apparent Broker of Record at Accelerated Realty Sales, she is officially unable to conduct any real estate transactions of any sort.

She can lose her license if she does.

In the Forked Reef Title Company, the title agent, and Reverend Henderson lock their hands together and pray, first for forgiveness, then for guidance. At different title companies throughout the Palm Beaches, this event unfolds thirteen more times during the afternoon. Praying is limited to the Forked Reef Title Company.

Severe swearing occurs at all the others.

At the Fort Lauderdale Airport, Anthony Silberg parks his Maserati in short-term, hourly parking, even though he will never return to drive it back out of the airport.

He already has a ticket to Provo in the Turks & Caicos Islands. He laments losing the additional funds he wanted to add to his account, but he still has more than enough to enjoy the rest of his new life in luxury.

He listens to the ending of Eric Clapton's *I Shot The Sheriff*, turns off the radio, and gets out of the car.

He sees a young man nearby who can't be more than twenty-five years old.

"It's your lucky day," he says to the kid, throwing him the key to the Maserati. The key falls on the pavement.

Silberg pulls out the worthless check and adds: "And now you're a multi-millionaire." He holds out the payment.

The kid holds out a gun with a silencer.

"It ain't your lucky day, pal."

"What is this?" Silberg says. He takes a swipe at the gun. The kid skips back, expecting the move, but does not pull the trigger. As Anthony Silberg's brain registers that he remains alive, a huge man pins him from behind.

The kid steps forward and whacks him with the butt of the gun, hard, on the side of his head. Silberg almost loses consciousness, and he vaguely remembers being put into a large, black Lincoln Navigator. The transfer requires three men. They roll Silberg into the back seat, and the huge man gets in next to him.

As Silberg begins to regain his senses, the big man says: "Jesus, you gotta lose some weight, buddy. It's just not healthy being so fat." Then he injects something into Silberg's arm, and their captive drops into a dreamless world.

"What about the wheels," the kid says.

"We're going to leave that beautiful Maserati right where it is," one of the men says, getting up off his knees. He is placing something under the Maserati, on the driver's side. He gets into the Lincoln Navigator's front passenger seat.

"Put the key on the roof, on the driver's side," he says to the kid. "Make it look like some idiot left it there by mistake."

"Some punk will steal it in a minute," the kid says.

"Yes, he certainly will," the older man says. "I hope he's a fat kid."

Chapter 13

Searching For a Beachfront Broker

The Luxury Partnership, Boca: Thursday AM

Frederick Phelps, the broker who owns The Luxury Partnership, hears the news of Silberg's theft about three hours after Brownstone's phone call from Angelo Rossellini. Martha Krumble tells Frederick Phelps about Silberg's stealing, but not right away.

"Freddy," she says to her broker, "How long have I worked for you?"

"Not long enough," Frederick says. A suspicious man by nature, he's afraid he knows what's coming. "You're the best agent I have, Martha."

"Had," Martha says.

"Shit," Fredrick says.

His boutique agency is already on the brink, and Martha abandoning it will send it over the edge. He has three empty offices, where six agents once worked.

Now he will have four empty offices.

"Come on, Martha. You've been with me for twelve years, and things will get better. I know they will. I'll jack your split up to ninety percent. How's that?"

"It's not all bad news, Freddy."

"It is if you're leaving," he says.

"Accelerated Realty Sales just lost its Broker," Martha Krumble says.

"Silberg? What are you saying? Please, tell me that an angry homeowner shot the son-of-a-bitch."

He has disliked Silberg from the start.

"Silberg just skipped town, and he took Accelerated Realty Sales' escrow money with him, almost but not quite all of it," Martha says.

Frederick Phelps jumps to his feet. "What a bastard! Boy, that figures! Oh, man!" He's very excited. "Martha, this is utterly fantastic." He starts strutting around the office. "Hell, we can't lose now. We can take dozens of high-end listings." He stops, focuses on Martha, who is smiling. "Today. Starting right now. My God, Martha. That stupid bastard has saved us!"

"I'm about to become the Broker of Record at Accelerated Realty Sales," she says. "Effective immediately. With a sizeable equity position in the firm."

Freddy slowly sits down in his chair. It's like watching a balloon deflate, including the high-pitched, squeaky sound of escaping air.

"I've accepted the offer," Martha tells him.

"I hate this business," Frederick Phelps says.

"No, you don't, Freddy," Martha says. "You love it."

"I hate this business," he repeats.

"Freddy, I've been authorized to make you fall in love with this business one more time."

Frederick Phelps looks at her. There was a time, years earlier, when he wanted to marry Martha Krumble, not long after her husband died of a massive and unexpected heart attack. Martha Krumble loved her first husband too much for anything to come of it. The timing was wrong, and after a while, she made him understand that, for her and Freddy, it would always be wrong.

But he still loved her.

"Will you marry me?" he asks.

She laughs, as she always does, and says, yet again: "In some other lifetime, Freddy."

"I hate this business," he says for the third time.

"Freddy," Martha says, "I want to bring The Luxury Partnership into Accelerated Realty Sales. You will be a separate division, keeping your name, with your people, right here in this prime location. You don't even have to change the signage, just add some lettering that says 'A Division of ARS.' That's all you have to do, Freddy. The FREC paperwork is easy."

She refers to the Florida Real Estate Commission. She watches him digest the offer she makes.

She sees that he does not believe in the concept quite yet. It needs more soft sell.

"You will have no shortage of staff, and no shortage of high-end listings," Martha continues. "I have a lot of people at Accelerated Realty Sales who would love to work in an office right here on the ocean, on the beach."

She words it in a way that makes it clear that she has left his office and become the boss of Accelerated Realty Sales. There is no turning back.

She gets up, goes to a window, and opens it.

The sound of waves crashing onto the beach filters into Frederick's office. Seagulls squawk in the distance.

She looks at him, throws a thumb towards the window. "That sure beats the sound of horns honking on Federal Highway," she says. "I know I'm going to miss it."

After about thirty seconds, she closes the window and puts her hand on Frederick's slumped shoulder, giving it a little buddy squeeze.

"So you want me to be a Division of ARS," he says. "You're going to make an arse out of me."

Martha laughs. "Not a chance," she says, going back to the chair in front of his desk and sitting down.

No question mark elevates his voice when he says: "It's not the end of my company, is it?"

"No, it's not, Freddy. It's the first day of your new company, our company, with more high-end listings than you or I ever dreamed of."

She wants him to know that they are in this together, just like they have been for many years. His mouth tightens, struggles between a grimace and a smile.

"Also," Martha says, "there's a sign-on bonus of three hundred and fifty thousand dollars. Cash. Payable to you, Freddy, personally."

Frederick Phelps leans back in his chair and smiles.

She looks at him and says: "I am the best salesperson you ever knew, isn't that right, Freddy?"

"No," he says. "Now, you're the boss."

"I'll be a perfect one, Freddy. And I promise I will always value your counsel."

Frederick Phelps puts his hands behind his head, something he always does when The Luxury Partnership takes a new listing.

"God, I love this business," he says, and they both laugh.

Fort Lauderdale Airport, Thursday Morning.

Torbjorn Petersson walks into Terminal Two at the Fort Lauderdale International Airport. He can remain anonymous and safe, as long as he does not follow his original plan. He tries to buy a First Class and one-way

ticket to Roanoke with a prepaid debit card that does not have his real name on it. It matches the fake but perfect Ohio driver's license in his wallet.

"That's not a very smart thing to do," the counter agent says to him.

Torbjorn Petersson does not like conversations at airports, especially not with people working there. He needs to remain anonymous, completely invisible.

"I don't understand. What is the problem," Torbjorn says to the agent behind the counter.

"Well, it would be so much smarter getting a round-trip ticket," the agent says, looking at him. "It's cheaper."

"Round trip," Torbjorn says. "Thank you. And I need to know where the First Class lounge is."

"Of course," the agent says. "No luggage, sir?"

"Just this carry on," Torbjorn says, holding it up.

It takes a while before the agent hands him the ticket, saying, "Now you can come back and revisit us." He gives the passenger a friendly smile.

"Thank you for your help," Torbjorn says in as flat a voice as possible. He steps away from the counter.

He does not go immediately to the First Class lounge. He walks over and takes a seat in the spacious waiting area, watching the agent who sold him his ticket.

Torbjorn might end up going to Miami if he gets a bad feeling. He pays attention to every intuition that he gets from his surroundings.

His awareness is what keeps him alive and unhurt during his time in Afghanistan.

It also works very well in his current civilian job.

He watches the agent.

The man is a severely overweight person who shifts from side to side as he serves his customers. He's very uncomfortable in a job that requires long periods of standing on his feet.

Most of the passengers seem frustrated, but with the system, not with him.

The agent appears well-organized and reasonably efficient. That means he will probably have a good memory.

Torbjorn is about to get a refund on the ticket and head south to Miami International Airport when something happens. It makes him much more comfortable.

A man steps up to the counter. He gets into an argument with the person who sold Torbjorn his ticket to Roanoke. The commotion is loud and abusive, from the passenger, not the ticketing agent.

The customer, at one point, throws his credit card at the agent, apparently angry over additional charges for his overweight luggage. The card misses the agent and flutters behind the counter.

A lot of impatient people watch the spectacle. Some of them hoot and whistle. Another agent, further down the baggage line, holds up the tossed credit card, which took a trip on the luggage beltway.

"Who's credit card is this?" she says, waving it above her head and looking at the passenger who threw it at her co-worker. She smiles at him.

Other passengers, suddenly in on the game, tentatively raise their hands.

Humiliated, the credit card owner takes it back and hands it to the agent, paying the charges.

"Have a pleasant flight, sir. I hope you have a wonderful time in Dallas."

As the passenger stomps away from the counter, he shouts at the agent: "I'm sure I will, FAT BOY!"

Torbjorn feels quite confident that any memory of the round-trip ticket buyer to Roanoke will quickly vanish from the agent's memory banks. He sees no point in going to Miami International.

Torbjorn stands up and goes to the First Class Lounge. He uses the office materials available to him there to package the contents of the black bag and send them back to George McKlane at 13752 Coconut Palm Court in Boca Raton.

He returns five of the six framed "Thank You" notes that he has taken off the wall.

One, he keeps.

He will return it later to the man who's existence his ancestors has saved for the second time.

He flies to Roanoke, Virginia. It's a 75-mile drive from there to Hot Springs, through Clifton Forge and Covington, and then another twenty-two miles through the Richardson

Gorge. He returns to the farm his family has owned in the Virginia mountains for over 200 years. It is time to become a farmer once again.

13752 Coconut Palm Ct., Boca Raton, Thursday AM

George McKlane gives his recollection of the break-in to a team of federal agents, with his advisors in tow.

Standing in the War Room, he points at six empty spaces on his wall of "thank you" notes. Federal agents read many of the letters.

A young agent named John Dempsey suggests they take them all off the wall and bag them as evidence.

"Evidence of what?" Judge Broadslate asks. "Compassion? Concern for the men Captain McKlane tried to save? How about the Medal of Honor on the back of the center island there, young man?"

Judge Broadslate slaps the counter hard.

"Maybe you need that as proof of the courage of Captain George McKlane."

Judge Broadslate shows a lot of anger. The young agent leans over and looks at the Medal of Honor. One of John Dempsey's superiors ushers him out of the War Room and sends him downstairs.

The agent in charge, Scott Larsen, apologizes to George McKlane for John Dempsey's attitude.

"And thank you for your service from a grateful Nation, Captain McKlane."

"I'll chalk it up to the passion of youth," George McKlane says. "Some of the men on that wall suffered from the same sort of eagerness, long ago. It does not end well."

Agent Scott Larsen nods and says, "Thank you, sir. Do you have any idea why your attackers would take six of the framed letters?"

"I have no clue," George McKlane says.

"Can you remember who the letters were from?"

"I haven't thought about it yet."

"Mister McKlane, if you can remember any of the names, it might be constructive, sir."

"It was a long time ago, Agent Larsen," George McKlane says.

He thinks and then says, "It was over sixty years ago. If I can figure out any of the names, I will certainly let you know. But I wouldn't hold your breath."

"Is that your gun safe?"

"It is."

"Do you mind opening it?"

Agent Larsen looks at the judge as he finishes the sentence.

"I don't mind," George says.

He does not add I *have nothing to hide* because he knows that such a claim always carries with it an unmistakable scent of suspicion. He glances at the judge. Broadslate shrugs, and George opens the safe.

"So you found them," Sharonda says, looking in the safe.

George McKlane says. "Holy smokes, I wonder how the heck those got there?"

The agents crowd around the safe, hoping for a revelation. They see a lot of guns, some ammunition, and one and a half family-sized chocolate bars.

Sharonda narrows her eyes at the captain and wags her finger at him, smiling.

Only the Doctor, Sharonda and George McKlane understand what is going on. Doctor Klein explains it to the judge, who smiles and shakes his head.

George says: "A chocolate bar may have saved my life."

The judge turns to the special agent in charge and suggests returning the Captain's .45 Colt to the safe. They have it in an evidence bag.

"You have the casings, and you have the bullets or at least one of them. I see no evidentiary purpose in keeping a gun that Captain McKlane is extremely well-qualified to use for his protection."

Agent Larsen says he will make sure that the .45 Colt goes back into the safe. The agents examine other guns, relics of the Korean War.

"Burp gun," George tells an agent holding a Soviet Shpagin submachine gun. "It holds seventy-two rounds, with a cycle rate of over 700 rounds a minute. That's what the Chinese Communist Forces used in Korea. It's loaded, but the safety should be on."

The agent suddenly decides to treat it like a stick of dynamite. He hands it cautiously to George, who puts it back into the gun safe.

"Obviously," George says, "I have permits for everything that's in this safe."

"With the sincere thanks of our great nation," Judge Broadslate adds, still a bit angry.

"You may lock the safe, sir," the special agent in charge says. "Why do you think one of the men took a home sale contract out of the safe, Captain McKlane?"

"I don't have an answer for that," McKlane says. "I can't figure it out."

"Would the contract implicate anyone conducting a criminal enterprise?" Agent Larsen asks. He watches George McKlane closely.

"What does that mean?" Judge Broadslate asks.

An agent rushes into the War Room with a cell phone and hands it to the special agent in charge, Scott Larsen, who steps back, keeping his eye on George McKlane.

Then Larsen turns his back, listening carefully to the caller, motioning to the other agents, who suddenly crowd around him.

He turns off the phone.

"Mister McKlane, do you think you could recognize the person who you shot?"

"He was wearing a ski mask," George says.

"I'll take that as a 'No.' Did you fire more than one shot at him, Mister McKlane?"

"I fired two shots. The second one blew out the window that you say we are not allowed to repair."

"But you only hit the man once," the Special Agent in Charge says to George.

"Unless the bullet through the window somehow hit the man, yes," George says.

"You can repair the window," Agent Scott Larsen says. He raises his voice and tells everyone in the room, "A body was just recovered from a canal up in Boynton Beach. The man had a serious hand-wound, with four fingers missing, but the man did not bleed out. That's not why he died. Two taps to the head killed him. I think we can leave now."

"I don't think so," Judge Broadslate says.

"I beg your pardon?"

"You asked Mister McKlane if the contract removed from the gun safe could implicate anyone conducting a criminal enterprise," Judge Broadslate says. "I assume that you are referring to money laundering, and I think that is why you are here."

All of the agents stare at him.

"I was a federal judge in New Jersey, gentlemen, which many people in the Federal Bureau of Investigation used to call the gateway to the Caribbean, the money laundering capital of the world."

"You have our undivided attention, Judge Broadslate," special agent in charge Larsen says with a faint smile.

"I think you need to listen to a recording made by George McKlane, who has a security system installed in this house for his protection. This system records conversations in most of the rooms of the house."

"And the guest house," Sharonda adds.

The agents all look at each other, and for about ten seconds, nobody says a word.

Some agents study their shoes.

"No recordings have been made anywhere in this house today," Judge Broadslate continues. "Mister McKlane operates, as we all do, under the assumption that you are here to protect us, and not to endanger our lives."

Several agents stop looking at their shoes.

"And this recording is what?" special agent in charge Scott Larsen asks.

"A conversation between Mister Anthony Silberg, the broker of Accelerated Realty Sales, and a Mister Gustavo, whoever, who was supposedly a Brazilian buyer looking at this home. His name is on the sales contract, which the thieves stole from the safe."

"We would be very interested in listening to this conversation," the special agent in charge says. Everyone goes downstairs. Nobody takes the elevator.

Sharonda sits down at George's desk and opens a drawer, revealing the Magic Wand surveillance system. None of its lights blink.

She turns it on, and red, yellow, and green diodes spring to life. She dials a number on the keypad of the system. As laughter fills the room, she turns on the computer. As the conversation concludes, she says something quietly to the judge.

"Would you like a copy of this conversation?" the judge asks Agent Larsen.

"Yes, please," he says.

"Will it help in your investigation?" the judge asks.

"Perhaps," the agent says. "Mister Anthony Silberg has disappeared, and we want to talk to him."

"Disappeared?" George McKlane asks.

"Yes," Agent Larsen says. "Along with most of the escrowed funds from Accelerated Realty Sales. This tape might have some use as soon as we arrest him."

"Some use?" the Judge asks. "Agent Larsen, a recording like this can nail your case closed. If any federal prosecutor came into my court with this sort of evidence, the only thing that might save the defendant from going to prison would be a fatal heart attack. How much money did Silberg steal?

"More than $300, judge." That number represents the amount that turns the theft from a misdemeanor into a felony, using Florida State Statutes.

Special agent in charge Larsen looks at his team. "We're out of here. If we have any more questions, Mister McKlane, we will contact you. Thank you for the tape. And your service to this great nation."

As the agents file out the door, they walk past a full bird colonel in a Marine Corps flight suit.

The special agent in charge of the case immediately recognizes him as a younger and almost identical version of Captain George McKlane.

Accelerated Realty Sales,
Thursday Afternoon

Martha Krumble stands on a podium hastily built at the front of the bullpen at Accelerated Realty Sales. Most of the agents know who she is, and many of them have worked with her on real estate deals. Anyone who has likes her. She is one of the most respected real estate agents in Boca Raton.

"As of this moment, we all remain in business, and our licenses are legally active with Accelerated Realty Sales," she says. "I am your broker, the Broker of Record at Accelerated Realty Sales."

The crowd applauds this news.

"As of tomorrow morning, the escrow account of Accelerated Realty Sales will be fully-funded."

A higher level of applause fills the bullpen.

"For that, I would like to thank Mister Angelo Rossellini, one of Boca Raton's foremost developers, and now the principal owner of this company."

A silver-haired gentleman with a very kind face stands up and waves. Many people in the room know Angelo Rossellini. They also know he is a lot tougher than his grandfatherly appearance, but he has also apparently saved the company, and many of them, from total disaster.

More applause fills the bullpen.

"During the next few weeks," Martha continues, "you will be renegotiating your contracts with this company. All of your extraordinary contributions to Accelerated Realty Sales will receive a careful review. In most cases, there will be no changes in the splits you operate under."

Not so much applause.

"There are fourteen closings that should have occurred today, which did not," Martha Krumble tells the gathering. "On Friday, those closings will move forward."

More applause.

"When you leave this office today, you do so as representatives of Accelerated Realty Sales. There are reporters and camera crews outside the office right now. I will not tell any of you what to say."

She smiles.

"Just remember that your contracts with Accelerated Realty Sales are in the process of being renegotiated."

Some people laugh.

A lot don't.

"Most of you know Frederick Phelps," Martha continues. He stands up and smiles at the group. "Freddy has joined Accelerated Realty Sales and runs our new beachfront division, which will retain its name as The Luxury Partnership, a division of ARS."

Applause. People who know Frederick Phelps, like him. Some of them used to work for him.

"The Luxury Partnership will be nicknamed our Suntan Division." Silence. "That's a joke," Martha says. "We all need to lighten up a little here." A few people laugh. Others think the nickname might catch on.

"If any of you wants to work out of our new oceanfront offices, talk to Freddy Phelps."

She pauses, looks over the entire group. "There are a lot of rumors out there right now. We need to deal with nothing but facts, people. I'd like to introduce Special Agent in Charge Scott Larsen, who works for the Federal Bureau of Investigation."

Agent Larsen takes over the podium, and he looks exactly like who and what he is. Martha assumes he has a lot to tell the group.

"If anyone here has any knowledge of the whereabouts of Anthony Silberg, or if you have any thoughts on the matter, my team is in the conference room," he tells them. That's it.

Agent Larsen steps off the podium.

Martha Krumble hesitates for a moment; she had hoped for much more information.

Stepping back on the podium, she says: "All of you know that Mister Silberg has disappeared with the escrow funds of this company. If any of you can help the authorities with information, please do so. And thank you for supporting and being the backbone of Accelerated Realty Sales. We will continue as the largest real estate firm in Boca, and I, and hopefully, all of you, intend to make us the best and most trusted real estate company in Florida. That will take some work after the damage that Mister Silberg has done to your reputations. Let's get to work."

As the meeting breaks up, a lot of people congratulate Martha Krumble as their new leader.

Freddy Phelps does a brisk business with people who recognize the possibility of a new beginning, including some of the women who work in the Goldfish Bowl.

Barbara Rossellini decides not to leave the Goldfish Bowl. She goes into her office and tapes her *Goldfish Never Drown* sign back onto the glass partition.

Alice Koenig also decides to stay in the Goldfish Bowl. She has been the top producer at Accelerated Realty Sales for two years running, and she's comfortable in her position.

Barbara Rossellini goes and spends a few pleasant moments with Angelo Rossellini, who welcomes her with open arms and leans down to kiss her on both cheeks.

Most of the agents who see this have already assumed that the tiny woman and Mister Rossellini are related.

The FBI, sitting around the conference table, does no business at all. After fifteen minutes, the special agent in charge, Scott Larsen, gets a phone call from the District One Miami-Dade state trooper command center saying that they think they have the body of Anthony Silberg.

The agents leave through the garage, avoiding reporters and cameras surrounding the front of the building.

Quite a few of the realtors® grandstand for the press as they leave the building through the company's Federal Highway exit. Almost without exception, they emphasize that their primary goal in life is to re-establish their reputation as someone to trust when you buy or sell a luxury home.

They all knew that Silberg was a crook, and they resent the fact that he has besmirched their otherwise exceptional reputations.

Very little of the footage gets airtime on the five o'clock local news. None of it gets on the ten o'clock news, which focuses instead on a triple homicide-suicide in Wellington and an explosive, traffic-snarling automobile accident on the Florida turnpike.

Chapter 14
Check The Wreck

Fort Lauderdale Airport, Thursday Afternoon

Charles Summers works at the check-in counter of Delta Airlines at the Fort Lauderdale International Airport. Because of his weight, his feet usually start to hurt after about fifteen

minutes. After eight hours, edema makes his ankles swell, and his feet become numb but still painful.

Charles Summers makes frequent trips to the employee lounge to visit the men's room, where he catheterizes himself, trying to rid his body of the poisons that he thinks his bladder no longer eliminates.

Catheterization does not, and will not work. Summers has a kidney, not a bladder problem. His doctor has suggested kidney dialysis, but he steadfastly refuses. He needs his job, not a dialysis center that will require three to five-hour visits, three days a week.

Charles Summers smiles at the customer who refuses to pay overweight charges for his luggage. He says: "I am very sorry, sir. I do not make the rules. If you want the bag to arrive with you in Dallas, Texas, I need your credit card. Your luggage is ten pounds overweight. Perhaps you ...."

"Listen, you fat tub of lard," the passenger says. "How overweight are you — 40, 50 pounds? Listen, pal, I've been a customer of ...."

"Sir, there is no need for ad hominem attacks. I do not make the rules for the airline."

The ad hominem thing confuses the passenger. He does not know what it means, but he's reasonably sure he has been personally insulted.

"I want to speak to the supervisor!"

"Fine," Charles Summers says. He steps back, turns slowly around in a circle, then steps back to the counter and says: "Yes, sir. May I help you?"

"I said I wan ...."

"I am the supervisor, sir. Your bag is ten pounds over the limit, and I need your cred ...."

Pushed by catcalls from customers in the line behind him, the passenger angrily flicks a Platinum American Express Card at him.

It floats past Charles Summers' right ear, catches a slight updraft, and flutters down, landing on the edge of the moving luggage belt.

The supervisor and the passenger both watch it. Charles Summers makes no move to retrieve the card as it heads for destinations unknown.

An agent further down the line plucks the credit card off the belt just before it disappears. She knows where it comes from because she was watching and thoroughly enjoying her colleague's altercation.

She raises the card in the air and attracts the attention of dozens of impatient customers by shouting: "Whose credit card is this?"

The disgruntled passenger, humiliated, raises his hand. So do a lot of other people. She returns it to the rightful owner with a pleasant smile.

Charles Summers registers the charges, returns the credit card, and says: "Have a pleasant flight, sir. I hope you have a wonderful time in Dallas."

"I'm sure I will, FAT BOY!" the passenger shouts over his shoulder as he heads for Concourse B.

Charles Summers smiles at him, waves, and then he very carefully sends the man's overweight bag to Chicago. He checks his watch. He steps away from his station.

He goes to the employee lounge, walking like a man ten years older than his actual age, buys some junk food out of the candy machine, and makes another visit to the men's room. His shift is only half over.

When his workday finally grinds to an end, he repeats his junk food visit to the lounge, with yet another bathroom break, which includes catheterization. Then he walks painfully out of the terminal to a spot where the employee parking bus always stops.

He leans against a cement pillar and scans the cars in short-term, hourly parking. As usual, a lot of BMWs and a Jaguar, the latest model. Then he spots a Maserati with something twinkling in the sun on its roof.

Oh, my God, he thinks. He looks back up the roadway to see if an employee parking bus is coming. No. He looks back at the Maserati. He sees a forgotten key on the roof. The owner might reward a good deed. It seems worth a try.

He walks carefully across the road, to the Maserati, steel gray and sleek. Charles Summers knows cars., and he recognizes the GranTurismo MC Centennial Edition.

Although he dislikes the Maserati logo, which always reminds him of Satanic rituals, he recognizes that he is standing next to a slumbering and costly beast.

"The Granturismo has a top speed of one hundred and eighty-five miles an hour, and a price tag of over one hundred and sixty-six thousand dollars," he says out loud, somehow making what's happening real. The owner has left the key on the roof. The car lock moves up, soundlessly.

He opens the door. He squeezes in, surprised at how easily the car accepts his extra-large frame.

Then he looks on the passenger seat, leans over and picks up what he thinks he sees, and says softly, but out loud: "Holy Mother Queen of Grace."

In his shaking hand, he holds an endorsed, co-signed check for seven and a half million dollars. He opens the glove box and pulls out a steel gray driver's booklet. It matches the color of the car perfectly.

Charles Summers finds the insurance card. It has a name and address on it.

He sits, very excited, and tries to think. He decides he will collect his just rewards in person. He will not let airport authorities sink their teeth into what seems to be an assured, life-changing event. He has visions of early and unexpected retirement. He may even get a kidney transplant.

It takes him a few seconds to figure out how the car starts. The slumbering beast awakens, purrs, and then transfers its power into the body of Charles Summers.

His feet do not hurt.

They no longer display any numbness.

He feels his toes wiggle in his shoes, a sensation unknown to him for years.

Charles Summers drives carefully to the parking exit, hoping the car has not been at the airport for too long. As he approaches the gate, it rises automatically. The vehicle has a Florida Sun Pass.

Charles Summers decides to drive the long way to the address in Boca Raton.

He flies past the turnoff to I-95 North and heads towards the Florida Turnpike. It is the most exhilarating ride he has ever had.

He cannot even imagine how thankful the owner will be. Then doubt creeps into his dreams.

He suddenly realizes that the owner might be on a plane flying elsewhere.

The jerk who called him fat boy drifts through his mind. No, that's not likely.

Perhaps it was the younger gentleman, the one who never smiled, the one he persuaded to buy a round-trip ticket to Roanoke, Virginia.

That passenger was a tall man, perhaps six-foot-three, weighing about 195 pounds. He also had a Marine Corps tattoo on his wrist.

Charles Summers looks in the mirror and sees a bunch of state police cars flashing their party hats far behind him.

He looks at the speedometer, drops 15 miles an hour, reluctantly reining in the Maserati masterpiece to the legal speed limit of 65.

The soundproofing of the car is excellent, and he does not hear the helicopter directly overhead.

He is surprised when it drops into view in front of him, with a warrior in a flack jacket pointing an automatic rifle directly at him.

Christ, he thinks, the owner must have been picking someone up at the airport and reported the car stolen. He did not understand enough about this journey to his just rewards.

Charles Summers slows down quickly and pulls into the emergency lane on the far right of the Turnpike. Fingers shaking, he turns the car off.

His last thought is that no good deed goes unpunished. His final feeling is that of being pushed by the Hand of God, through the roof of the Maserati.

The spectacular car explosion appears on many cameras, from both the helicopter and in four State Trooper cars converging on the Maserati.

The car bomb, wirelessly armed to accept one start and one stop of the ignition, blows a perfect smoke ring into the evening sky.

Recognizable parts of a human being appear to lead the smoke ring's trajectory, along with a lot of twisting, twirling pieces of metal.

Charles Summers falls back to earth in many pieces.

The helicopter, rocked backward by the blast, makes a safe landing beyond the Turnpike barriers.

The pilot has already called for an ambulance before he touches down.

The gunner in the helicopter doorway has suffered severe leg injuries from the exploding debris.

The pilot is not confident if the helicopter is airworthy. Otherwise, he would head to a trauma unit immediately. He calls and suggests an airlift, fast.

The gunner is losing a lot of blood. The pilot grabs some rope in the back of the chopper, and he ties tourniquets below the knees on both of the gunner's legs.

Later, in official police reports, he is credited with saving the man's life.

All of the State Troopers get out of their vehicles with handguns drawn, or shotguns pointed at the wreckage. They slowly lower all of their weapons.

The Maserati is dead.

A Nursery Near The Florida Everglades: Thursday Night

Anthony Silberg does not know where he is, although he smells a mixture of dirt and flowers. He's groggy, and badly blurred vision makes it difficult to discern anything in the dim light. Silberg hears garbled sounds, cotton voices strangely muffled, and shadows move back and forth in a slit of light at the bottom of what might be a door. He tries to move, and he can't. Silberg realizes that he has been shrink-wrapped in a chair. Plastic ties secure his hands behind him, attached to the metal neck joining the back and the seat of the office chair he's sitting on. He shifts his weight, and the chair moves slightly. It's on wheels. It's on a hard surface, with no carpeting.

Duct tape covers his mouth. Something stifles his vision and his hearing. He realizes that shrink wrapping covers his entire head as well as his body and legs. He is sweating profusely. The Florida heat has tightened the wrapping. He vaguely sees something white at the bottom of his vision. He gradually figures out what it is. Thick plastic straws pierce the shrink wrapping. They have been shoved into his nose so he can breathe.

He cannot perceive what the people beyond the door say. He thinks he hears something about TV reception, but he can't be sure. He tries, unsuccessfully, to relax.

He closes his eyes. He waits, with his senses dulled by whatever the large man, who bear-hugged him in short-term parking, shot into his arm. He remembers it vaguely, at first with anger.

Then the rage slowly seeps out of him into the pool of sweat, forming a puddle beneath his chair. After a while, it mixes with the smell of urine. Finally, caught in the overpowering fear of helplessness, Silberg passes out.

Bright lights wake him up. The door is open. Light pours in, forcing him to squint. Someone cuts and then yanks the shrink wrap off his head, and the nose tubes come with it, which gives him a severe nose bleed. The duct tape stays over his mouth, and it's difficult to breathe. He thinks he might drown in his blood.

"He's choking," the man who pulls off the shrink wrap says to the others.

"Let 'im," a voice beyond the door answers.

Silberg sees a large television monitor in a room beyond the door, several men, no women, all of them looking like farmers. He glimpses long rows of plants and flowers under artificial light.

He's choking badly, but someone rips the duct tape off his mouth. He gasps for air, spits out blood and phlegm.

"Thank you," he sputters. "Thank you." He can finally breathe again.

The man walks out, half closing the door.

The door swings open again, another man walks around behind him and starts pushing him into the next room. Silberg thinks he's in a nightmare. He is in a nursery, and he smells marijuana.

Five men watch as the sixth man wheels him into what looks like an office.

They are unshaven, rough-looking, and relatively young. Someone hands something to one of the men, a computer disk. He's also on the phone, and he says, very politely, "Yes, sir. I just got it." He listens and then hangs up the phone.

"Boss says he wants to show you how you died," he says to Anthony Silberg.

He takes the computer disk and puts it in a CD player on a shelf below a large flat-screen television.

The Ten O'clock News comes on.

The station's main anchor has a severe warning for viewers. What they are about to see is very graphic and may not be suitable viewing for young children.

A female reporter stands next to a blazing car, thanks to the projected magic of a Green Screen. The picture dissolves into the Maserati logo on the front of the vehicle. The emblem appears intact, although it's so well-defined that it may have been photoshopped.

Silberg recognizes his vanity license plate: **ARS4U**.

"The question remains," the reporter says, "whether or not the police helicopter, which swerved in front of this crumbled wreck of a luxury sports car, shot a guided missile into it. Some witnesses have come forward and said that they saw the trail of a rocket, fired from the underbelly of the police helicopter, destroy this two hundred thousand dollar luxury vehicle."

She emphasizes her producer's inflated price of the sports car.

Recorded footage shows a Maserati rolling to a stop in the emergency lane on the Florida Turnpike. The recording seems to be shot from an aerial camera about a hundred feet away.

The long-distance shot shows a person in the front seat, two hands on the wheel.

As the camera starts to move slowly in on the driver, one of the driver's hands comes off of the wheel. The camera never has a clear shot of the driver's face.

The camera shot rocks backward as the car explodes, and the footage dissolves into another view, further away, taken from an approaching police patrol car.

The explosion tears the front of the parked car apart, sending what looks like two bodies into the air along with a lot of metal debris.

An almost perfect smoke ring chases the bodies, which fly out of sight, off-camera.

The recording has sound, which the TV station has enhanced considerably.

As the noise of metal and debris rains down on the turnpike, a young woman's voice replaces the resonance of explosive destruction.

The young girl's "voice over" runs for several seconds before her face crossfades onto the screen, full-frame.

She's a pretty girl in her early twenties who chews gum with enthusiasm.

She explains she was driving well behind the sports car, and she saw the helicopter drop slowly from the sky and take aim at the destroyed vehicle.

"I saw that police helicopter fire a rocket into the sports car," she says. "Just like in the movies. My eyes don't lie." She cracks her gum to prove the point.

The camera dissolves back to the smoldering wreckage and the field reporter.

"The authorities strongly deny these charges," the reporter says.

A decorated police commander, with lots of stars on his shirt collar, fills the screen with an official denunciation of what he calls "a conspiracy of paranoia."

The commander says: "Once we fully investigate this event, we will release a detailed report that refutes this ridiculous rocket conspiracy theory."

The camera shot dissolves back to the scene of the accident's inferno. The screen fills with a slow zoom into the license plate of the burning car. Then the screen fades into a rewind of the Maserati's explosion.

"The police say there was only one person in the vehicle," the reporter says during her voice-over wrap. "The videotape suggests otherwise. The driver and his passenger remain unidentified, pending notification of the next of kin. Back to the studio."

The station cuts to the evening news anchor, who solemnly repeats: "Just like in the movies. We will certainly bring all our viewers updates on this extraordinary event."

The television station turns its attention to a murder-suicide in Wellington. It fades from the screen in front of Silberg when they turn off the CD player.

Silberg looks at the CD operator and says: "You got any popcorn to go with this show?"

"Nope," he says. "But we got a lot of dead fish."

One of the men sets a putrid bucket of fish in front of Anthony Silberg.

"And we got us a very nice Gator Pole." He throws a notched, six-foot pole, sharpened on one end, next to the stinking bucket of rotting fish.

Silberg suddenly knows how he's going to die.

He thinks he would prefer being in a fatal car explosion. But as long as he's alive, a chance of survival exists.

"Who was in the car?" he asks.

One of the younger men starts snapping his fingers, and another rhythmically slaps his pants.

They've been working on a rap song during the boredom of waiting for something to happen.

The finger snapper rap-talks the answer for Silberg:

> ***Just an ol' fat guy***
> ***sumpin' like you,***
> ***an ol' poboy,***
> ***gettin' bit in two.***
> ***Gonna slip his soul***
> ***to an alligator shoe,***
> ***an' he sure gonna make***
> ***a fine alligator stew.***

Everyone has a good laugh, except for Anthony Silberg.

"Let's go, boys," the CD operator says.

They start to wheel Silberg out of the office, into a star-filled night with no moon.

The sounds of the Everglades overpower the noises of men lifting and pushing Anthony Silberg into the front of a flat-bottomed airboat.

Miami-Dade District One State Troopers Command: Thursday Night

Special agent in charge Scott Larsen and his men sit in the headquarters of District One of the Miami-Dade State Troopers. They watch all the accident footage from the helicopter and the police vehicles. Despite the reports circulating in newsrooms, it's

evident that only one person was in the Maserati. They freeze the explosion, clicking forward frame by frame. They can see the head, the torso, and the lower half of a single body shoot skyward in two separate pieces, in front of a slowly forming smoke ring. As the body parts move higher, they disappear off the screen. Then they fall back into the picture, but not shredded into so many pieces by the explosion that it may be impossible for anybody to put the human puzzle back together.

They still do not know if the body is Anthony Silberg, although it appears that it might be.

In Boca Raton, federal agents enter Silberg's home at The Royal Coconut Yacht and Country Club, with a warrant.

Still, they do not find suitable bodily fluids for a definitive DNA test. They do discover some Kleenex tissues in a wastebasket in the bathroom, and they hope that they will produce a sound sample. But even if they do, the DNA backlog at the Federal level, combined with an insufficient number of laboratory analysts, make a quick check impossible. Once the tests begin, it will still be almost three days before any evidence produces hard facts.

Prison records show that Silberg's blood type is O-Positive. The blood at the accident scene is the same. It is the most common blood type in America.

In the accident debris, investigators discover a partially-burned body part that they recognize as a male sex organ. A female investigator finds it.

The investigator tags it, putting it in what she jokingly calls her "Bobbitt Bag." It is a reference to a famous incident in June of 1993 when a woman named Lorena Bobbitt cuts off her drunken husband's penis with a carving knife after he assaults her and passes out.

Authorities find his severed manhood on the side of a wintery highway, where Lorena Bobbitt tosses it after rolling down the window of the car she uses to escape from the scene of her crime.

Doctors later reattach the organ. The owner tries, and fails, as a male nightclub dancer.

A tasteless but unforgettable story is born.

Another field officer at the scene quips: "You know, investigative humor in the field has a very sharp edge to it." His teammates laugh. He leans down and picks up an Accelerated Realty Sales bank check. It shows a definite number on the recipient's line, but the fire has destroyed the signatures, and the exact value is not discernible, although the word "million" is.

In the Headquarters of District One of the Miami-Dade State Troopers, the special agent in charge, Scott Larsen, asks his men: "Why was Silberg driving North on the Turnpike? Why would he be driving away from the Miami International Airport, which would be an obvious escape route?"

"And if all the escrow money is missing, gone from the CitiBank account," another agent asks, "why does the check even exist?"

"I don't think it was Silberg in the car," special agent in charge Scott Larsen says. "I think he wants us to think it was him, but I imagine that he's long gone. I think the check is bogus, a red herring. The number on that check is probably going to be a fake."

"Silberg may be a pretty smart guy," one of the federal agents says.

Agent Larsen looks at him and nods. "Most crooks are."

Special Agent in Charge Larsen does not denigrate the enemy. You catch bad guys with respect, not bravado.

"Speaking of red herrings, how about the Bobbitt Bag?" another agent asks. The joke has caught on, spreading laughter through every department of the local, state, and federal police forces.

A female state trooper laughs and says: "You see one, you've seen them all." Some of the men appreciate her humor. Others do not.

Special Agent in Charge Larsen says: "Let's find out who he was banging. Let's see if we can get a positive ID."

People laugh but quiet down because he means it.

Chapter 15

Late-Breaking News

The 10 O'clock News, Boca Raton, Thursday

Bill Brownstone thinks he will probably spend the rest of his life in prison. He co-signs the check that Anthony Silberg uses to clean out the escrow account of Accelerated Realty Sales. Brownstone becomes an accessory, an unwitting and unwilling partner in criminal activity. He watches enough crime stories on television to know where and how it ends up.

On Thursday afternoon, he goes downstairs to see if he can confess to something and offer evidence as a government witness. He walks into the conference room with a brave face, ready to confront the FBI people, but they have already left. Martha Krumble finds him an hour later, crying in his office. She does not know him, and he has never met her. His whimpering embarrasses her. She tells him to go home and return to the office on Friday morning.

"We have a lot to talk about, Mister Brownstone, and as the Office Manager, your primary responsibility will be to give me all of the facts that I need to evaluate where Accelerated Realty Sales goes from here."

He almost spills the beans then and there, but she leaves his office too quickly, saying: "Get a good night's sleep, William Brownstone. You're going to need it."

Martha Krumble does not hear him say: "I'm sorry. Yes, yes, I am so sorry." He says it with a voice that barely achieves the level of a whisper.

Bill Brownstone gets home at around 6:30 in the evening, and his wife has left him a note saying that she will be back around nine-thirty, perhaps a bit later. His dinner is in the refrigerator.

He does not think she will agree to go into a witness protection program.

When she gets home at a few minutes before ten, she walks from the garage, through the kitchen, opening the refrigerator door for a late-night snack.

She sees that her husband has not touched his supper.

"Billy Boy?" she shouts. "Where's my Billy Boy?"

She sees light flickering into the darkened living room, coming from the den, where he must be watching television. He has probably fallen asleep. He works so hard.

She goes back to the refrigerator, eats a chilled Snickers bar, then takes out his dinner. She also pulls out another Snickers bar. She puts Bill's dinner on a tray, organizes it nicely on a real plate, but with plastic utensils, and walks with it, into the den. Sure enough, he's sound asleep, even though the television is quite loud. She puts down his food, opens a portable tray, sets it up in front of him on the couch, and glances at the television.

The Ten O'clock News anchor says: "A word of warning. What you are about to see is very graphic and may not be suitable viewing for young children."

A reporter, seemingly standing much too close to a flaming car wreck, says something, and then the camera focuses on a vanity license plate, which Bill Brownstone's wife immediately recognizes.

Her husband has shown her "the boss's car" several times in the underground garage at Accelerated Realty Sales. Each time she has put her foot down and said that there is no way her Billy Boy will ever waste money on such a vehicle.

"Unless, of course, it is a company car. You should ask for a company car, Billy Boy."

Then he can have a fancy sports car like his boss, Anthony Silberg.

On the television monitor, she watches Silberg's car pull to the side of the road, stop, and, as the camera moves closer, explode. The sound is enormous.

"Billy Boy!" she shouts, pushing him on the shoulder. An almost empty bottle of whiskey rolls out of his lap and onto the floor.

"My God, Bill Brownstone, you're DRUNK!" she shouts. She glares, first at him, then back at the television.

A young girl says: "I saw that police helicopter fire a rocket into the sports car. Just like in the movies. My eyes don't lie."

Then a Police Commander starts talking about conspiracies, and Bill Brownstone's wife is punching her drunken husband on the shoulder, shouting: "What's going on here, Bill Brownstone? What have you done?"

He does not respond.

Then she sees the orange pill container, missing its screw cap, opened on a side table next to the couch. It is her collection of oxycodone tablets, a pillbox filled with powerful, codeine-related drugs that she has avoided taking during six months of painful dental procedures.

She's finally perfecting her smile with dental implants. She's enthusiastic about the procedure because she thinks it might get her to eat less food while it's going on.

She has been on a diet of one sort or another since her thirteenth birthday.

The dental implant procedure does nothing to curb her appetite. It cannot even stop her from pulling frozen Snickers bars out of the freezer.

She knows the habit-forming danger of oxycodone. She thinks that she is much stronger than any pain her dentist can give her, although she does fill all the prescriptions. She just never uses them.

Well, maybe she swallowed a couple after the third visit to the dentist, which uncovered a large abscess in the back of her mouth. But that was a moment of weakness, an exception in her life of stoically bearing any pain with Irish toughness.

The orange container is now empty, lying on its side, with the screw cap missing. There had been at least 24 pills in it, maybe more.

She shakes her husband harder and harder. She leans into <u>Bill Brownstone</u> and puts her ear next to <u>his</u> mouth. She was never any good at finding a pulse on men.

The television anchor promises to keep everyone up to date with updates on the car explosion.

Bill Brownstone's wife begins to scream.

After a few minutes, she dials 911.

She eats the Snickers bar, but will not remember doing so. When the police come, she is sitting in the den with her dead husband, eating his dinner, and crying.

Accelerated Realty Sales
Boca Raton: Friday AM

The following morning, the special agent in charge, Scott Larsen and his team interview the new broker of record at Accelerated Realty Sales. Martha Krumble never worked for Anthony Silberg, but she has some candid opinions about the man.

Distinctive Homes & Services

"Silberg was a criminal, very dishonest, unscrupulous, competitive to a fault, and a disgusting womanizer," she says. "Other than that, he was a wonderful guy."

They stare at her without smiling.

"I am speaking facetiously, gentlemen. Anthony Silberg was a rotten and very dishonest bastard," Martha says.

"And Mister Brownstone?"

"What about Mister Brownstone? I don't know where he is," Martha says. "He was supposed to be here this morning for a meeting. I called his home, but the telephone company has disconnected his line."

"Bill Brownstone is dead," agent in charge Larsen says.

Martha leans back in her chair. "How?" she asks.

"The coroner will let us know later today."

"Was he shot? Did Silberg shoot him before he died in the car explosion on the turnpike?"

"What do you know about the car explosion," another agent asks. It is Agent John Dempsey.

His voice assumes a very accusatory tone.

Martha looks at Agent Dempsey, then at the special agent in charge, Scott Larsen.

"Really?" she says. "We're going to be the bad guys in all this, and you're going to act like big, tough, good guys? Is that how this is going to work?"

Scott Larsen holds up his hand to agent John Dempsey, who starts to speak.

Larsen says: "I'm very sorry, Missus Krumble. We're all under a lot of pressure, looking for answers."

"Well, I hope you find them, agent Larsen," she says. "For what it's worth, my father was a supreme court judge in New York State, and quite a famous one, so I know how the system works. But you won't get far with me or anybody in this building if you intend to treat all of us as suspects, as criminals. Do I make myself clear?"

"Yes, you do."

Martha asks, again: "Did Silberg shoot Bill Brownstone, before Silberg died in the car explosion?"

"He did not. We believe that Mister William Brownstone committed suicide."

The special agent in charge considers adding that they remain uncertain about the victim in the car explosion, but he holds that back.

"I never met Mister Brownstone until I took over this company yesterday," Martha says. "His suicide might suggest that he and Silberg were in this together."

"That's certainly a possibility. I would like to go back to your description of Mister Silberg for a moment. You said he was a disgusting womanizer?"

"That was his reputation, and I, myself, had to beat off his advances a long time ago when I almost went to work here. He locked that door over there and tried to fondle my right breast."

She sees almost all of the men focus on her right breast. The one who doesn't focuses on her left one. *Dyslexia.*

They all quickly look back at her face.

"I distinctly remember walking out of the office and telling Silberg he was a cheap, lecherous crook," Martha says. "Those were my exact words, gentlemen. Do you know what his answer was?" They want to know.

"He said he was not cheap." She stares at the men. "In other words," Martha adds, "by default, he admitted he was a lecherous crook, but a generous one."

Scott Larsen nods. "Do you think there are women here at the company with whom he might have slept, women that he had a sexual affair with?"

Martha presses a button on her phone. "Sarah, could you come in here for a moment?"

As Sarah Golden steps into the office, Martha Krumble introduces her as "Mister Anthony Silberg's former, and now my executive secretary."

Sarah Golden approaches her imminent retirement with an almost insatiable fondness for cream pastries. Martha can see all of the men mentally crossing her off their list of Silberg's possible sexual partners.

"Sarah, who was Silberg screwing in this company?" Martha Krumble asks.

"What do you mean by screwing?" Sarah answers, a bit shaken by the possibilities.

"Who was he banging, Sarah? Who did Anthony Silberg have sexual relations with?"

"I don't know how to answer that," Sarah says.

"We're off the record, gentlemen, is that correct?" Martha asks.

"Absolutely," Scott Larsen says. "*Absolutely not*," he and all of his men think.

"So who was Silberg screwing, Sarah?"

"The Goldfish Bowl," Sarah Golden says.

"All of them?"

"Not the men," Sarah Golden says.

"Thank you, Sarah. That's all."

Sarah quickly backs out the door. She phones Alice Koenig, who she saw earlier in the Goldfish Bowl with Barbara Rossellini.

Sarah knows that most of the other women in the Golden Harem are interviewing this morning with Frederick Phelps at the new ARS Luxury Partnership branch located on the beach.

With the probable exceptions of Koenig and Rossellini, the Goldfish Bowl women want to join the Suntan Division. They want a fresh start.

"Get ready for the Feds," Sarah says when Alice Koenig answers her phone.

Sarah hangs up quickly, with a tight smile, as all the FBI agents head out of Martha's office, led by Krumble.

In the Goldfish Bowl, Alice knocks on Barbara's glass door and says: "The Feds are coming." She sits down in one of Barbara's chairs, and they both watch the men, led by Martha Krumble, marching towards them.

"What have we done?" Barbara asks.

"I think they know that Anthony Silberg was our boy toy." She smiles, and Barbara smiles. They both know that neither one of them will miss Anthony Silberg.

"Let's make sure we stick together," Barbara says. She's starting to like Alice Koenig.

They both stand up as everyone crowds into Barbara's office. Martha introduces Alice Koenig, with whom she has closed many luxury home sales over the years. They do like one another.

She then introduces Barbara Rossellini, with whom she has never done any business.

Martha Krumble explains to the Feds that Barbara is a member of the family of Angelo Rossellini, the new majority shareholder of Accelerated Realty Sales.

Then Martha says: "Gentlemen, if you'd like to use the conference room, please do so. I'll be in my office upstairs. Ladies, speak the truth." She turns and leaves.

Barbara and Alice tell the Feds they would like to be interviewed together. The Feds say that some of the questions might be very personal. The women say that's fine, and they have no secrets. They all go to the conference room and sit down, the federal agents, all men, on one side of the table, and the two women on the opposite side.

Special Agent in Charge Larsen starts by saying: "We know you both had, uh, personal relations of a sexual nature with Mister Anthony Silberg."

"Who told you that?" Alice asks.

"That's not important," Larsen says.

"Maybe not to you, but to us, it is crucial."

Another agent, the same one who irritated Martha Krumble earlier, and who also suggested taking George McKlane's thank you letters off the wall of his War Room, as evidence, says: "Do you deny you had a relationship with Mister ...." Agent Larsen's hand, held up, silences the man. He turns to another agent and says: "Get Dempsey out of here." Two agents disappear from the room.

"Wow," Barbara Rossellini says. "It's a little early for Good Cop, Bad Cop, isn't it?"

Special agent in charge, Scott Larsen sighs, shakes his head. "Ladies, we need your help. We found a male body part, fully intact, at the scene of the explosion, and if you have had sexual relations with Mister Silberg, you might be able to identify it. I'm sorry for your loss."

The women both look at each other, turn to the agents and ask, in unison: "How big is it."

Embarrassed, Special Agent in Charge Larsen holds out the index fingers of his hands as if he's telling someone about a fish he recently caught. A relatively small fish.

"Not a chance," Alice Koenig says.

"No way," Barbara Rossellini says. She holds out both of her index fingers, about four times wider than agent Larsen's demonstration.

Agent Larsen, feeling somewhat inadequate, says: "Really? Are you serious?"

"Really," both women say, again in unison. The other agent looks at Rossellini, a petite woman, and wonders how that could work. He says nothing. The thought intrigues him, however. "Well then," he says, "I guess we won't have to take a trip down to the county morgue."

"Thank God for huge favors," Alice says. "No pun intended, of course."

Barbara smiles.

"I guess that we're done here, ladies," Special Agent in Charge Larsen says. "I'd like to thank you very much for your time. And your honesty."

The women leave. The two other agents return. One of them immediately says: "I'm sorry, sir."

Special Agent in Charge Larsen says: "You certainly are, Dempsey." Then to the group, he says: "I think we all knew it wasn't Silberg in the car. The evidence we have just heard, admittedly anecdotal, suggests that the car explosion might be a carefully-planned deception. Silberg is still alive. I want all the flights out of Miami checked. Unless he has a fake passport, which I recognize as a distinct possibility, his name is going to be on someone's manifest."

"Should we check Fort Lauderdale International Airport as well, sir?" agent John Dempsey asks. "The explosion was north of five-ninety-five. The car might have been coming from the Fort Lauderdale airport."

"That's possible," agent Larsen says. "Good thinking, Dempsey. You're going to be in charge of that part of this important investigation."

Special Agent in Charge Larsen knows that any car going north from the Fort Lauderdale airport would almost certainly use I-95 and not the Florida turnpike. However, the troublesome agent's suggestion will keep Dempsey out of the way for a few days.

In Alice Koenig's office, Barbara Rossellini says: "That means that Silberg is not dead."

"No, he's not," Alice Koenig says. She reaches over and presses the Silberg button on her speed dial, which connects her directly to what is now Martha Krumble's office, bypassing her executive secretary.

Alice then puts the call on speakerphone.

"Yes?" Martha says, not sure why her phone rings without any warning from Sarah Golden.

"Hi, Martha. Alice. You're on speakerphone. I'm with Barbara. The Feds are gone. Who told them we were in bed with Silberg?"

"They asked me if anyone here was sleeping with Mister Silberg. I asked Sarah Golden, in front of them, who he was screwing. Sarah Golden answered: 'The Goldfish Bowl but not the men'."

"Yeah," Alice says, "I guess she would know that."

"What did the Feds want?" Martha Krumble asks.

Barbara Rossellini says: "Anthony Silberg is still alive. That wasn't him who got blown up on television last night." Alice Koenig and Barbara Rossellini explain.

It's a strange conversation, but all three women seem to bond a bit because of it.

Afterward, Martha Krumble phones George McKlane, the third name on her long list of valuable customers to call, but the first one she phones.

McKlane answers himself sees the caller ID as Anthony Silberg, and motions to his son, who is sitting across from him in George's office.

"Mister Silberg," George says. "I thought you were dead, and you probably thought I was dead."

He puts the call on speakerphone, and he quickly turns on the Magic Wand recording device.

Martha Krumble's voice suddenly fills the room. "Excuse me, Mister McKlane?"

"Who is this?" George McKlane asks.

"It's Martha Krumble, George. I think it must be the caller ID on this phone system. We have not changed that yet at Accelerated Realty Sales. I am now the broker here, as well as one of the owners."

"Well, you gave me quite a shock, Martha. I thought I was about to talk to a dead person who tried to kill me early yesterday morning."

"What in the world are you talking about, George?" Martha asks him.

"Silberg," George says. He tells her about the break-in and the attempt on his life.

"We need to talk," Martha says. "I suggest you get some 'round-the-clock protection, George. I have reliable information that Anthony Silberg is still alive."

They set up a meeting at George's house for lunch. "You'll meet my son," George says.

Martha steps out of her office and looks at Sarah Golden. "I want every caller ID on every phone in this company removed," she says. "Someone just thought I was Anthony Silberg when I called them. I am most definitely NOT Anthony Silberg."

Sarah Golden looks at her and says: "Thank God for that." Even to her, it sounds like she's sucking up to Martha, but Sarah's pension is only six months away, and she's scared that it might vanish.

In George's office, Colonel McKlane looks at his father. He says: "When I touched down at the Boca Airport, I a team of what you used to call Marine commandoes met me, Dad. Nowadays, they're part of the Marine Raider Regiment. They're at my disposal while I'm here. If you don't mind, I'd like to offer them room and board for a few days."

"That sounds like an excellent plan, son."

When Martha Krumble pulls through the gate to George's house an hour and a half later, she's impressed by the number of Marines, in battle gear, standing guard in different areas of the driveway. She has to show her license to one of them as she enters. He says: "The colonel is expecting you. Missus Krumble. Welcome aboard."

Martha wonders when and how Captain George McKlane became a colonel. She also notices a Boca Police car in the parking area. George McKlane is well protected.

Chapter 16

The Gator Pole

People who disappear with the help of criminal organizations do so in many ways. Some people murder them openly, lessons, and warnings for their peers. The ones who vanish without a trace, the ghosts never found, follow a path of tradition.

Chicago favors cement, and New York City likes crushed cars. Las Vegas demands long walks in the desert.

In Palm Beach, Florida, the criminal hierarchy prefers something called a Gator Pole.

Three men load Anthony Silberg onto an airboat at two o'clock in the morning.

They secure him in a seat at the front of the boat, still shrink-wrapped around his chest, stomach, and legs. He locks like a cellophane mummy.

"You know, most people have to pay a lot of money for a front-row seat like this," one of the younger men tells Silberg. "This trip is a gift for you. Maybe I should take your watch as payment."

"Leave it," the pilot of the airboat shouts, seeing the man digging through the shrink wrap for Silberg's watch. The kid spits tobacco over the side of the boat and steps back. It's just an old military watch, probably worthless.

In 1921, a South Florida developer and aircraft builder, Glenn Curtis, invents airboats. People initially call them "frog boats." Curtis bolts an airplane propeller onto a small fishing boat and opens the door to millions of acres of wetlands, impenetrable before the deafening roar of his shallow-bottomed contraption.

Airboats become an industry in the final quarter of the 20th century.

Florida companies build almost all of them. They fly up the Congo River in Africa, across unexplored ice and snow in Russia near the Ural Mountains, through the swamplands of Louisiana.

Nobody knows how many airboats exist, although a good guess, just for the state of Florida, is 20,000. Most of them are registered incorrectly as conventional powerboats.

The airboat on which they strap Anthony Silberg has no registration at all. Nobody has ever applied for it.

It's a modified Diamondback model, creating a loud amount of noise because the men privately upgrade the craft. Two of them sit in bucket seats directly in front of the propeller cage, one of them the pilot, one riding shotgun, a 12-gauge, sawed-off version. They both wear noise-blocking headphones. A third man sits on a lower chair in front of them, also wearing noise blockers. Silberg sits in the forward chair. Perched at the front of the airboat, Anthony Silberg gets no headphones.

The shallow-bottomed machine glides across the Everglades, the River of Grass, smoothly.

Silberg twists his neck around, trying to understand how the pilot steers the airboat. The man behind him hits his face hard and tells him to keep his eyes straight ahead.

Occasionally, the pilot follows a long stretch of canal. Then he slips smoothly over grass into brief, open water. The surrounding Sawgrass is tall, spotted with islands, some of which move a few inches every day. The boat's roar drowns out the night sounds of the Everglades. Silberg cannot hear the low, rumbling bellows of alligators along the shoreline and in the Sawgrass, although he sees their splash from time to time in the starlight.

Silberg has no idea where he is, but the airboat pilot knows their exact position. After almost forty-five minutes, deep within the Everglades, they slow down in front of an island. The moon climbs into the stars, and Silberg sees what looks like a small stretch of sand. The airboat slips up on the beach. The prop stops. The silence seems to be ringing at first, and then Silberg's ears begin to recover.

One of the men jumps out. He walks up and down the sandy area, stopping and checking some previous Gator Poles sunk into the ground, sticking a half a foot above the sand. He pulls them out quickly. They have rotted in the tropical decay of Florida. The small island hasn't seen any activity for seven months. The beachcomber walks back to the airboat and takes the new pole, finds some solid ground, and starts to wiggle its sharpened tip into it. The Gator Pole goes through the first few feet of the island with no problem. After that, the pole needs a sledgehammer to sink it into the tangled roots. The top of the pole widens from the hammering it requires to beat it into the island.

The man takes some black nylon rope and runs it through a hole drilled six inches from the frayed top. He stands up, tugs on it, leans backward.

The pole does not budge.

They untie Silberg, still shrinkwrapped, and tip him out of the boat, slamming him hard into the beach.

"Hey," the Pilot says. "Be careful. Those gators don't like their meat bruised."

They all laugh. The songwriter tries to repeat what he had created earlier, but he can't remember the words. He's been smoking marijuana on the way out.

They tie Silberg to the pole, with about two feet of play in the rope. They tighten the rope around his feet in a series of figure eights, then wrapping the center of the eight, tightly.

One man takes a barbecue lighter and melts the final knot of the rope, burning Silberg in the process. Silberg shows no pain.

He is angry, and he is still alive. He feels his feet starting to go numb.

They cut off the hand ties securing him. "So you can give your new friends a hug," the man says.

Finally, the songwriter takes box cutters, slicing the shrink wrap off of Silberg as a second man pins his arms in the sand. The man with the box cutters does not do his job very carefully, and Silberg is bleeding afterward from shallow flesh wounds.

The other man crumples up the shrink wrap and says: "Don't want to give any of your new friends indigestion."

They take the wad of shrink wrap and toss it into the flat-bottomed boat.

"Hear that low grumbling sound?" the Pilot asks.

Deep and menacing sounds surround the island.

"It's gator mating season."

Another man says: "One of those big 'ole boys gonna come up here and make you his girlfriend."

The third man says: "Gonna ask you for your hand ... although he'll probably start with your legs."

They laugh at their cleverness.

Silberg is still alive.

Finally, the pilot goes to the boat, takes out the pail of rotten fish, and splashes it over Silberg. He leaves a putrid trail of fish down to the water's edge, putting the bucket back in the boat.

The men push the airboat back into the water, clambering aboard. The propeller turns smoothly, and the airboat roars off into the night. Silberg hears it cut its engine, and then it starts up again. The roar turns into a whisper as the airboat disappears.

Silberg knows they have probably dropped off one of the men on another island, maybe a hundred yards away, certainly within view of the Gator Pole. Silberg is not ignorant about Gator Poles, although this is the first time he has been on the receiving end of one.

He tugs on it, and it barely moves. He slides around and tugs on it from the other side. It barely moves. He does this from each quadrant and finally gets it to move a bit. He looks up and sees a cloud moving over the moon.

In the increased darkness, he lies flat on the sand, belly up, with his butt against the pole. With the rope wrapped around his feet, he pushes upward, his feet pointing at the sky. Silberg has sturdy legs, one of the reasons he was a good boxer. The weight he has gained over the years has maintained the power of his leg muscles. The Gator Pole rises almost 12 inches. He scurries around, wiggles it back and forth, and drags it entirely out of the hole as the moon reappears. The pole lays flat on the sand. He wonders if whoever was dropped off by the airboat saw the Gator Pole as Silberg pushed it up with his legs and then dragged it out of the ground.

As the moon peeks through fast-moving clouds, Silberg sees a large log in the water, moving towards the beach. He estimates that it is at least four or five feet long, and that's just what is showing. The Gator itself will be at least two times that size. A cloud suddenly covers the moon again. Silberg crabs his way back into the brush, dragging the Gator Pole behind, attached by the nylon rope to his feet. He bumps into a tree, tries unsuccessfully to pull his weight onto the first branch. *How the hell did I get so badly out of shape?*

He inches his way further into the undergrowth. He finds a tree he can get up into, but only about four feet off the ground. He stares in the direction of where the airboat disappeared. He sees the soft glow of a cigarette far off, near a bend in the canal. *I know he's smoking dope*, Silberg thinks.

The moon continues to hide behind clouds. The glow of marijuana turns on and off, on and off. Then the pinprick disappears. The moon remains hidden, and a lighter flickers and then glows on a distant face as the watchman lights up another joint.

Silberg takes the sharpened end of the Gator Pole and goes to work on the rope around his feet. It takes time.

Something dark and menacing moves up on the beach, but Silberg, on a low branch, is twenty feet away. Every time he looks up, he watches for the distant glow, and then he stares at the shadow on the beach. He finally frees his feet.

The Gator Pole becomes his weapon, but hardly a match for an alligator that must be at least ten feet long.

He wishes he had the spear in McKlane's War Room. Sharonda enters his thoughts, and then she quickly vanishes

The full moon reappears.

On the beach, a large gator lifts its snout, bulges its neck, and bellows. The sound reverberates across the Everglades. Silberg moves off his perch, skittering further into the undergrowth, quietly.

He sees a python slither off, but he's not afraid.

Silberg is still alive.

Suddenly, a gunshot rings out from the bend in the canal, then another, and finally the third shot. It is a signal. The monster on the beach lumbers back into the water, moving slowly away.

Silberg thinks that the pothead might believe the monster has eaten him. He crouches in the underbrush.

After about fifteen minutes, he hears the airboat. It surprises him, coming from the other direction, running up on the Gator Pole beach. They will pick up the watchman after they make sure the alligator has done its job.

The pilot remains in his seat as the second man steps off the airboat, onto the beach. Better odds, Silberg thinks, two to one.

While Silberg prepares for what might be his final fight on earth, George McKlane is at home, in bed, with the television flickering off the empty tinfoil wrapper of his second chocolate bar. Once again, George drops into another time, another place. It is a battle every bit as dangerous as the one Silberg is about to face.

North Korea: The Bridge Drop, Dec 7-10, 1950

George McKlane and his Marines get ready to continue their fight to the coast of North Korea. An essential link to their successful escape drops from the sky, floating into the perimeter at Koto-ri.

An earlier test drop, from an Air Force C-119, crumples in failure on December 6th at Yonpo.

A special crew of Army parachute riggers and over a hundred other Army engineers works all night to prepare for the new drop into the protected Koto-ri perimeter. More giant parachutes are flown in from Japan.

Starting at 0930 on December 7th, 1950, eight sections of a steel Treadway bridge, each weighing well over a ton, drop out of the back of C-119 transports. Huge parachutes billow spectacularly in the frozen sky — the first three land safely within the Koto-ri perimeter. Buffeted by strong crosswinds, one drops into enemy hands. Another suffers severe damage.

By noon, three more airdrops make it into the perimeter. Only four sections are needed.

About four klicks south of Koto-ri, a sixteen-foot gap, requiring twenty-four feet of bridging, has become one of the Chinese communist's favorite targets.

The CCF blows up the bridge crossing three times, first when it was concrete, and then its wooden replacement, and most recently an M-2 Steel Treadway span installed by the Army Corps of Engineers.

The bridge spans four large steel pipes that discharge water from the Chosin Reservoir. The water tubes make an almost vertical descent down the mountainside, feeding the turbines of a power plant in the valley far below. The road leading up to the gap is a mountain on one side and a sheer drop on the other. It is the only exit available to the machinery, the tanks, the artillery, the trucks, and the long, trudging columns of marching Marines. They inch, like a broken centipede, towards their coastal embarkation point, fighting the bitter cold as well as the Chinese regulars.

The new bridge is in place by December 8th, and the road has cleared. Each portion of the long line of men and machines fight and protect the new bridge.

Each group defends it long enough for the Marines and machinery following them to take their place.

The final group across will include a platoon of demolition experts. They will blow up the bridge and prevent the CCF from shooting the retreating columns of Marines in the back.

As they approach the bridge, Captain McKlane and his men jump off their trucks and fire into the hills and down the sharp embankment.

A Marine Corps M46 Patton tank is part of their entourage as they approach the bridge.

The M46 tank starts to slide on the narrow road, and the driver quickly and unexpectedly swivels its turret in an attempt to maintain balance and traction.

"Watch out, captain!" Sergeant Chapman shouts.

Forty-four tons of steel, plus a five-person crew and a bunch of troops hitching a ride, barely nudges the captain. Sergeant Chapman grabs hold of the captain's parka.

Both men fly off the side of the mountain, toy soldiers tossed by a metal monster. They disappear.

His men shout, yell, look over the edge into the valley far below, some of them chaining hands to lean precariously over the rim of the winding, rutted road.

The captain and the sergeant are gone.

One man sees what he thinks is a machine gun skip off the mountainside and disappear towards the valley far below. For a few minutes, shouts of "Sergeant!" and "Socks!" echo in the hills. Only echoes answer

They must go on. Marines cross the bridge, fire more than necessary into the hills, protect the crossing for the last group. Nobody fires into the valley. One of the men tries to shoot the tank, but cooler heads calm him down. Some men cry, saying it's the cold.

The sergeant is still alive, almost forty feet down the mountainside. He is not sure about the captain, who hangs over the small precipice on which the sergeant has found a foothold. The sergeant has an iron grip on the captain's parka. He hears men calling faintly, but the wind howling up from the valley does not permit their sound to translate into words. All of Raymond Chapman's strength focuses on pulling the captain onto the thin rock shelf jutting out from the mountain. He lifts him inch by inch, almost losing his footing and tumbling further down the hill. It would mean certain death for both of them.

The captain has a machine gun strapped around his chest. The sergeant pulls on it, the strap breaks, and the gun clatters down the mountainside, hits a rock, flies out into oblivion. Gradually, Sergeant Chapman inches the captain onto the precipice. Captain George McKlane starts to regain consciousness. His arm flops over the side of the rock shelf.

"Don't move a muscle until you know where you are, Socks," the sergeant shouts.

The captain freezes. He's disoriented. He waits to regain better bearings. The sergeant does not release his grip on McKlane's parka.

"Where are we, sergeant?"

"I'd say we were right on the edge of hell, Captain McKlane. Right on the edge of death."

"What happened?"

"We tried to trip a tank," Sergeant Chapman says. "You think anything's broken?"

"I don't think so."

They yell at each other to hear one another over the howling wind. The captain finds a handhold and gradually gets to his knees, thankful that the wind pushes him against the cliff rather than trying to tear him off of it. He moves slowly to his feet, facing the mountain, then turns carefully around. "The edge of death," he says.

"The shelf runs around the corner there," the sergeant shouts. "Let's inch our way over there and see how it looks."

After about fifteen feet, which takes a long time, the precipice widens enough for them to sit down, stretch out, and catch their breath. They both almost fall asleep.

Adrenaline helps save them, but when it dissipates, it sucks the strength out of their bodies. A colossal explosion awakens all their senses.

"There goes our trip home," Captain McKlane says. "They just blew the bridge."

The Everglades, Florida Before Sunrise, Friday

After the airboat slips up on the beach in the Everglades, the man who jumps out onto the sand says: "Hell, that gator musta used the pole as a toothpick. Everything's gone." The airboat pilot  stands up on his bucket seat, holding the propeller cage, looking at the shadows of the undergrowth. He sees Silberg break through the brush, rear back, and throw the Gator Pole at him.

Shocked, he has no time to duck.

The pole hits him in the neck and knocks him from his perch, grasping frantically at it. The pole goes through his neck. The sharp end protrudes a foot and a half out the side of his throat, pumping blood from his jugular.

As the pilot splashes into the water, Silberg launches himself at the second man, who is reaching for something in the boat. Silberg wallops the second man and starts pounding him with devastating blows to his cheekbone.

Silberg hears bones crunch, and the man howls. He breaks the man's nose with a solid punch and then drives the palm of his hand upward, sending bone fragments into the man's broken sinus cavity.

The man stiffens, then relaxes, dead.

Silberg moves cautiously onto the airboat and looks over the side. The pilot is motionless, face down in the water, the gator pole still lodged in his neck. The pilot's holster holds a sawed-off shotgun.

"The Black bitch would be proud of me," Silberg says out load, imagining Sharonda and thinking again of the spear in McKlane's War Room. A distant voice shouts out from the bend in the canal.

"What the hell is going on?"

Anthony Silberg crouches in the bed of the airboat. The second man was reaching for a rifle, and he picks it up: an old 30-06, with no scope.

He decides he will wait for sunrise.

He rolls over and looks at the sky. It starts to lighten faintly behind him, so he must be facing west. The pot smoker, further west, will be looking into the sun.

"What the hell is going on?"

Silberg reaches over the side and tries, without success, to retrieve the Gator Pole and the shotgun. He wants to shove the pilot further away from the boat.

He creeps out of the airboat and takes the shirt off the body of the second man, throwing his own blood-stained shirt, sliced by box cutters, into the water.

He takes the man's pants, checks it in the moonlight. It contains a wallet, identification, and several hundred dollars, mostly twenties. The clothes fit, but not well.

"What the hell is going on?"

He pushes the body of the second man towards the loose shirt he took off, crouching back into the airboat. He checks the water periodically for alligators.

The airboat shudders, and Silberg looks over the side. The pilot and gator pole are gone. Minutes later, a struggle occurs in the water as two alligators fight over the floating body of the second man.

"What the hell is going on?"

The pot smoker marooned at the bend in the canal periodically shouts in Silberg's direction.

As the sun pierces the horizon, Silberg sees him, perched in a tree, smoking. There's a white chair on the ground, under the tree.

The watchman tries to climb down and take cover when Silberg starts to shoot at him. Silberg's third shot drops him out of the bottom branches of the tree. The man falls next to the white chair, where he does not move much while Silberg shoots him three more times.

Anthony Silberg stands up as the sun slowly rises.

He has no idea how to drive an airboat.

He sits in the seat closest to a long handle that he can move backward and forward. An air rudder behind the propeller cage turns left and right as he pushes or pulls the rudder stick away or towards himself. So if he pushes it forward, he will probably turn right. If he pulls it back, he will go left, and if he holds it upright, in the middle, the flatbed airboat should go straight.

He sees gauges between the bucket seats and a metal flap that, when lifted, shows a set of keys, one in the ignition. He checks the fuel: three-quarters full.

He climbs down from the bucket seat. The sun breaks free from the horizon. He pushes the boat slowly off the beach and hops aboard.

The airboat drifts out into the water. Silberg looks down at the bend and sees the pothead being jerked slowly into the canal by an enormous alligator. He turns the key. The engine roars to life — some of the logs floating near the airboat sink below the surface.

He presses a pedal in front of the bucket seat. He does it too hard, and the airboat butts back onto the beach. It takes him twenty minutes to get it back into the water. He does not know how to reverse the airboat.

He drifts to the center of the canal and tries again, gently. He pushes the handle forward; he slides right. He pulls back. He slides left.

He moves up the canal, cautiously turning after a few hundred feet, bumping into the bank. Gradually, he learns how to coordinate his steering stick and the throttle.

The flat-bottomed airboat turns better when it moves with speed. He stops at the bend, where he sees a white chair and a rifle on a small patch of sand. He has no interest in owning a second weapon.

The canal here widens. Silberg drifts and thinks. If he heads into the sun, going east, he will eventually hit dry land somewhere along the border of the Everglades, where modern developments encroach on the River of Grass.

He heads east on a reasonably wide canal. As it starts to narrow, he turns around and backtracks to an extensive channel he crossed over earlier. He heads south.

Eventually, he sees an even larger canal, at a 45-degree angle to the one he's on. He heads southeast. He gets the hang of it and starts to enjoy himself, fishtailing a bit on the wide canal. Then he swerves into a channel going due east, and he can see the outlines of large buildings in the distance.

Anthony Silberg, wearing earmuffs, guns it. As he comes near to the end of the canal, where it forms a 'T,' going north and south at the top of the 'T,' he eases back on the throttle. He shuts off the boat and drifts into the shoreline of a grassy berm. He hears traffic in the distance.

He climbs the berm and looks across yet another canal.

Beyond that, he sees Friday morning traffic on what he thinks is the Sawmill Expressway, north of Miami.

He goes back to the airboat, starts it up, and moves slowly north along the berm until he runs into a cut leading into the final canal and dry land. He moves north on that canal when he sees some fishermen in the distance. He cuts the throttle as he gets close to them, pushing the airboat up onto a shallow embankment.

He walks towards the fishermen with his rifle. He suggests they trade their rusted, solitary truck parked on the embankment behind them for a gleaming new airboat.

"It's almost half full of gas," Silberg says, holding the rifle across his chest.

Nobody argues, and as Silberg drives off in their dilapidated pickup truck, the fishermen feel satisfied that they have received the better side of the deal. They jump in the airboat, crank it up, and head for a docking area on Alligator Alley, where they know they will find some of their friends.

They'll borrow a trailer from one of their buddies and take their prize home. The airboat is the best and biggest catch they've ever made in the Everglades.

Chapter 17

Getting Even

Located in Sunrise, forty minutes north of Miami, Sawgrass Mills is the 7th largest mall in the United States. Anthony Silberg upgrades his wardrobe with money out of the wallet he took from the

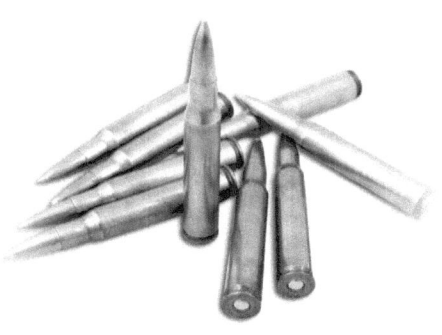

man who tied him to the Gator Pole, the man he pummeled to death. He buys a fake alligator belt to celebrate his victory.

In a men's room at the mall, he throws away the clothes he stripped off of the dead man.

He still stinks of dead fish, and he washes up in one of the toilet stalls with some toiletries he bought at a booth in the mall. The girl working there wrinkled her nose at him.

His shirt and pants get slightly stained with dried blood from his superficial box cutter wounds. He puts some newly-bought Neosporin salve on long slice lines down his left side and left leg. His wounds no longer bleed, but they hurt.

He puts on his new clothes, checks himself in the mirror, and approves his rugged, unshaven look. He has lost almost 12 pounds in 36 hours, mostly water from his shrink wrapping. He buys a floppy straw hat. He puts it on and thinks he looks like a farmer from the Panhandle. He goes to a costume shop and buys a mustache that matches his hair color. He no longer looks like Anthony Silberg.

He walks into a food court in the mall, saying "Howdy" and "Yup," and he eats three cheeseburgers with extra catsup, pickle relish, and mustard.

He's so hungry that he almost eats his new, fake mustache by mistake.

Anthony Silberg goes into an electronics store and buys a prepaid cell phone with a credit card taken from the dead man's wallet.

He pays at the cash register located closest to the entrance, in case he has to escape into the crowd of shoppers.

The charges for the new throwaway cell phone go through with no problem.

The young person at the cash register does not ask him for identification.

He walks out into the parking lot and makes a phone call to his old friend, Gregory Richards, more recently known as Gustavo Oliveira from Brazil.

"Hello, Snake," he says.

For a moment, the man who pretended to buy George McKlane's house remains quiet, and then he says: "You're not alive Pop."

"Who killed me?" Silberg asks.

"I don't know, Pop."

"Yes, you do." Silberg knows Rossellini wants him dead.

"Where are you?" Snake asks.

"Orlando," Silberg lies. Disney World and Universal Studios are about 215 miles north of Sawgrass Mills.

"Never been there, Pop," Snake says.

"And you never will be, Snake, unless you help me. You know those guys on television who say, 'I'm going to Disney World'? You will never walk among them unless you listen very carefully to me right now, Snake."

"I don't know if we should be talking to each other."

"Don't hang up, Snake. Think about it. Somebody burned me, and I am still here. And the people who tried to burn me are no longer breathing." He makes his voice as menacing as possible. "I know where you live, Snake."

Snake does not hang up.

But he does not say anything, either.

"I need a charter boat to do some deep-sea fishing, Snake. And if you help me get it, you are going to make well over two hundred thousand dollars. Cash."

"Oooh-kay," Snake says, stretching the word thoughtfully. They continue talking, and in the end, Snake says he will call back.

"No," Silberg tells him. "I'll call you in twenty minutes. And don't be stupid Snake. I have nine lives, and I haven't used even one of them yet. You, Snake, only have one life. Do you understand?"

He does.

An hour and a half later, after falling asleep in the rusted truck he traded for the airboat, he phones Snake. An all-day fishing boat is ready for the following morning at eight o'clock, the *Wholly Mackerel* out of Delray Beach, skippered by Captain Holly Smolkes.

Silberg returns to the Mall, goes into a sporting store, and buys a deep-sea fishing pole.

The salesperson says: "You're going to need a first-class reel with that rig."

Silberg says: "Nope. Got one."

He returns to the truck, takes the pole out of its canvas carrying case, and replaces it with the rifle he used to kill the pothead in the Everglades. He does not like the way it looks. He takes one of the two fishing pole sections and puts it back in the canvas bag with the rifle. It looks much better.

He returns to the mall, finds a gun section in another sports store, and buys two boxes of Golden Bear 30-06, 145 grain, full metal jacket ammunition, forty rounds in each box. He also buys a gun-cleaning kit. He drives to a secluded section of Sunrise and spends time cleaning and oiling his weapon, a Winchester Model 70 with no scope, and a magazine that holds ten rounds. Then he gets on the Sawmill Expressway and drives towards Boca Raton, Florida. He finds a cheap motel and sleeps until the sun goes down.

Nursery Hunting In Boca Friday Evening

Silberg drives up State Road 441, which borders the Everglades to the west of Boca Raton. He passes a county dump and keeps going. Then Silberg sees a sign for a nursery turns his truck into a dirt road leading away from 441, towards the Everglades. He recognizes nothing. It is a hunch. As his vehicle gets into the nursery area, he turns off his lights, driving in the starlight. He makes a sharp right on the dirt track, almost running off the path and into the brush.

He sees it in the distance, well lit. He feels his heartbeat, deep in his chest.

He recognizes the place where they had taken him. He feels it in the hair standing up on the back of his neck, like an angry, hungry animal.

He turns off the engine, glides slowly to a stop, two football fields away. He gets out quietly, listening for voices, hearing only night sounds, mostly from the Everglades. He listens to the throaty grunts of alligators. The sound angers him, but it is anger he can control.

He takes the Winchester Model 70 out of its canvas bag, chambers a 30-06 round, and adds another to the clip. He gets more bullets and puts them in his shirt pocket.

He does not care that the rifle has no scope mounted on it. He wants to get up close, wants to see their eyes, wants them to see his. He has no fear, only a commanding, vicious need for vengeance and retribution.

It takes him ten minutes to get within hearing distance of the men in the open-door office. There are no guards. They perceive no danger.

They are sitting on wooden chairs, watching the large television on which they showed him how he supposedly died in a car explosion. The big man gets up and turns the huge screen off.

"It's been too long. Something is wrong."

"They don't answer their cell phones."

"No service out there. No signal. No towers."

"We wait."

"Why not run out there and see what's happening?"

"Wouldn't take more than a half an hour."

"Should have gone in the daylight."

"How many shots did we hear?"

"Three, then nothing. Then maybe six or seven more shots just after the sun came up."

Sound carries a long way across the River of Grass, but the wind is going west during the night, and the gunfire is a whisper, not a roar.

"Should have gone out there after sunrise."

"We were told to stay here."

"Been sitting here the whole frigging day."

"Should have gone out there at sunrise."

"We wait."

They have repeated this conversation half a dozen times during the day without reaching a decision.

But this time the phone rings, an old-fashioned one that lifts off a receiver. Silberg, twenty feet away, in darkness, tenses slightly at the sound of the telephone, but the men in the office remain relaxed.

They have nothing to fear, except maybe the caller.

The big man, the apparent leader, lifts the phone to his ear. He listens and then says: "Nothing. We're thinking maybe of taking a run out there to check." As the man listens to the phone caller some more, Silberg raises his Winchester in the darkness, sights it into the light of the office. It's a simple shot. "Okay," the man says, "then we'll ..."

The explosion is loud. The phone shatters as the bullet passes through the man's hand, snapping his head away from it, throwing blood on the wall of the office. A second man starts to stand up then he suddenly spins backward as the next shot hits him in the chest.

The third man has his back to Silberg, who has moved forward, no more than ten feet away. He stands up slowly, his hands in the air.

"Turn around," Silberg says. The man turns around slowly. His mouth is open; his eyes are wide. He is afraid.

"Who are you?" he asks.

Silberg laughs, only it is not a laugh. He takes off his straw hat, throwing it aside, stepping into the light.

"Who are you?" the man asks again.

Silberg peels off the fake mustache.

The man recognizes him.

"Jesus," the man says.

"Not today, I'm not." Silberg studies the man, keeping his gun leveled on his chest. "You're the guy who ripped the duct tape off my mouth," he says.

The man nods.

"I was choking to death."

The man says nothing.

"You saved my life."

The man nods, faster this time.

"You're the only guy here who did me any favors."

The man stops nodding. He sees it in Silberg's eyes even before Silberg pulls the trigger, sending him backward, tripping over the big man's body, slamming into the wall. The man is dead before he falls to the ground.

The person on the other end of the shattered phone hears the gun explosions. The bullet does not destroy the bloody mouthpiece on the phone. After the first explosion, he hears buzzes and electrical sounds, and then another explosion, then something that might be human voices, but incomprehensible, and then a third explosion.

After about ten seconds, he hears three more explosions, all of them evenly spaced.

He's about to hang up when he suddenly hears a television and a familiar tune. The listener pulls back the sleeve of his white silk shirt and looks at his expensive, gold Rolex timepiece.

It's just before seven-thirty, and in the Palm Beaches, the theme song of the quiz show, Jeopardy, always comes on a few minutes early. The killer is watching television.

The man on the phone slowly hangs it up.

A Farm in Bath County
Saturday morning

"Pancakes!" Gammy yells, followed by "Blueberry!" and Torbjorn moves from the bottom of the staircase into the kitchen, where he will fulfill her request. The breakfast table against the wall has a framed letter on it, with an official Marine Corps photograph of his grandfather in its bottom right corner.

Ernestine Petersson comes into the kitchen in her pale, blue housecoat and says: "I heard you come in late last night, son, heard the tires on the gravel. I thought maybe you'd come and tell me what happened. I'm scared to ask."

"That's an awful lot of words spilling out of you this early in the morning, Gammy," Torbjorn says. He flips a flapjack, turns, and smiles at her.

"Over there on the breakfast table," he says.

She sits down and takes the frame into both hands, reading it carefully.

Torbjorn keeps flipping flapjacks.

He hears her say: "I had much nicer handwriting in those days, son."

He turns because she sounds a little funny, and he immediately realizes she's crying softly.

He turns off the gas on the stove and goes over to sit next to her, not across from her.

"You saved Captain McKlane again, Gammy."

She bursts into tears, and he holds her gently until she quiets down a bit.

"Oh, Lord, I wish I could save my own blood and not the blood of others, son. Look how handsome Jackson was." She touches his official Marine Corps photograph with fingers that tremble.

Torbjorn can imagine her sixty-five years earlier, bending over the letter in the hallway, crying as she reads the Captain's thank you note hanging next to the Bronze Star.

With the morning light falling through the window onto the framed letter in her hands, he sees other, original teardrop stains on the note she sent to Captain McKlane.

"Look how serious he looks," Gammy says, holding the frame up to Torbjorn. "Your Grandfather was the sweetest man I ever knew. He was never that serious."

"I wish I'd known him, Gammy."

"Oh, you do, Tor," she says, using a nickname for her grandson that she rarely uses. "You look a lot like him. His blood is running all through you."

"I know it is Gammy."

"Look how nice my writing was back then," she says, looking back at the framed note.

"Like a schoolgirl's writing," Torbjorn says.

"Teacher always gave me an A-Plus for my cursive, son. Heck, I was a schoolgirl when I wrote this."
The letter is dated February 21, 1951.

Dear Captain George McKlane,

Thank you for the kind words you wrote about my Jackson. I miss him a mighty amount, and I wish he would be here when I give birth to our baby come the end of March. I'm about big as a barn right now and I guess it's the last gift he'll ever give me. I am awful glad, as you said in your note, that he gave you and a lot of other Marines, who are fighting over there, the same gift of life.

Yours truly,

Mrs. Ernestine Petersson

P.S. I will pray that you come home to the people who love you.

"People don't write 'Thank You' notes anymore," Gammy says to Torbjorn. "It was always the proper thing to do."

After a while, Torbjorn breaks the silence.

"Gammy, I think we should send this back to Captain McKlane. I made you a copy of it over in Roanoke, and I got a frame pretty much like this one here. The color copy looks almost identical to this. But I think we should send this one back to the Captain."

She smiles at her grandson.

They usually think alike. "Get me a pen, first," Ernestine says, and when he does, she holds the pen a long time before she writes something on the back.

She writes almost as nicely as she did as a schoolgirl. Torbjorn smiles at her message to the Captain. "That's about perfect, Gammy," he says.

The next day, he drives down to Roanoke and parks his car near the Marine Corps recruiting station at 5375 Peters Creek. He does not have to wait long before he sees a kid walking towards it with a sense of purpose.

"Gonna sign up to be a Marine?" Torbjorn asks.

"What's it to you, fella?"

"I got a package I want you to give to the recruiting sergeant in there," he says to the boy, who still suffers from a teenager's complexion.

"What kind of package?"

"This one here."

In large print, it says:

Captain George McKlane, USMC
Medal Of Honor Recipient
Korean War
13752 Coconut Palm Court
Boca Raton, Florida

"How do I know it's not some kind of a bomb," the kid asks. "You might be a terrorist."

"Recruit," Torbjorn says, sounding very much like a drill instructor on Parris Island, "I am a Marine Corps sergeant, who's won a pocket full of medals over in Afghanistan. You will do as I say, and you will deliver this package to the desk sergeant on duty. Do you understand me, recruit?"

"Yes, sir!" the boy says.

"Shit, they might even send you to officer candidates' school for doing this. You're holding a package addressed to a Medal Of Honor winner in your hands, boy."

"Yes, sir!"

The youngster embraces the package carefully as if it were a folded American flag. As Torbjorn drives off, he sees the recruiting sergeant in the rearview mirror stepping out of the doorway, holding the package, a long way off.

Torbjorn turns a corner. The sergeant returns to his desk in the recruiting station.

"Did that man have a name, son?" the sergeant asks.

"I'm sure he does, sir, but he didn't give it to me. Just the package there, sir."

The sergeant connects to the internet and searches for a Captain George McKlane. He gets multiple hits, all of them the same person, all of them a Medal Of Honor winner.

The sergeant stands up. "Attention!" he says.

The authority of his voice makes the recruit snap to attention, something he has practiced in front of his mother's full-length mirror, ever since he was a small boy.

The sergeant nods approval at the youngster and says: "Salute this package, recruit. This man is a recipient of the Medal Of Honor, our great nation's highest military award!"

Both the recruit and the sergeant salute the package, the snap of the Marine impressive, the recruit's attempt a work still in progress.

Then the sergeant takes his return address label and puts it in the upper left-hand corner of the envelope. He never opens the package. That would dishonor Captain George McKlane.

The package goes by military courier to the Medal of Honor recipient in a war that ended sixty-three years earlier

The sergeant sits back down behind his desk.

He looks at the recruit and says: "At ease, son. How many years were you thinking of signing up for?"

Chapter 18

The Breakfast Club Meets Again

13752 Coconut Palm Court,
Boca: Saturday Brunch

When Martha Krumble walks into George McKlane's house, she sees him coming out of his office wearing his Marine Corps fatigues.

He has grown several inches taller and at least thirty-five years younger.

And he's been promoted to a full colonel in the United States Marine Corps, with flight wings on his chest.

Her heart skips a beat when she sees him.

It is a feeling she has not had for over a decade.

"Missus Krumble," he says. Even the voice matches. "My dad's out on the patio. We're going to have lunch under the lanai."

"You're a carbon copy of your father," Martha says.

"I sure hope so, ma'am," he says, with the same extraordinary smile, taking her arm and leading the way to the patio through the Birdroom.

Judge Ralph Broadslate comes over and hugs her. "How's your father?" he asks.

"Still teaching at Columbia Law in Manhattan, Judge," she says. "He raises a brand new batch of ornery prosecutors every semester."

"Best supreme court judge New York ever had," her father's friend says.

Martha Krumble has known Judge Broadslate since she was a teenager growing up in Riverdale, New York.

"Welcome back," Sharonda says to Martha, with a genuine and friendly smile.

"Congratulations on taking over Accelerated Realty Sales," the original George McKlane says. "I'm George One, and he's George Two." He points a fork at his son. "Sharonda, I can't eat this salad. It tastes like straw."

"I'm Doctor Gunther Klein," a man roughly the same age as George One says, standing up and shaking her hand. "And this is my wife, Rachel, who is trying very hard to turn George One into George New, with a special diet of twigs and bark."

"Eat your salad, George," Rachel says, smiling at Martha.

"I'm Sharonda's husband," a large, uniformed police officer says, standing up and waving across the table at Martha. "Sergeant Samuel Nelson."

"I am not going to eat this salad," George says. "Not even if it's covered with chocolate."

"What would you like for lunch?" Sharonda asks. Before she can run through the menu, Martha says: "I'll have some twigs and bark."

George stabs his salad with his fork, but he's grinning. "Let the lunch begin," he says.

Martha listens as they all discuss the break-in, and the shots fired. They discuss the appearance of the FBI and the probability of money laundering through luxury homes.

They backtrack to the recording that started it all. Judge Broadslate reiterates the legality of the Magic Wand as a protective device for Captain George.

"Are we being recorded right now?" Martha asks.

George holds up his fork. His hand is not shaking as severely as she remembers from their first meeting. "Speak into my fork," he says.

Martha takes his hand in both of hers, steadies it, leans towards the fork, and says: "Testing, one, two, three, testing." She lets go of his hand, and they smile at one another. He likes Martha. She makes him feel younger.

Ralph Broadslate says: "No. The Magic Wand is off." He looks at Colonel McKlane. "Some of us are quite dangerous, but not to each other." The colonel smiles, but only slightly.

"And why are you here, Sergeant Samuel Nelson?" Martha asks.

"I'm here to make sure my wife doesn't shoot anybody," he says — everyone at the table, including his wife, laughs. The joke still works.

Martha noticed the weapon on Sharonda's hip when she first walked out on the patio. "I'm in the Honor Guard of the Boca Police Force," Samuel Nelson says.

"And a good friend," says Captain George.

"And a good Marine," Colonel McKlane adds. He looks at Martha. "You told Dad that Silberg was still alive. Please fill all of us in on that."

"He has undoubtedly left the United States with all the escrow money," she says. "But here's how we know he was not the person killed in the accident that I'm sure we've all seen on television."

"Over and over," Rachel Klein says. "In slow motion. Now they're even drawing red circles around body parts."

"But not Mister Anthony Silberg's body parts," Doctor Gunther Klein says, smiling patiently at his wife. "Please, continue, Martha."

"Well," she says, "speaking of body parts ...." She tells them the whole story that Alice Koenig and Barbara Rossellini explained over the speakerphone earlier. She makes the story quite graphic and oddly funny, including finger measurements and embarrassed FBI agents. Colonel McKlane laughs heartily at her storytelling ability.

"Was Barbara Rossellini involved in any of this?" Captain George asks.

"I don't think so," Martha says, "If she were, she wouldn't still be here. She'd leave town. But I think the office manager, a man named Bill Brownstone, was most definitely involved. He committed suicide last night."

"Intentionally?" Doctor Klein asks. Sergeant Nelson shakes his head at the Doctor's comment.

Martha smiles. "Yes, according to the FBI."

"Barbara Rossellini is my Goddaughter," Captain George says.

"I didn't know that," Martha says, showing genuine surprise. "I thought she was related to Angelo Rossellini." She explains that the well-known developer is now the principal shareholder of Accelerated Realty Sales. "He's invested a lot of money in Accelerated Realty Sales. He has already replaced all of the escrow funds stolen from the firm by Silberg."

"Why would he do that?" Judge Broadslate asks.

"Because he's buying the firm for about thirty cents on the dollar," she says. "I am assuming that we will keep most of our customers, despite the negative stories circulating throughout Boca Raton right now." She looks at George One and smiles. He smiles back and tells her to finish her twigs and bark. Then he adds: "If I'd listened to the judge in the first place, I would have listed with you at the other brokerage. Then we wouldn't be going through any of this, would we?"

"You are listed with me now, George," Martha says. She turns back to Judge Broadslate. "I think Angelo Rossellini will recover all of the money he has put into escrow very quickly. Plus, he now owns a company that makes a great deal of money. Eventually, assuming insurance covers Silberg's theft of the escrow funds, the money he has funded us with will turn into a cash windfall, for him and all of his shareholders. I'm one of those shareholders."

Sharonda says: "Barbara was married to Angelo Rossellini's son, Roberto. Their marriage was annulled after a few months."

"Angelo was at our staff meeting on Friday, and he and Barbara seemed very friendly." Martha turns back to George One and says: "I didn't know she was your goddaughter."

"Barbara Rossellini's father saved my life in Korea when Army engineers blew up a bridge during our retreat from the Chosin Reservoir. It was a long time ago."

FBI Miami Division in Miramar, FL, Saturday

The Federal Bureau of Investigation catches a break from an unlikely source.

Special agent in charge, Scott Larsen and his team sit in the conference room on the seventh floor of their relatively new glass and aluminum office building at 2030 SW 145th Avenue, in Miramar, a city with a population of over 120,000 just north of Miami.

The FBI team operates as a unit focusing on asset forfeiture and money laundering. They work very closely with the Internal Revenue Service.

Unlike most competing government enforcement offices, they rarely stumbled over inter-agency politics or jealousy in their pursuit of unlawful activity.

Since Fiscal Year 2011, the asset forfeiture unit has investigated over 300 cases: 37 indictments and 45 convictions net the Department of Justice over $20,000,000 in restitution, recoveries, and fines.

Special agent in charge, Scott Larsen looks at his unlikely source and asks: "Did you confirm this with your own eyes?"

"Yes, sir. His name is on the manifest," Agent John Dempsey says.

He pushes a copy of the Delta Airlines flight record, to the Cayman Islands, across the table. "And I have also learned that he had a connecting flight to Providenciales in the Turks and Caicos."

"But, you cannot positively confirm that he was on either one of those flights?"

"No, sir, I cannot. The island flights do not follow acceptable manifest procedures."

"You ever been to Provo, Agent Dempsey?"

"I don't know what Provo means, sir."

"Providenciales. The airport. The tourist center of the Turks and Caicos Islands."

"No, sir, I have not."

"Pack a bag. Do not dress casually. Suit and tie. Find a bank that has an account with this number."

He passes across a copy of the mutilated check found at the scene of the car explosion.

Working with the IRS, the FBI has started to turn secret offshore banking into a spectator sport. The people and the companies getting caught for tax evasion or money laundering have shifted from a trickle into a flood. Some are professional crooks. Many just enjoy the fruits of cheating.

To retain their banking license, the institutions that once promised absolute secrecy revert to an open book policy that sends a lot of crooks to jail.

Agent Larsen looks at Dempsey and says: "Tell them that you work as a special liaison between the Department of Justice and the Internal Revenue Service. Don't talk to anyone lower than the bank manager. I want you to tell them that you're going to shut them down, put them out of business if they don't cooperate."

He looks at another agent, one of the most senior men on his team.

"Jenkins will go with you," Agent Larsen says.

Jenkins nods, but not happily.

"And Dempsey?"

"Yes, sir?"

"You are the lead agent on this assignment." Jenkins rolls his eyes, then quickly recovers under the withering glare of special agent Scott Larsen.

"Sir?" Agent Dempsey asks, more in wonderment than as a question.

"Well done, Agent Dempsey. Jenkins will help you in whatever capacity you need him to help you. It is your big chance, Agent Dempsey. Now get out of here."

"Yes, sir. Let's go, Jenkins," he says with some authority.

"I'll make sure the plane is ready," Jenkins says.

"Yes. Absolutely. The plane."

After they walk out of the conference room, Agent in Charge Larsen tells his men to make sure that Jenkins, not Dempsey, gets a complete list of all the banks in Cockburn Town on Grand Turk.

"Wait until Jenkins drives Dempsey past the salt ponds on Turk," Agent Larsen says. "He'll think that God broke wind in his face."

Everyone laughs, although several of the agents don't know what their boss is saying. He immediately recognizes their confusion.

"White gold," Larsen says. "Salt ponds. Used to be the island's most important industry until it collapsed in the early 1960s. They stink worse than your fat uncle at an annual cauliflower festival."

Everyone laughs.

13752 Coconut Palm Ct., Boca, Saturday Brunch

At the late breakfast at George's house, Judge Broadslate runs through the chain of events that led up to the firing of shots two days earlier. He cannot understand why a bogus sales contract on a six million dollar house leads to Captain George's attempted murder.

"I wish we had a copy of the contract," the judge says. "There has to be something in there that we're missing, or that we just do not understand."

"There must be copies of the contract on our computers at the office," Martha Krumble says to the group. "Let me get hold of one."

She phones Sarah Golden, her secretary, who calls Martha back and says that the contract is not in the system.

Sarah Golden has checked the office network and all the personal directories on Silberg's computer. She even checked his computer's recycle bin.

A cyber shredder has erased all of Anthony Silberg's computer files.

Nobody can recover the files.

Martha phones Barbara Rossellini, the agent who wrote the contract. She discovers that she never actually did so. It was Anthony Silberg who handled it.

Barbara had a copy of the contract. Now she cannot find it. She thinks she might have given it to Jimmy J. Johnson, three offices away in the Goldfish Bowl, but she cannot be sure. Martha tells her to get it.

Barbara Rossellini calls back and says that Jimmy J. Johnson never had the contract.

She thinks he's probably right.

She vaguely remembers putting it in her top drawer after Silberg initialized his change to the "no inspection" clause. That's the last she saw of it.

"After he did what?" Martha asks her.

"He changed and initialized the inspection contingency," Barbara says. "It matched all the other initials that were on the sales contract."

Barbara says that she was confident she put the contract in her top, right-hand drawer. If she did so, someone removed it.

"When I came to work on Thursday morning, Bill Brownstone came out of my office and tried to throw me out of the building. I think he took it," she says.

Martha Krumble thanks her and hangs up. To everyone at the luncheon table, she says: "Silberg deleted the paper trail on the contract, and it looks as if he signed the contract himself as the buyer."

"Can he do that?" Doctor Klein asks.

"No, he can't," Martha says. She turns to Captain George. "Not unless he told you he was the buyer when he wrote the contract. A licensed agent has to reveal their expert status if they make an offer for any real estate purchases on their account."

"He didn't," George says. "According to Silberg, the Brazilian buyer made the offer."

"So I think we can assume that all roads lead to Silberg," Judge Broadslate says.

"And also to Bill Brownstone, our office manager who committed suicide," Martha says. "He was apparently in Barbara's office on Thursday morning. According to agent Larsen, he committed suicide on Thursday evening. I was supposed to talk to him on Friday morning. On Thursday afternoon, he was crying like a child in his office."

Martha tells them that Barbara Rossellini thinks Bill Brownstone is the one who took the contract that she put in her desk drawer.

"Silberg is still alive," Sharonda says.

"So, all of this was Silberg-driven?" Doctor Gunther Klein asks. "Why worry about a bogus six million dollar contract if you're going to rob millions from a real estate company's piggy bank and take off to parts unknown?"

"Silberg appears to be the subject of a money-laundering investigation by the FBI," Judge Broadslate says. "It undoubtedly amounts to a lot more than the money stolen from the escrow account. The contract, with his signature and initials on it, would be substantial evidence of guilt. The fact that he also cleaned out a real estate company's escrow account, that's just one more charge in a federal indictment against him. He appears to have had his hands in a lot of different cookie jars."

"And he also still has the watch that he stole out of the War Room," George McKlane says. "I feel a little foolish saying that, but the watch is significant to me."

"Silberg is still alive," Sharonda says again.

Judge Broadslate nods. "And since it was not him in the car explosion, he probably has a murder charge added to his lengthy indictment."

"And attempted murder," George says. "And I don't understand why I'm alive."

"What do you mean?" Martha asks.

"The man who took a shot at me up in the War Room did so from, what, ten feet? Maybe less. And I think we can all agree that he was a professional killer. They don't miss a ten-foot shot."

"And you have no idea who the killer was?" Rachel Klein asks him.

"None," he answers. "He was young, moved like a young man, in good shape. And he was a pro. If they found his partner, the one I shot, dead in a canal with two bullets in his head, it's a pretty good bet that the guy was in the business of killing people."

"You're lucky to be alive, Dad," his son says.

"Yes, I am. But it also makes no sense." He thinks a moment. "And the letters they took off the wall. That makes no sense, either."

"This entire case put together with loose strings and false windows," Judge Broadslate says.

"Silberg is still alive," Sharonda says for the third time.

"I'd like to talk to him," Colonel McKlane says.

Chapter 19

Suicidal Tendencies

Rhondo Homes, Boca Delray, Saturday night

Barbara Rossellini hears the buzzer in her condo. She goes to the intercom and asks: "Who's there?" She now knows his voice, and she's a bit stunned. "Come on up," she says. She checks

herself in the mirror and then looks through the peephole on her condo door.

Jimmy J. Johnson turns the corner by the stairs and walks down the hallway. She opens the door with a smile before he rings the bell.

"What's up, Jimmy? Come on in."

"You hear anything from Silberg," he asks as he steps across the threshold, looking left and right.

Barbara closes the door.

"Mister Silberg and I are no longer on speaking terms, Jimmy," Barbara says.

He laughs. "Mister Rossellini asked me to come over and keep you company," Jimmy says.

"Why's that?"

"He's concerned about you."

"Is Angelo turning into a matchmaker, Jimmy?" She sees him blush slightly. Christ, men are easy. "You want a drink?"

"No, thanks," he says.

"So you're going to be a cheap date, huh?"

He takes off his suit jacket. He's carrying a gun. "Barbara," he says, "no messing around, okay? Mister Rossellini has reason to believe that Silberg is in the neighborhood. Angelo wants to make sure you're all right."

"Silberg is here?" she asks, suddenly serious.

"Near here," Jimmy says. He takes his gun and places it on the table. "Maybe I could use a glass of water."

She gets him one, with ice. She gets herself a glass of Jameson Black Barrel, no ice.

"I thought he'd be long gone," Barbara says. "He's got an awful lot of people looking for him, and I don't think any of them want to be his friend."

"Copy that," Jimmy J. Johnson says.

"So, are you going to spend the night here?"

"If I have to," he says.

"I only have the one bed, Jimmy."

"I'm not here to sleep, Barbara. You want to hit the sack, do so. I'm comfortable right here."

Barbara's cell phone rings. She steps into the kitchen to answer it, whispering. When she returns, she says: "Well, I guess a lot of people want to protect me from Mister Anthony Silberg tonight."

"What does that mean?" Jimmy asks.

"My Godfather, Captain George McKlane, wants his big strapping son, Colonel McKlane, to come over here and take me to the McKlane compound for the night. He's even better-looking than you are, Jimmy, at least that's what

Sharonda told me on the phone. They have a bunch of Marines over there to protect me."

"That the Sharonda, whose old man is a cop?" Jimmy asks. "She works for McKlane, right?"

"Yes, she works for Captain McKlane, Jimmy. She's kind of like a doctor. She's a Nurse Practitioner."

"They know I'm here?"

"Yes, they do. I told McKlane you were."

"Good," he says, although he doesn't look like he means it. "We'll wait for the colonel, and then I'm off duty. I got to make a phone call to Mister Rossellini."

He gets up and goes into the bathroom.

The condo buzzer rings and Barbara goes to the intercom and says: "That was fast. Come on up." She buzzes the colonel through. She opens her front door a crack and goes into her bedroom to pack an overnight bag.

When she walks back out, Anthony Silberg is picking Jimmy Johnson's gun up off the dining room table. He has a rifle as well. He uses it to move her into the living room. She barely recognizes him.

Silberg has a floppy straw hat on his head, and he's grown a perfect mustache. But she knows it's him.

She tastes the metal from the fillings in her teeth. She considers making a break for the door.

"Don't even think about it," Silberg says. He closes the door quietly. He hears talking in the bathroom.

Jimmy J. Johnson steps back into the living room, pockets his cell phone, and suddenly freezes. He sees his gun i no longer on the dining room table.

"Hello, Jimmy Johnson," Silberg says. "I guess Angelo has you working overtime, huh?"

Johnson takes a few steps, looking as if he's going to sit down, and then he rushes at Silberg. It's his only chance, and he takes it.

The gun makes a lot of noise, but the bullet reaches his brain before the sound ever does. He drops to the floor, briefly on his knees, then topples over.

Barbara Rossellini does not scream, although she wants to. Her legs feel weak, and her mouth goes dry. Everything starts to move in slow motion, even Anthony Silberg's voice as he tells her to sit down at the cheap dining room table.

She says, barely audible: "I wish I had never met you." She does not want to use his name. If she doesn't use his name, maybe he will go away.

It is an absurd thought. Barbara wants to distance herself from his being, his presence, however possible.

The neighbors hear the first shot, and then they hear a second shot as well. They remain in their condo units, unsure of what to do.

A young couple, a few doors away, thinks somebody turned up a television way too loud.

Rhondo Condos have thin walls; the people living in an adjacent apartment dial 911.

As Colonel McKlane, and the raider regiment sergeant driving him, turn into the Rhondo Homes complex, they see a farmer in a straw hat, with a mustache, driving out in an old, beat-up truck. They meet at the entryway, both cars with their windows lowered in the coolness of the evening. The farmer waves at them, and gives them a thumbs up, shouting: "Howdy, and thanks for your service, boys." He tips his floppy hat.

They wave back.

The colonel and his driver park in a space marked Guest Parking, across from Barbara Rossellini's condo. People are coming out of the building, talking excitedly. Suddenly, Boca and Delray Beach police cars surround the entrance to Barbara Rossellini's condo. The police get out of their vehicles, some with weapons drawn.

"Something's wrong," Colonel McKlane says into his cell phone. His driver starts to get out of the car, and the colonel grabs his arm, and then he lets go. "We'll find out what's happening." He nods to the driver, and they walk towards a Boca police car, surrounded by men with weapons in their hands. A patrolman signals them to stop, motions them lower.

"What's happening?" Colonel McKlane asks the cops. The colonel and his driver crouch down.

"Who are you?" the police officer says.

"We're good friends of sergeant Samuel Nelson," Colonel McKlane answers.

The police officer looks back at the building as men start to approach the condo. "Shots fired," he says. "At least two shots. That's all we know so far. Stay down. Stay put." He looks back at the colonel, and the sergeant with him, repeating: "Stay where you are."

The colonel and sergeant eventually move back to their vehicle, get in, and wait.

An ambulance arrives, then another. Police tape suddenly appears Plainclothes detectives quickly show up, badges on their belts.

"Stay in the vehicle," Colonel McKlane says to his driver. He gets out and walks over to the police line. They will not let him through. He gets on his cell phone again.

He turns and slowly walks back to their vehicle, gets in, still talking on the phone. He hangs up and says: "Back to Captain McKlane's."

Sharonda meets them in the driveway. She has returned after leaving for the day. She walks into George McKlane's home with them. Her cell phone rings, and she answers it, moving into the kitchen. Captain George is in his office, and so is Martha Krumble.

Martha looks at the colonel and says: "I got here as soon as your Dad called. I phoned Barbara, but she does not answer her cell. Now I'm calling her home phone."

The room listens to her side of the conversation.

"Barbara, is that you?"

"Could I please speak to Barbara Rossellini?"

"My name is Martha Krumble."

"I am Barbara Rossellini's boss. She works for me at Accelerated Realty Sales."

"I am the Broker at Accelerated Realty Sales. Please tell me who I am talking to."

"I would like to speak to Barbara Rossellini, detective."

"Why not?"

"Why can't she come to the phone?"

"What has happened, detective?"

Martha listens, and then she holds the phone away from her and turns it off.

She tells the phone: "Someone shot Barbara." She looks at Captain McKlane. "Your goddaughter is dead."

She looks back at the phone. "The detective just hung up on me."

Sharonda comes into the office. She has spoken to her husband, Sergeant Samuel Nelson.

"They're talking about a lover's quarrel," she says. "According to Sam, Barbara shot a ... "she refers to a piece of paper " ... someone named James J. Johnson. The gun was apparently in her hand. They think she committed suicide after she murdered him."

"My God," Martha says. "James J. Johnson works for Accelerated Realty Sales as well. He works just a few offices away from Barbara's office."

"I spoke to Barbara on my cell phone when you were leaving here to pick her up," Sharonda says to Colonel McKlane. "She said that a Mister Johnson was there, in her condo with her. She called him 'Jimmy' It didn't sound like she was stressed. She seemed happy."

Everyone looks at Sharonda.

"She told me that Jimmy Johnson was there to protect her," Sharonda says.

"To protect her from Silberg?" George asks.

"Silberg, yes," Sharonda answers. "She said he was protecting her from Silberg, who someone repor6ted as being in the neighborhood."

Colonel McKlane looks at Martha. "Did Silberg have a mustache?" he asks her.

"No," she says.

"How well do you know this person Jimmy Johnson?" Captain George asks Martha.

"I haven't even met Jimmy Johnson yet. My office has scheduled a broker meeting with me on Monday. I think he's one of our top people, a top producer."

"Could they be a couple?" Sharonda asks.

"I have no idea. I guess Jimmy and Barbara could be," Martha says. "It appears that they were."

A leather-faced sergeant, a member of the colonel's team, rings the doorbell and enters the unlocked front door. It does not need to be locked when three members of the Marine Raider's regiment stand guard in the driveway, and four more surround the estate.

"Some old guy, looked like a farmer, was driving back and forth in front of the perimeter, sir," the sergeant tells the colonel. "We tried to stop him, but he took off when we photographed him, sir. He was in an old, rusty truck. Made a very impolite gesture to us when we tried to talk to him."

"Did he have a mustache?"

"Yes, sir, he did. And an old floppy hat that covered most of his face. Here's the flash." He gives his iPhone to the colonel.

"That's the same guy I saw driving out of Barbara Rossellini's development," the colonel says. The iPhone passes from person to person.

Martha says: "That could be Silberg."

Sharonda says: "That IS Silberg." She looks at the colonel and the sergeant. "Is it okay if I send this to my husband, Samuel. He'll get it to the right people in the Boca police department."

"Do it," the colonel says.

Three hours later, Boca police people surround an old truck in a parking lot on Federal Highway, north of Yamato, but short of the Delray Beach town line. It's in the mostly-deserted Comcast parking lot, long after closing hours.

The police approach the truck carefully, with their guns drawn. The vehicle is empty, but there's broken glass in the empty parking spot next to it. Silberg's growing list of crimes now includes auto theft.

The Wholly Mackerel
Delray, Sunday AM

Holly Smolkes knows a lot
of bad people. Few of
them ever try to take
advantage of her, and
those who do usually
regret it. She is a still-
beautiful woman, scarred
by life. It includes a jagged
five-inch slash across her

left cheek, which she gets in a barroom brawl in Key West,
Florida when she is barely 20 years old and starting to model
swimwear.

The scar ends that career.

"The other dog in the fight, a pedigree bitch, looked a
whole lot worse," she tells friends.

Holly's voice possesses the rich, smoky sounds of too
many cigarettes and too much brandy, although she neither
drinks nor smokes. She spends too much time in bars. Her
laughter surprises strangers with its timbre, coming from deep
inside of her, oddly infectious, somehow mysterious.

She loves the ocean, the water, the sounds of seagulls,
and the smell of seaweed, sand, and sun.

She buries three husbands, one of them still alive, far out
in the Atlantic Ocean.

She is 34 years old, the Skipper of a fishing boat for here
in Delray Beach, the *Wholly Mackerel.*

Most people pronounce the name of her ship, "Holy
Mackerel," and think it's a clever joke. She explains to

strangers that it sounds like her name, Holly, with a "W" in front of it. "Wa-Holly," she says.

She tells people that the name comes from the East Indies, and it means "gale-force winds." She then says to them that she suffers from strong breezes come from indigestion, not from the forces of Mother Nature. This tasteless revelation always melts into her dark laughter.

It is all a complete fabrication, borne from the fact that the person who painted the name on her boat was an idiot. During the painting, the man was almost always drunk.

"When he sobered up, he was still an idiot," she says. "My third husband, may he rest in peace."

She initially does mean the name of her boat to be a joke – *Wholely* Mackerel – but her husband drops a vowel, inadvertently putting her first name on the ship. It works out fine, she says, for a screw-up that never cost her any money, just a marriage doomed by musical barstools.

When she gets the call from Snake the previous day, she says she's busy, even though they are professional friends.

'You have a Charter?" Snake asks.

"I have to visit my Granny," Holly says.

"Holly, you don't have a Granny," Snake says.

"Listen, Snake. I need some time off."

"Let me tell you what it's worth, and who it's for," Snake says. He does, and she changes her mind.

At six-thirty in the morning, a black Navigator pulls up to the dock where Holly moors the *Wholly Mackerel*. A white-haired gentleman steps out and walks to the boat.

"Welcome aboard, Angelo," Holly says.

"One of my favorite people," he says to her. "Let's go inside, where we can talk without seagulls watching us."

"Of course," she says.

Holly Smolkes and Angelo Rossellini had known each other for a long time, since before she graduated from Miami University. They had mutual respect for one another, and, for Holly, some fear as well.

For Angelo, she has turned the Russian euphemism, "wet work," into a double entendre. Originally coined by the KGB as a synonym for spilling blood, Holly has expanded the "wet" part of the phrase to include swimming with sharks, far out at sea.

For Holly, her relationship with Angelo has given her a life of permanent financial comfort, including the *Wholly Mackerel*, debt-free, and a mortgage-free penthouse at the Astor Condos in Delray Beach.

She does not wisecrack or joke with Angelo, the way she does with most people. She listens.

"Someone named Anthony Silberg has chartered your boat in a little over an hour," Angelo says.

He speaks carefully, slowly.

"He will be armed, and he will be dangerous. He will try to kill you and steal your boat to escape from many people who are looking for him. They include the Department of Justice, the Police, and myself. He has already killed some of my friends, and he has stolen a great deal of money from me. Do you understand everything I am saying, Holly?"

"Of course," she says. "But the man who has chartered my boat is George McKlane."

Angelo smiles, appreciating Silberg's dark humor.

"His real name is Anthony Silberg," Angelo says. Then he waits for Holly to ask the obvious question, which she does when he does not continue.

"What do I do with him?"

"You welcome him aboard," Angelo says. "And then, when you clear the harbor, you have a little surprise for George McKlane."

An hour later, an overweight man, bald with a very dark mustache, wearing no hat, walks up to the *Wholly Mackerel,* carrying a deep-sea fishing pole in a canvas bag.

He says he is George McKlane, looking forward to a day of deep-sea fishing.

"Welcome Aboard, Mister McKlane," Holly says with a smile, looking at his canvas bag. It sounds a little cumbersome when he places it on *Wholly Mackerel's* deck.

"We have all the equipment you need," Holly says.

"I like to use my gear," the man says.

"Fair enough, Mister McKlane."

She hops out of the boat and unties the mooring ropes, jumps back aboard, climbs the ladder to the bridge, leaving the door secured open, and then she starts the powerful inboard engines.

As they pull away, she shouts down to him: "You ever drive a boat like this, Mister McKlane?"

"Call me George," he answers. He climbs the ladder and joins her on the bridge. "Yes, I have. But please, give me a refresher course, Holly."

He stands next to her, thinking she's a nice-looking woman, even with the scar.

Maybe they can have some fun before she takes her last swim. Silberg watches as she goes through some effortless nautical maneuvers.

She shuts off the engines, restarts them, reverses the boat, and then she goes forward again.

She guides the boat through some buoys onto open water. The chop is light. She steps back, smiles at her passenger, and says: "Try it, Mister ... sorry, George."

He takes the wheel.

"How far can you go in a boat like this?"

"To the Bahamas and back," she says. She shows him the green specks of the Bahamas Islands on the radar in the wheelhouse. When they are about a quarter of a mile offshore, Silberg steps away. He wants to check his gear.

Holly takes the wheel as Silberg climbs down the ladder from the bridge.

Silberg bends down to unzip the canvas bag. A voice stops him.

"Hello, Tony."

Angelo Rossellini has opened the main cabin door and holds a strange-looking rifle in his hand.

"Angelo," Silberg says, straightening up. The two men face each other, no more than seven feet apart. "I had no idea you enjoyed deep-sea fishing."

"I only do it for huge trophies," Angelo says, without smiling. "Back up to the railing, Tony."

An orange Coast Guard helicopter flies high overhead, going towards Miami. Neither man looks up as it chops the air. Silberg steps back to the railing.

Holly cuts the engines.

Silberg looks at the shoreline. Holly starts to walk out of the door on the bridge, carrying something that might be a rifle. Silberg watches Angelo's hands, not his eyes, the way a good boxer would. He sees the trigger finger tightening. He bobs to the left and yanks himself overboard as a dart from Angelo's tranquilizer gun grazes his back. None of the sedatives enters his body. He is underwater, swimming towards the shoreline, holding his breath as long as possible.

Holly is on the bridge, aiming a rifle at Silberg as he bobs to the surface and starts stroking towards the shore.

"Don't shoot!" Angelo shouts. Other boats in the area would hear it, although none are nearby.

"You want me to run him over?" Holly asks as she slowly lowers her weapon.

Angelo climbs the ladder to the bridge. "That would be hard to explain," he says. They watch Silberg.

"He's a good swimmer," Holly says, as Silberg switches from the crawl to a much less strenuous breaststroke. "Maybe a shark will catch up with him."

"I don't think so," Angelo says. He considers telling her that the sharks won't bother him as a professional courtesy, an old joke, but he does not utter it aloud. He finds nothing funny about Anthony Silberg's remarkable ability to escape.

Silberg has no value to Rossellini if he's alive. As long as he breathes, he represents a potential disaster to the Rossellini Empire. If the Feds capture him, he might testify against Rossellini and his associates and then disappear into the relative safety of the witness protection program.

As a ghost, however, Silberg can make Rossellini a fortune. If the authorities think he's alive, on the run, then every step Silberg takes can make millions of legitimate dollars for Rossellini. Silberg must become a legend, a money-laundering poltergeist.

"The beach is still empty," Holly says.

Angelo has already phoned his men onshore. After he hangs up, the black Lincoln Navigator starts to move down the highway to a landmark that Angelo gives them.

Silberg comes out of the water exhausted, but alive. His mustache is gone. He moves towards the sea grapes, then through a break in them leading up to the road. He recognizes a building on the beachside of the A1A Highway, although its signage surprises him. He did not know that The Luxury Partnership was now a part of Accelerated Realty Sales.

He almost makes it to the parking lot when three people jump him, the largest one pinning him down. They are the same three men who kidnaped him at the Fort Lauderdale International Airport.

Silberg does not have the strength to fight them. He looks at the kid and says: "Hello, again."

One of the men puts a needle in his arm and says: "Goodbye, again."

He pushes the plunger.

They carry Silberg, unconscious, breathing heavily, to the SUV. They roll him into the back seat.

"He's lost some weight," one man says.

Then they drive away.

Chapter 20

Dunking For Dollars in the Turks & Caicos

Turks & Caicos Islands
All Day Sunday

Agent John Dempsey spends the morning on Turks & Caicos convinced that his partner, Agent Jenkins, has arrived at the stage of life where fierce gastric juices trump politeness.

The windows of their rental car are up as far as possible, and the air conditioning runs full blast. Agent Jenkins keeps smiling at John Dempsey. The smells he makes are horrifying. Jenkins leans forward and flips the air conditioning off. Agent Dempsey has no choice but to roll down the window. When he does, he starts to choke at the stench. Agent Jenkins bursts out laughing and tells him that they are in the island's Free Farting Zone.

"The what?" Agent Dempsey asks.

Agent Jenkins stares at him. He shakes his head. "How the hell did you ever make it through Quantico?" he asks.

"They didn't teach us anything about Free Farting Zones," Agent Dempsey says. He's serious.

"There's no such thing as a No Free Farting Zone, you moron," Jenkins says. "That smell is from the abandoned salt lakes on the island. They smell like shit!"

"Oh."

"Sweet Jesus, it's a joke, Dempsey!"

Agent Dempsey says: "I graduated Quantico at the top of my class."

"I'll bet you did. Turn around. We're going back to town." Agent John Dempsey does as he's told.

"It was just a joke, John. It's Sunday, and not one of the banks is open. We can take the rest of the day off."

As they drive into Cockburn Town, Agent John Dempsey says: "That bank isn't closed."

They see a well-dressed man walking out of a small, but a modern bank, waving goodbye to someone who closes the green-tinted glass doors and starts to lock up.

They pull over, in front of the bank, and walk to the entrance. Jenkins taps on the plate-glass door.

The man inside, who has just turned off some internal lights, waves them off.

Agent Dempsey pulls out his FBI identification and slaps it on the glass. The man inside approaches and looks at it. Then he reluctantly opens the door.

"Now what, my dear fellow?" he asks.

"You're not exactly working banking hours, are you?" Agent Jenkins says.

"I would if you bloody people would stop your incessant, pestering tactics," the man answers.

Jenkins shows the man an oversized photo of the account number in question.

"Is this account associated with this bank?"

"Not any longer," the man says. "But you fellows jolly well know that, don't you?"

"Not any longer?"

"Well, your colleague over there sucking a bleeding pint of lager has removed it all," the banker says, pointing across the street to a man who waves a tall glass of beer at them.

"Stay here," Jenkins says to John Dempsey. He walks across the sand-swept street and identifies himself to the gentleman drinking beer, who then identifies himself to Agent Jenkins.

The senior FBI agent sits down and talks to him for a few minutes. Then he gets up and walks back across the street to Dempsey and the banker.

"Twenty-three and a half million dollars?" Jenkins asks.

"That's correct, and, I might add, absolutely no charges whatsoever for the Cashiers' Check," the banker says, "which would have been thousands of dollars, dear fellow, tens of thousands. Now I hope you people will leave us alone. I have signed all the release forms for you, and we are in full compliance with your bloody Internal Revenue Service. And, I might add, you buggers should focus on Internal American business, and not try to ruin all the banks here on the Turks and Caicos Islands."

"A Cashier's Check?" Jenkins says, dumbfounded.

"That's what you bleeding people demanded!" the banker says, frustrated into a total loss of politeness.

"You gave the Department of Justice a Cashier's Check for twenty-three and a half million dollars?"

"Indeed. And now I am done with you fellows. Good day, gentlemen. And goodbye!"

They leave, and the banker closes and locks the doors.

Agent Jenkins looks back across the road. The beer drinker has disappeared, without finishing his beer, and both FBI agents run across to his empty table.

Nobody knows what happened to the man, although he left a sizeable tip.

"He was an American," the waitress tells them, "and a wonderful person."

The size of the tip that he left for her influences her judgment. She admits that she has never seen him before, but she can remember his name. He repeated it twice, asking her to remember it.

"Anthony Silver, I think he said. Or maybe it was Silberg. I'm not sure. I see a lot of tourists every day, and I guarantee that he was a tourist. Can I get you gentle people anything to drink?"

Agent Jenkins tells John Dempsey: "That's not the name that was on the guy's DOJ card. His ID was a perfect counterfeit of a Department of Justice ID."

Agent Dempsey shows the waitress a picture of Silberg.

"Was this the man?"

"I don't know," she says. "Like, that doesn't look like the customer to me. So do you guys want anything to drink?"

They spend the rest of the day trying to locate the bogus Department of Justice agent. Dempsey spends the night at the airport. Jenkins goes to the hotel and reluctantly phones Special Agent in Charge Scott Larsen.

Agent Jenkins spends much of the Larsen conversation holding the telephone at arm's length, trying to prevent damage to his ears.

The next day they return to the bank and talk to the man they spoke to previously.

They try to find out who received the Cashier's Check, but the banker, who is the Manager, refuses to divulge any more information. Case closed.

They have no further jurisdiction on Provo, if they ever had any in the first place.

He does show them the paperwork, which appears official and legitimate in every respect.

The signator for the Department of Justice is, in fact, a real agent. Both Jenkins and Dempsey talk to him on the phone. He has never been to the Turks & Caicos Islands.

He works in Des Moines, Iowa. His name is Charles Maloney, and he has never heard of Anthony Silberg.

Pouring Cement In North Miami Beach, Monday AM

Anthony Silberg remains unconscious, and Angelo Rossellini glances up at him occasionally. Then he goes back to studying the blueprints spread out on the table in front of him. They are the plans for Rossellini Towers, the latest and probably the most expensive hi-rise condominium complex in North Miami Beach.

The construction site remains quiet.

The sun will not rise in the east for another four hours.

Someone taps three times, then twice on the door of the construction trailer.

Angelo Rossellini tells him to enter.

When he does, he looks at Angelo, not at Silberg, who is in a chair in the corner wearing two sets of handcuffs.

"We've cut the rebars, Mister Rossellini. Four down, five across, and when we put them back, there's no need for welding. There will be no structural weakness once the cement falls in place. No point in getting the welder here. Just an extra set of eyes. Not necessary."

"Good. Will that fat man fit?"

The Site Engineer looks at Silberg for the first time.

"Yes, sir."

"Are you ready to pour?"

"No, sir."

"Why not?"

"Cement truck is on its way. Should be here in about ten or fifteen minutes."

"Good. Thank you."

The man leaves the trailer. Rossellini gets up, walks over to Silberg, and lightly slaps his face."

"Ah, Anthony," he says. "You're still with us."

Silberg raises his head slowly. The dream he was having disappears, never captured in his memory, gone forever.

"Can you hear me, Anthony?"

"Fuck you," he says, but the words stumble out of his mouth because of the sedatives.

"Yes," Angelo says. "That would be your first choice of a greeting. Let me explain the rules, Anthony. We are going to have a conversation, and if you disrespect me one more time, at any point in our conversation, then we will stop our little chat, and you will die. That's the only rule."

Silberg says nothing. He tries to test his restraints, but he has no strength, no coordination.

"So, Anthony," Angelo continues, "I believe that everyone should leave this earth without a lot of questions troubling them. Do you have any complicated questions I can answer for you?

"I never disrespected you," Silberg says.

"Of course you did."

"I never disrespected you," he says again, more clearly.

"You stole over seven and a half million dollars from me, Anthony Silberg."

Anthony has a hard time understanding what's Angelo says. The seven and a half million dollar check was bogus.

Angelo goes over to him and holds an iPhone in front of him. He flicks some pictures, first the bank in the Turks & Caicos, and then a crisp photo of a Cashier's check for $23,537,623.14.

Silberg looks at the check, has a hard time seeing it clearly, then suddenly recognizes it: "My money."

"No, that is my money, Anthony. It is the money you have stolen from me during the last twelve years. Tomorrow it will be in a safe deposit box in Switzerland, a loophole in their government's regulations that require no reporting to the IRS or any other government office, American or Swiss or Russian or Chinese. It is truly my secret money."

"I built the largest real estate company in the Palm Beaches," Silberg says, shaking his head, desperately trying to think more clearly.

"I allowed you to build it for me, Anthony. You may not realize this, but I am now the owner of Accelerated Realty Sales. Your friend, Martha Krumble, a person of honor and integrity, has replaced you. Do you have any idea how many millions of dollars have become legitimate in this process? And all because you tried to steal seven and a half million dollars in escrow funds."

Silberg says: "I never disrespected you."

"You disrespect me by killing people who work for me, Anthony." Angelo shakes his head. "Did you know that I heard you as you murdered the men in the nursery? I heard you shoot each man twice. That was me on the phone, Anthony. And then you killed Barbara Rossellini? A Rossellini! And Triple-J, Jimmy J. Johnson. Jimmy was a great man who served this nation in Iraq. You have ruthlessly murdered all these friends of mine, Anthony Silberg."

They hear three taps, and then two, on the construction trailer's door. The site engineer sticks his head in the office and says: "Ready to pour, Mister Rossellini."

Angelo waves him off.

Silberg feels his heart starting to pound in his chest.

The door closes.

"Then, Anthony, you try to murder my friend, Captain George McKlane, a great American hero."

"What are you talking about?" Silberg asks.

"You hired a killer to eliminate George McKlane and steal the contract on his house for six million dollars?"

"I never did any such thing."

"Well, Anthony, I don't think agent Scott Larsen would agree with you."

"I don't know an agent named Larsen. He never worked for me. I never —"

"Ah, Tony. He's an FBI agent, not a *real* estate agent. He thinks that you tried to kill George McKlane."

"That's bullshit."

"No, Anthony, that's you being a predictable criminal. You should know that it is not the first punch that wins a fight. It is the final punch."

Angelo Rossellini shakes his fist in Anthony Silberg's face, smiling. Enraged, Silberg spits on his fist.

Angelo Rossellini smiles at him and says: "So, there we are with your disrespect. And now, our conversation ends."

He goes to the door and opens it. The three men who tackled Silberg earlier, outside The Luxury Partnership offices in Boca Raton, step into the trailer.

One of the men has some box cutters, and he bends down to free Silberg's feet.

For a moment, Anthony thinks he might have a chance, one more life left in him.

Then he feels the sting in his shoulder as one of the men administers another shot. At least he will not feel the cement as it crushes and suffocates his life. He says something as he drifts off.

"What did he say?" Angelo asks.

"He said, 'Thank you.'"

Angelo steps over and puts his hand on Silberg's head, gently, as if he were blessing a child.

"You're welcome, *Antonio*," he says.

Angelo Rossellini knows that this is a name that Silberg hates. Perhaps he will carry it into his miserable afterlife.

Chapter 21

Welcome Back Corporal Petersson

Colonel McKlane walks into his father's office and says: "Dad, this was just delivered by Marine Corps courier to my men at the front gate."

He hands it to his father. "We have not opened it. We did scan it. I think it's your last missing 'Thank You' note from the wall upstairs."

The previous afternoon, five of the six stolen, framed letters arrived via FedEx.

The package they came in contained a printed note explaining that they had been left at the airport in Fort Lauderdale. The accompanying letter has no signature.

The FedEx Package comes from the Delta Airlines passenger lounge.

George McKlane phones agent Scott Larsen and tells him that the framed memorials have returned. He does not say that one is still missing. He explains that cleaners discovered them in a men's room at the Fort Lauderdale International Airport. Agent Larsen's only comment is that the shooter was obviously in a hurry.

George McKlane studies and tries to remember each of the Marines represented in the returned frames.

They die young, and they remain so in his memory.

As he carefully places them back on the wall in the War Room, he says a prayer for each man.

Alone, he salutes each frame.

He knows that the missing Marine, the sixth frame, belongs to Jackson "Smartass" Petersson.

Sitting in his office, he hefts the courier package his son gives him. Welcome back, Corporal Petersson.

"Are you going to open it?" Colonel McKlane asks.

"Later," George says, putting the envelope aside.

He does not know why he does this, but the package feels private, somehow sacred, nobody's business but his own. It surprises his son, who shrugs it off.

His father is getting old.

George steps out of his office and says, "Sharonda, I'm going upstairs. I'll be in the War Room."

She comes out of the kitchen, where she's been reading and smiles at him. "Want a snack of carrots and celery?"

"Undisturbed," he says.

"Understood," she replies.

George takes the elevator to the second floor, carrying the package. He opens it at the desk in the War Room, reading the letter Ernestine Petersson wrote to him sixty-four years earlier. He still remembers the postscript she wrote:

"I will pray that you come home to the people who love you."

How difficult it must have been for her to write that, knowing that her loved one would never return. George goes to put it on the wall, turns it over, and sees new writing in the same schoolgirl cursive that the original letter contains.

P.S.S.. My original prayer was answered, Captain McKlane. Now my grandson has also returned you to your loved ones. Take no one else from my family.

He hangs the frame on the wall. He says a prayer, sending another Marine to everlasting peace. He opens the gun safe, takes out the last chocolate bar, and sits down in his comfortable leather chair.

So it was her grandson.

He tries piecing it together. He will never understand all of it. But he also realizes that, by luck, by chance, by the Grace of God, her grandson was the only person on earth in a position to save him five days earlier.

He knows the killer missed him on purpose. Now he knows why. He also understands that his silence is the only way he can ever repay the sacrifice of Ernestine Petersson. Then he slumps in the chair, returning to Korea.

The Funchilin Pass, December 10, 1950

The Marine Corps M46 Patton tank has tossed

Captain George McKlane and Sergeant Raymond Chapman off the side of the mountain road.

After tumbling down the mountainside almost 40 feet, they find themselves perched dangerously on a ledge that overlooks the valley below, just south of Koto-ri. They hear an explosion destroy the bridge that is their only escape route, seemingly their last chance to rejoin the most celebrated retreat in military history.

Sergeant Chapman says: "We aren't going to die here. We've been through too much shit together, Socks. Let's see if we can get back up to the road."

It takes them almost an hour and a half to slowly make their way back up the mountainside. They have to backtrack several times, finding new footing leading higher. They do finally make it.

They move very cautiously as they approach the road.

They can hear a lot of voices on the road above them, and the soft shuffle of large numbers of feet. Hundreds of refugees move towards the destroyed bridge.

"I think they know something we don't know," Captain George McKlane says.

"I sure hope so."

"What have we got for weapons?" the Captain asks.

"Your handgun and my fists," the sergeant says.

"And this," Captain McKlane says.

He walks over to an older woman, resting on the side of the road. She has a Soviet Shpagin machine gun sticking out of her backpack, the spoils of war.

She gives it to the Marine captain with a smile. He checks the clip, and it's half full.

She hands him two more full clips.

Another refugee walks up to them and hands them another burp gun and additional clips of ammunition.

The refugees willingly surrender their weapons of war to the professionals who can protect them and who know how to use them.

The captain and the sergeant fall in with the refugees.

As the straggling line of men, women, and children approach the blown bridge, they turn right and claw their way up the steep hillside.

After a problematic 250-foot climb, they turn and walk under the steel pipes, without ducking, and then they return to the road below, on the other side of the destroyed bridge.

"Won't take China too long to figure this one out," Captain McKlane says. "I think that this might be a good place to camp for the night, sergeant."

Reluctantly, the sergeant starts to dig a foxhole that overlooks the steep, 250-foot climb that they have just struggled up.

"One way or another, captain, you are going to get me killed," Staff Sergeant Raymond Chapman says.

Captain George McKlane has no answer.

They pile rocks in front of their foxhole. Some of the refugees help them with the earthworks, then move on, hoping American warriors will protect them. Some of them leave weapons, even a few Chinese hand grenades.

"Fifty percent alert," Chapman says. "I guess we're going to save a lot of lives, captain. You sleep first."

"Yeah," Captain Socks says. "I'm pretty sure that our Marines will appreciate it."

They start piling up bodies in front of their position at about 0400. After each firefight, either the sergeant or the captain bellies out to the growing pile of dead Chinese and returns with machine guns and grenades.

The captain gets shot first. "Flesh wound," he says. He says this two more times before the Corsairs move into the valley at dawn, protecting the most celebrated retreat in the history of the Marine Corps.

The Marine Wing Commander shouts: "ABORT! HANDS OFF THE PICKLE! NO DROP!" None of the pilots press the bomb drop button, the pickle. Corsairs roar fifty feet above the heads of the sergeant and Captain George McKlane. The planes turn, make strafing runs at the wave of men trying to swarm over the two Marines fighting at the top of the hill.

All of the fighter bombers mimic the Wing Commander's maneuver. Every pilot keeps his thumb off of the bomb drop button.

The Wing Commander is shooting and talking at the same time. "You got two Marines at the top of the hill near the blown bridge, and they must have three or four hundred dead Chinese piled up in front of them, maybe more. Jesus Christ, I've never seen anything like it."

Marine Headquarters phones the field commander of the retreating column.

In less than ten minutes, a full platoon of Marine commandoes is airlifted by helicopter to within 200 yards of the fighting. They reach Captain McKlane and Sergeant Chapman just as their position is about to be overrun. Hand-to-hand combat turns into ultimate victory as the Commandoes do their job. They take both the captain and the sergeant on stretchers back to waiting helicopters and airlift them to safety.

Then the Corsair fighter bombers drop their fire on an enemy defeated by the blood and guts of two Marines.

Within half an hour, Captain George McKlane's men hear about it. There's a good deal of cheering and shouting among them.

The story spreads quickly about how Captain George McKlane and Sergeant Raymond Chapman hold off wave after wave of CCF. Just the two of them. Those who embellish the details cannot exaggerate very much.

As the captain and the sergeant destroyed hundreds of Chinese by firing down on them from their mountainside perch, the Marines who made it across the airdropped bridge finally secure their escape.

Nobody knows how the captain and the sergeant survived being tossed off the mountain by an M46 Patton Tank. That story surfaces much later, during debriefings on a hospital ship and in Japan.

On the day of the event, during a break in the retreat, a corporal says: "Even when they weren't with us, they covered our ass. Captain Socks and Chapman."

He repeats the final four words a few times, and gradually it grows into a chant among all the men. *CaptainSocks and Chapman.*

It requires an explanation to Marines who do not know about Captain Socks and the sergeant. When they understand, they join the chorus. *Captain Socks and Chapman.*

Both men are alive, wounded, Captain Socks the worst, shot three times with a knife gash down his back. He might not live, but the captain does — his men her about it. And the day finally comes both the Captain and the sergeant rejoin their unit and lead them once again. But that comes almost a year later, long after the most celebrated retreat in Marine Corps history comes to a successful conclusion.

They return to Korea at their request, less than a month after Captain George McKlane receives the Medal of Honor. Raymond Chapman wins the Silver Star.

Captain McKlane tells the sergeant that it should have been the other way around.

He is not humble.

It's what he feels.

"If you'd let me go on the ledge, it would have been you," he tells the sergeant.

"No, sir," the sergeant answers. "I would not have done what you did. I would not have stayed there."

13752 Coconut Palm Ct.,
Boca Raton, Monday PM

George McKlane hangs up the phone in his office and says: "That was Angelo Rossellini, and he says he would like to visit me." George is talking to his son, who has spent most of the afternoon with Martha Krumble.

They seem to like each other.

"Rossellini is the new owner over at Accelerated Realty Sales, where your friend Martha Krumble is the Broker." He smiles at his son, who smiles back.

"What does Mister Rossellini want to talk about?" Colonel McKlane asks.

"Anthony Silberg."

"I think I'd like to be part of that conversation," the colonel tells his father.

"I think that would be a good idea. Ask Sharonda to come in for a moment, son."

As Sharonda steps into the office, George says: "We're about to have a guest, Mister Angelo Rossellini, and the colonel and I will be talking to him in the Birdroom. I think the Magic Wand should pay very close attention to everything we talk about."

"Okay," Sharonda says. "This is Mister Rossellini, whose son was briefly married to your goddaughter?

"Yes."

"That will be an interesting conversation."

"Yes, it will be."

Angelo Rossellini arrives thirty minutes later in a black Lincoln Navigator driven by a huge man who opens the rear door to let Mister Rossellini out. The apparent bodyguard looks around at the Marines, leans into the vehicle to say something, and then backs away as Angelo steps out. The bodyguard rings the doorbell and stands in front of Angelo when Sharonda answers it. She's wearing a gun, the first thing the bodyguard notices.

"It's all right," Angelo says. He holds out his hand to Sharonda and introduces himself, bowing slightly.

Angelo Rossellini is an impressive man with a quiet voice and a full head of white, slightly wavy hair. His face is younger than he is.

"Mister Rossellini," George says, stepping forward. "I'm George McKlane. Martha Krumble has spoken well of you. Of course, I know you are a major developer in this area. Welcome to my home."

"Thank you," Angelo says. "And I think this gentleman must be your son. You look the same."

"Yes," George says. "I think I used to look something like that thirty-five years ago."

"Yes," Angelo says, smiling.

"I was hoping I could join your conversation," the colonel says.

"No," Angelo says. "That will not be possible."

An awkward silence settles between all of them. Angelo says: "What I have to say is for you, and you alone, Captain George McKlane."

"George, please."

"George."

"Well, just you and I then, Angelo. I have a place I call the Birdroom –"

"In your office, please, George."

Another awkward silence.

Sharonda says: "I'll organize the furniture, so you're both comfortable."

"No," Angelo says.

Sharonda stops. "No?" She glances at George.

Angelo says: "No recordings."

Colonel McKlane coughs and is about to say something, but Captain George holds up his hand.

"No recordings," he says. "Just you and I. In my office. Would you like a drink, Angelo."

"Only if you have one," Angelo says.

"I'll have a Guinness, Sharonda."

"I, too, will have a Guinness, Missus Nelson."

Sharonda does not remember telling him her last name.

"Please," George says, pointing the way to his office. Sharonda brings them their Guinness on a silver tray, setting it down on George's desk. She steps out, closing the door.

Angelo Rossellini's bodyguard places himself in front of the closed door.

He's a huge man, and the colonel and all his Marines take note of his size.

In the office, Angelo asks to see the recording system. George pulls out the drawer holding the Magic Wand. A few lights are blinking, although it's not recording.

"I would like to see all the lights go off," Angelo says.

George smiles and throws a switch, and then he starts to close the drawer.

"Perhaps ... "

"Fine," George says. "The drawer stays open, Angelo."

"Thank you."

Angelo looks around the room. He stands up and walks down the wall of photographs, sipping his Guinness."

"You have known many famous people."

"One of the benefits of a long life," George says.

"Yes," Angelo says.

He raises his glass of Guinness. "A long life."

He comes back and sits down. "We are both old warriors, George, although I have never been in the military. And I think you have lived a little longer than I have, but not by much."

"I was only in the Marine Corps for three and a half years," George says.

"But you were, you are a great war hero."

"I was lucky."

"Yes," Angelo says. "You are lucky." He smiles.

"It's been a difficult week and a half," George says.

"I am very sorry about your goddaughter," Angelo says. "She was an innocent."

It's an odd phrase, George thinks. An innocent. He says: "The police think she may have killed Mister, uh ...."

"Johnson," Angelo says.

"Yes, I think James Johnson," George says.

"I called him Triple Jay," Angelo says. "Jimmy J. Johnson. He was one of my most favorite people, George. He was almost like a son to me."

"I'm very sorry," George says.

"Your goddaughter did not kill him," Angelo says.

"How do you know?"

"Anthony Silberg killed him. And afterward, Anthony Silberg killed your goddaughter."

George is silent.

"This is why your recording machine is off, George."

"You know Silberg did it? For a fact?"

"For a fact," Angelo says.

"Shouldn't the police know about this?"

"No, they should not."

"But Silberg is a dangerous person."

"No, he is not."

George thinks he knows what he has just been told, but he remains quiet.

"I have a gift for you," Angelo says. He produces a small, wrapped box, taped but with no ribbon. He puts it on the desk, in front of George.

"Please," Angelo says. "Open it."

George does. He holds it up, turns it over, reads the inscription.

> ### *To Capt Socks from*
> ### *the men he saved and*
> ### *those he could not*

"Silberg is dead," Angelo says.

"You know this?"

"By my own hand."

Angelo glances over at the Magic Wand.

It is off.

"And now you know this," Angelo Rossellini says. "My secret is your secret."

"The police?"

"The police do not know this. The police do not know how to keep secrets."

George, after a moment of silence, says: "You live a very dangerous life, Angelo Rossellini."

"No," he says, "I live a very safe life. But it is a life of secrets. And it is the secrets that keep us safe."

Angelo Rossellini looks at George. His words carry no threat, no demand. He simply defines the reality of a life of power and decision.

"I believe that you also know how to keep secrets, Captain George McKlane."

George considers this.

He thinks about Angelo Rossellini saying: "It is the secrets that keep us safe."

In the end, he answers: "Yes, I do, Angelo, I know how to keep secrets."

The End

Epilog

Six Months Later

George McKlane never does sell his home, taking it off the market when Martha Krumble asks him to renew his listing at the end of their six-month contract. George says: "Those twelve days in June changed my mind about selling this place, Martha." His son also no longer

wants him to get rid of the estate at 13752 Coconut Palm Court in Boca Raton.

"I'll probably die in this house," George tells Martha.

"Take your time," Martha says. Her quick candor always makes George laugh.

George McKlane does not stop eating chocolate. He also keeps drinking Guinness, although he does try to follow Rachel Broadslate's bland dietary advice.

Time travel back to Korea disappears once George finally stops taking Prednisone.

Sharonda remains George McKlane's Nurse Practitioner. She hires two caretakers for George, so they have a 24-hour hospital shift.

The breakfast group gathers every Saturday morning under the lanai or in the Birdroom. It includes Sharonda's husband, Samuel, as well as Martha Krumble. George's son also stops in once or twice a month. He says he needs flight hours. Captain George knows better.

Initially, Sharonda wears her Glock every day. George finally persuades her to disarm after three months. He tells her that he knows that Silberg is no longer a threat. He never explains the source of his certainty, just as he never gives any details about the mysterious reappearance of his watch in the War Room.

Accelerated Realty Sales continues as the largest, and arguably the best real estate agency in the area. Martha Krumble goes to Washington, D.C., to give an important speech on ethics to the National Association of Realtors®. The NAR remains the second-largest lobbying group in the nation. Her address receives polite, but light applause.

Martha spends her spare time during the Washington visit with a man she finds very attractive: originally Colonel and now Brigadier General George McKlane.

The General's first wife died in a car accident in Cleveland, Ohio, over twenty years earlier, and Martha meets, and likes, the General's son, George McKlane III. The youngest George, called Mac, also resembles his grandfather.

"But you might all work on originality when naming your children," Martha tells them.

George McKlane III works at Homeland Security. He is the leader of an Antiterrorism Unit, called CWMD (Countering Weapons of Mass Destruction). He serves two tours in Iraq and one in Afghanistan before leaving the Marine Corps to run the unit.

Frederick Phelps continues to run the Luxury Partnership branch of Accelerated Realty Sales, with great success. Occasionally, he thinks about the morning he looked out his beach office window and saw three men tackle and abduct a bald guy coming off the beach, who looked sort of like Anthony Silberg.

He never talks to anybody about the abduction. He's reasonably sure that the kidnappers were federal agents.

Angelo Rossellini will soon have a Topping Out Party at Rossellini Towers in Miami. The event will signify the last beam laid on the top floor of the third and final building. "Topping Out" is an ancient ceremony, with its roots tied to the old Viking practice of putting the top of a tree on every new building.

The Norsemen did this to appease the spirits of men whose souls were misplaced.

Agent Larsen and his team feel cursed by the disappearance of Silberg and all the money he stole and allegedly laundered. Their estimate goes far beyond the seven and a half million dollars he took from the real estate company's escrow account. The Department of Justice thinks that Silberg's crime amounted to tens of millions of dollars, perhaps as much as a hundred million. They will track down and arrest Anthony Silberg, sooner or later. He remains on their Most Wanted list. They do have leads in the case. Anonymous tips send agents to different parts of the world, keeping the search alive, and sometimes in the news.

The Asset Forfeiture and Money Laundering Unit of the FBI recovers a little over two million "Silberg" dollars in the six months following his disappearance.

They have a photograph of Anthony Silberg in a coffee shop located in an underground cave in Cappadocia, Turkey. He's holding a newspaper that shows a date and news events that occurred over four months after he vanished. The picture is severely out of focus. When they enhance it, they can't tell whether someone has photoshopped it or not.

The Feds recover almost half a million dollars in low-grade diamonds in Johannesburg, South Africa, following an anonymous tip that Anthony Silberg rented a safety deposit box at a branch office of Barclays Bank. The signature on the rental agreement seems genuine.

Torbjorn Petersson continues farming in Virginia, doing an occasional out-of-state job. The duplicate of Ernestine's letter to George McLane hangs on the back of a closet door in her bedroom.

In late October, before the first snow of winter melts into the Jackson River, the Peterssons receive an official letter from the Federal government: a Notice of Eminent Domain.

The Tennessee Valley Authority, which governs waterways in Virginia, will force them to sell their farm.

The TVA is building a dam on the Jackson River, below the Petersson place, on the old Gathright spread. The Petersson acreage will sink underwater when a lake forms behind the dam.

The Peterssons will not move off their land without a fight. Of course, that's another story, not yet written, called "Poison Heartbeats."

Temple Emmet Williams
Boca Raton, Florida

Acknowledgments

Thanks to the first professional writer who took me under his wing and dared me to make a difference with words, fifty-one years ago: Hayes Jacobs at the New School for Social Research. He wrote in *The New Yorker.*

Thanks also to all the great newspaper and magazine people who turned me into a journalist. Richard D. Peters became my first editor at the *New York World-Telegram & Sun*, and Otto Krause at *News/Check* magazine in South Africa became the last.

Neither the publications nor the people exist any longer, except through the fingertips of the hundreds of men and women that each of them so selflessly influenced.

Thanks also to the extraordinary people who turned me into an editor many years later: Ed Thompson and Mary Lou Allin at *The Reader's Digest*. Their lessons, their wisdom still influences both how and why I write.

Thanks also to the great copywriters and art directors who taught me the power of words and pictures combined, especially Steve Trygg, David Ogilvy, Leo Burnett, and Rudy Perz (who invented the Pillsbury Doughboy). I can no longer write without a camera clicking away in my mind.

Thanks to all the people who make a book possible, especially the readers who use their time and their intelligence to put a stamp of approval or even disapproval of what a writer has to say. I refer not just to the people who buy a book, although they remain the most vital part of the process.

I specifically address the extraordinary people who contribute time from their busy lives to look at a book before publication: proofreaders, beta readers, fellow authors, and friends who let me invade their lives.

I have a proofreader with the eye of an eagle. I can review my book a half a dozen times, assure myself that it is spotless, and **Judy Greenman** will swoop down on it and discover dozens of mistakes.

To me, this borders on magic, and I thank her for her time and her extraordinary care.

Thanks to an old friend who I have known for a long time and who lifts my spirits and gives me the confidence to continue. She worked for many years as a Psychiatric Social Worker, and she knows right (and wrong) characters when she reads them. Her opinions and friendship are highly valued. Thank you, **Jennifer Andrews**.

Thanks to Ronald A. Feldman, the author of **little secrets, BIG LIES**, an exceptional writer who helps me by example as well as in person. He shows me what putting your heart on a page can do.

Thanks to Robert Eggleton, who wrote a satirical, science fiction novel called **Rarity in the Hollow**. The book is a gem, and his generosity inspires me. He is a spirit lifter, a man who has spent a lifetime smoothing out wrinkles in other lives. Read his book.

David Haight, the author of a marvelous book of short stories, called **Lemon**. Thank you for your counsel. You continue to write beautiful short stories and novels.

A special thanks to Marsell Morris, the author of many books, especially the **Alien Contact series**, whose advice never fails to amaze me with its accuracy and simplicity. He is one of the world's good storytellers. I think it has something to do with the water that they drink in Detroit.

A heartfelt thanks to ***John Imperial***, a good friend, whose comments after reading an early manuscript led to significant improvements in the final book. John does not read much fiction, but he page-flipped through Wrinkled Heartbeats and gave my writer's compass a good spin, for the better. Thank you, John.

I would also like to acknowledge the ***United States Marine Corps***, of which I have been a proud member. I offer my thanks mainly to the authors of ***U.S. Operations In Korea 1950-1953***, Lynn Montross, and Captain Nicholas A. Canzona, USMC. Their series of well-researched, non-fiction accounts inspired many of the fictional military flashbacks contained in this novel. *Semper Fidelis*.

And finally, most importantly, I thank my Content Editor, a thoughtful critic of my work who never fails to make it better. Thank you, ***Kerstin "Kickan" Williams***, my soul mate for over four decades. You have the extraordinary ability to improve everything I do.

About the Author

Temple Emmet Williams

His first book was an award-winning, best-selling memoir called **Warrior Patient:** *How to Beat Deadly Diseases With Laughter, Good Doctors, Love, and Guts.* It's non-fiction.

It has received a B.R.A.G. Medallion, and it also won a 2015 Gold Medal at the Reader's Favorite Book Awards in Miami, Florida. At times, it has been #1 on several Amazon best-seller lists.

Temple grew up in Ohio. He was educated at The Hotchkiss School, and he attended Yale University.

As a journalist, he was nominated twice for the Pulitzer Prize as an undercover, investigative reporter for the *World-Telegram & Sun* in New York City.

He worked as an Editor at *The Reader's Digest* and was the managing editor of an international news magazine in Africa.

He was a creative director at big ad agencies around the world, living in Africa for six years and in Europe for almost as long. He and his wife, Kerstin, who is also his content editor, live in Boca Raton, Florida.

Wrinkled Heartbeats is their first novel, followed by **Poison Heartbeats**, and **African Heartbeats**.

Can You Review My Books?

Book reviews are the critical lifeblood of authors. They remain a valuable yardstick of their work to readers, so book reviews are essential to a writer.

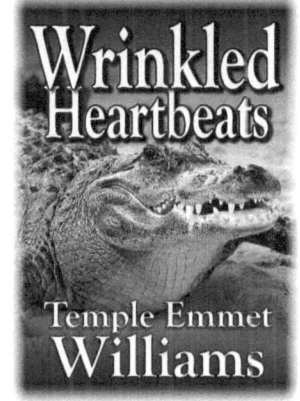

If you liked Temple's novel, *Wrinkled Heartbeats*, please review it on Amazon, Goodreads, Barnes & Noble, or Smashwords. Even a short review helps.

Wrinkled Heartbeats was one of six finalists for **Best New Novel** (under 80,000 words) at the Next Generation Indies Awards. It also has **Awesome Indies Approval**, and it won the **Silver Medal** in the crowded Action Fiction category at the Readers' Favorites Book Awards in Miami, Florida.

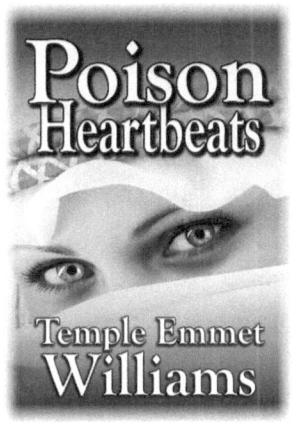

It is the first novel in the "Heartbeats" Series. The second book is *Poison Heartbeats*, published in 2017 It has already received **Awesome Indies Approval**, as well as numerous other awards, including a **cash prize at the Next Generation Indie Book Awards, held** at the Harvard Club.

African Heartbeats is the third novel in the Heartbeats Series. Shortly after publication, it received many five-star awards, five of which were "editorial" rather than reader awards, This book, although stand-alone, follows after *Wrinkled Heartbeats* and then *Poison Heartbeats*, both of which were widely acclaimed and remain relevant today. They are stand-alone

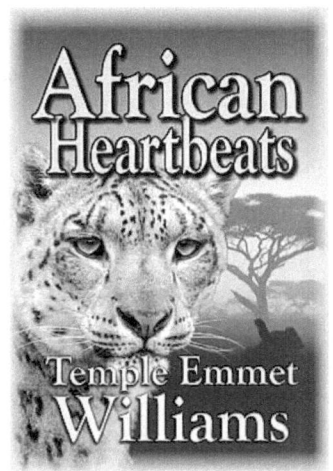

books. You do not have to read one to understand the other.

In *African Heartbeats,* Sharonda and Samuel Nelson have returned to their ancestral roots in the southern highlands of East Africa.

They secretly work for Homeland Security and Mac McKlane, and they prepare for an ISIS attack at one of the largest hospitals in Tanzania.

The terrorist strike will be the start of a multinational push to replace the lost oil fields of ISIS in Syria with a new cash crop in southern Africa, diamonds from the de Beers complex in Botswana.

ISIS also wants the eight atomic bombs built by South Africa during the time of Apartheid.

The author lived in Africa for six years. He spent three years researching this book. It's long, fast-paced, and absolutely The Africa of today.

Enjoy your trip through the southern nations of Africa. It will be a bumpy ride, filled with truth and surprising revelations.

Warrior Patient Heartbeats

"Live to laugh and laugh to live.

"This book may have saved my life!" That's how Robert Eggleton, the author of ***Rarity in the Hollow*** (an extraordinary science fiction satire), began his five-star review of the award-winning and best-selling memoir: ***Warrior Patient***.

Live to love and love to live. Enjoy the stunning and often funny story of someone who recovers completely from a relentless series of medical problems, many resulting from the system designed to prevent them. The book received a **B.R.A.G. Medallion,** and it won a **Gold Medal** at the Reader's Favorite Book Awards in Miami. Warrior Patient also won an **International Red Ribbon** from The Wishing Well Book Awards in Europe.